THE BEST GENERAL IN
THE CIVIL WAR

THE BEST GENERAL IN THE CIVIL WAR

A NOVEL

CONRAD BIBENS

Stoney Creek Publishing

Published by

Stoney Creek Publishing Group

StoneyCreekPublishing.com

ISBN: 979-8-9891203-9-0
ISBN (ebook): 979-8-9901289-0-3
Library of Congress Control Number: 2024910988

Cover design by Ken Ellis

"That left Thomas to pick up the pieces and save the army, and Thomas did all any soldier could have done."

Bruce Catton, "Never Call Retreat"

CONTENTS

INTRODUCTION
BY THE EDITOR OF THE THOMAS PAPERS

The discovery of the secret memoirs of General George Thomas has pleased and confounded historians of the American Civil War. Thomas, usually considered the outstanding Northern general after U.S. Grant and William T. Sherman, had said he would not write such a book, and, in fact, had his private papers destroyed to keep his life from being "hawked in print" by biographers.

Yet the *New York Tribune's* publication in early 1870 of a letter disparaging the general's great victory at Nashville over Confederate forces led by John Bell Hood angered Thomas, and he started writing these words in response.

The memoirs were found in 2020, tucked away in a storage area of St. Paul's Episcopal Church in Troy, New York. They were wrapped in oilskin papers and sealed in a tin box. The papers were in remarkably good condition for being 150 years old. Also in the tin box was a photograph of Thomas with his wife, Frances, apparently taken in San Francisco not long before he died in March 1870. Mrs. Thomas enclosed an epilogue as well.

Though Thomas had made clear to his wife that he did not want this manuscript to be released to the public, she preserved it, likely for sentimental reasons. Her husband's funeral had been held in St. Paul's, and she may have thought the church was a good place to conceal the work from nineteenth-century journalists.

Yet she may have hoped that it would be discovered in the distant future when all the principal actors of the war had passed from the scene. This book is full of the general's often scathing opinions about the notable men of the war, including Lincoln, Grant, and Sherman. Perhaps Frances Kellogg Thomas gave the tin box to an Episcopalian priest when she knew her life was drawing to a close in 1889, and the priest respected her request to hide it. If so, any instructions she had given him about future use of the contents of the box were lost, or the priest may have died before he could fulfill her wishes.

This is all conjecture, of course. After well more than a century, the box was found by a young priest looking for old church ledgers.

Readers should be warned that George Thomas' opinions on slavery, race, and ethnicity, while relatively progressive for the nineteenth century, may not be palatable for some twenty-first-century sensitivities. One should judge the man according to the times he lived in and by what he did for the United States when it mattered most.

While most historians have accepted the authenticity of the Thomas memoirs, a few have raised doubts. The first chapter of the manuscript is in the general's handwriting, of which there are several examples in government archives. In Chapter 2, his handwriting becomes shaky and less legible, but by Chapter 3, the manuscript is written in a firm, seemingly feminine, hand. It appears to be that of Mrs. Thomas, although there are few surviving examples of her handwriting for comparison. It seems likely the general dictated the bulk of his memoirs to his wife. Regardless of the questions expressed by a handful of my academic peers, I believe this manuscript to be genuine.

I thank St. Paul's Episcopal Church, especially the Reverend Shelby Vidal, for first bringing these papers to my attention, and I thank my fellow historians of the Civil War and the staff of the

University of Troy for their help and advice in preparing this book for publication.

George MacDonald Berger
Professor of History
University of Troy

CHAPTER 1

IN WHICH NAT TURNER ALMOST SLAYS MY FAMILY AND MYSELF

May God curse John Schofield, a damnable puppet of Grant. I must answer him. Or them. A reply to that letter in the *New York Tribune?* How to begin?

"It has come to my attention that a reader of your publication believes the Battle of Nashville was of little consequence, and that the Battle of Franklin was the true victory in that theater of the War for the Union ..."

Hang it all, how to explain it in a logical sequence? Yes, Franklin wounded the rebels, but they were still formidable in those hills above Nashville. It took courage more than generalship to survive Franklin, the grit to stand up to repeated charges. John Schofield was in command there in name only. While other Union officers were keeping the rebels from breaking through, Schofield was two miles away, cowering in safety.

And after Franklin, poor John Hood, dauntless John Hood, still chased Schofield all the way to Nashville. The rebels were wounded, but unlike their leader, their army still had two legs and two arms.

And Hood frightened Sam Grant. The North's "greatest" general was so nervous, fretting in his Virginia stalemate, that he nearly had me relieved, even though I had matters well in hand as I waited for the freezing Nashville weather to clear before I gave the order to attack. And then we utterly destroyed Hood's army.

That letter to the *Tribune* disparaged not just me but every Union soldier who fought at Nashville under my command, including the former slaves who fought as gallantly as their white comrades. Schofield didn't sign the letter, but it is clearly his handi-work. Grant must have approved it as well. Perhaps Schofield still wants revenge for his nearly being expelled from West Point—on my recommendation. He was a coarse and vulgar young man, not worthy to wear the uniform of a cadet.

But why does Grant still sabotage me? The president of the United States should have more pressing matters to contemplate. Does he fear I will run for president against him? Some thoughtful Americans have asked me to seek the White House, but I do not have Grant's thirst for power and recognition.

And shouldn't Sherman come to my defense? If he claims to be my oldest friend, why is he silent?

I must gather my thoughts. Why must I continue to fight for my reputation? No general in the Union Army was a better commander than George Thomas, which I say with unadorned honesty, not vanity. A general's value can be vastly overstated, but I believe the South would have won the late rebellion had I taken its side.

Am I a braggart to say this truth, even in these written words that I will lock away in my desk? I have never put myself forward in public, thinking such ostentatiousness lacks dignity and profes-sionalism. But I will not be slandered, especially by that cur Schofield.

Oh Lord, I have given up so much to stay true to the Union, save my honor. At least one of my brothers has forgiven me, but my two maiden sisters still consider me to have died in 1861. I've lost all knowledge of my other siblings.

Virginians have made a saint of Lee. They worship Jackson and Stuart. Even Bragg, that arrogant, bumbling Bragg, still has a handful of defenders in North Carolina. How Bragg wishes he were a Virginian! That I gave up my home state for the Union is inconceivable to him and all the other traitors. Stuart once called for me to be hanged, and many other Virginians still agree with him. I would not have done the same to him, as much as he and the others deserved it. I chose honor over birth.

And I was not born the son of a high and mighty plantation owner. No haughty aristocrat was my sire. John Thomas was a middling farmer of strong character who made time to serve his neighbors by overseeing elections and highways. He considered himself a yeoman at heart, willing to work in the fields with his dozen or so slaves, never mistreating them. It was the work that killed him, the farming accident that made my mother a young widow. If my father had been a lazy patrician, he might have lived a long life, sitting on the porch, sipping a mint julep while a houseboy waved a fan.

Many gentlemen lived that way in Kentucky, across the Ohio River from where Grant grew up. Surely that's how the hero of the Union imagines my upbringing in an even grander Southern state. Grant must have been envious, a tanner's son looking across the Ohio and cursing his fate.*

Just as well for him that he was born on the northern side of the river—growing up with Kentucky spirits close at hand would have hastened his descent into drunkenness. He would have been as shameful a failure at running a Southern plantation as he was at making a living in the North. He would have killed many slaves through his incompetence much as he killed brave Union soldiers at Cold Harbor. He was a greater enemy to me at Nashville than Hood.

Oh dear Lord and Savior, please allow our president to be honorable and capable in his sacred position. Amen.

It's time to put Grant out of my thoughts for the present. He has done me enough damage in life; let him not invade my mind. It was fate that put him in the North, just as fate made me a Virginian.

---

* Editor's note: Thomas seems to believe that Grant was raised in poverty. Grant's father usually made a decent if smelly living from the tannery business.

~

I FIND myself at cross purposes here. My intention was to answer Schofield's lies that were inspired by Grant, and instead I find myself drifting further back in the past. I have never intended to write my memoirs, preferring to let the passage of time be my judge. Yet now I feel the need to make myself understood about the war and slavery, especially to my fellow Virginians. I will write down my thoughts even if I never allow the public to read them. This will help me when I compose my response to Schofield's *Tribune* letter.

I inherited slaves in the same way that the South inherited slavery. My opinions have evolved on slavery, which we Southerners preferred to call by the more polite phrase the peculiar institution, "peculiar" meaning "unique" in our usage. And by custom we referred to our slaves as servants, another more decorous term.

Given time, as soon as our servants had been able to fend for themselves, I might have insisted that my family follow George Washington's example and manumit them. But my family, especially my sisters, were like too many in the South, too greedy to hire free white men to do their work and too afraid that freedom would turn their black slaves into a race of Nat Turners. Curse that day in 1619 when Africans were first unloaded in Virginia. Some gentlemen in Jamestown didn't want to soil their hands, and now our land has been washed in blood many times.

Nat Turner's rebels slaughtered nearly sixty whites across twenty-seven miles of Virginia's Southampton County in August of 1831. Some of his victims were my childhood friends. That chieftain of slaves might also have killed me, yet he gave me a kind of freedom. Before that terrible time, I thought of Negroes as little more than playmates. I was a constant guest in their quarters at my father's farm, trading sugar I had pilfered from the kitchen for raccoons and possums. I also shared my lessons in school, teaching the smartest Africans to read and write. My parents and siblings frowned on that, preferring slaves to be ignorant. Yet our wisest servants usually did the best work. And they were friendly to me. I saw no hatred in their eyes.

My kindness to our servants may have saved our lives. When Turner, that black preacher turned black demon, began his revolt, he found no eager followers at the Thomas farm.

A quest for freedom I can understand, but Turner wanted white blood more than an end to his bondage. A few months before the massacres began, Turner had seen a solar eclipse and interpreted it as a black hand reaching over the sun, a sign it was time to kill all whites whether they had slaves or not.

My memory of his fiends is chillingly fresh. Some of the seventy or so drunken brigands bore guns, but most carried farm tools that had become weapons. A neighboring farmer, James Gurley, had ridden to our home and warned us of their approach: "Flee, flee, all of you! Black devils are on the way! The Prophet Nat is leading them. They're murdering all their masters!"

"I knew this would happen, I knew it!" my mother said. "George, get the carriage!"

"Yes, Mother. Mr. Gurley, which roads are they using?"

"Only the back road from the Travis place. Turner's already butchered them like hogs. His own masters! I'm riding the main road to warn others."

Off he galloped. We loaded the carriage with my mother and siblings, and I drove the horses. My father had died two years before, compelling me to take on a man's role. My two older brothers already considered me their equals although I was only fifteen. They carried guns as my mother huddled with our crying sisters. As we departed, I shouted to Sam, our Negro overseer who had served our family loyally for years: "Don't fight them, Sam. Let them take what they want and keep yourselves alive. We'll see you in Jerusalem."

"God bless all you Thomases!" Sam shouted back. "May Jesus keep you safe!"

"We can never trust our servants again," my mother lamented as our carriage rattled over the dry dirt road. "Never again."

"We can trust Sam," I replied. "Our servants are good people."

So they were. After my family's exodus, Turner's scoundrels entered our dwellings and forced our slaves to accompany them. At their first opportunity, the Thomas servants escaped Turner, refusing to take part in his infamy.

Though I drove our horses as hard as I dared, the mounted marauders nearly caught up with our overloaded carriage. Their crude and profane shouts filled us with dread. We abandoned the carriage and ran into the forest, heading into swamps where horses couldn't go. We lost our pursuers but still had to trek through the wetlands to the county seat, Jerusalem, where we told the towns-people of the peril.[*]

When we were safe in the town, I volunteered to be a messenger and go by horseback into the countryside, taking communications to other farms so that a militia could be formed to counter the slave rebellion. My mother protested, but I knew the townspeople and my brothers would protect her and our sisters. My oldest brother gave me one of our father's one-shot pistols, which I prayed I wouldn't need.

Thank the Lord a fast horse was able to keep me from Turner's horde, well out of the range of their guns. Turner and his devils could only curse me as I rode on. My efforts, like those of Mr. Gurley, helped save the lives of more than a few Virginians that day, though no one in that state will give me thanks for it now.

Led by Sam, our slaves eventually reported to my family in Jerusalem. Our servants then briefly stayed in the county jail, not a place they deserved except that it was the safest lodging for them in the confusion of that horrible time.

Within a few days, the rebellion was crushed by the state mili-tia. I was considered too young for such military duty. Most of the rebels were executed, but whites killed at least two hundred other Negroes (including some freedmen) who had nothing to do with the uprising. The angry whites thirsted for any black blood they

---

[*]   Editor's note: The old Virginia village of Jerusalem is now named Courtland.

could find. In their savagery they were no better than Turner and his minions.

Virginians knew all too well of the recent slave rebellion in Santo Domingo, the former French colony that some call Haiti. The black slaves there had revolted, massacring thousands of whites as they set up their own nation.

Whites all over the South lived in trepidation that such an outrage could happen in the United States and were determined to prevent it. There already had been a few aborted uprisings, including near calamities in Louisiana and South Carolina. The bloodshed in Southampton County confirmed all the whites' fears.

Turner himself wasn't captured until six weeks after his revolt was put down. He was found hiding with the Nottoway tribe, some of the few Indians still dwelling in Virginia. Before he was hanged, drawn and quartered, he was asked if he repented for his deeds. "Was Christ not crucified?" he replied.

How did Turner and his murderous blasphemy give me freedom? By letting me see Negroes as men, subject to the same longings as their masters. Beneath all the blood lust, Turner's savages wanted freedom too. Do not misunderstand me—I hated Turner and his followers with all my heart and rejoiced at their execution, just punishment for the death of my young friends. Thank the Lord our servants turned away from murder, choosing loyalty over mayhem. Yet I could see in Sam's eyes that freedom also called to him.

"I had heard the Prophet Nat preach," Sam told me days later when we were back at the farm, clearing away the wreckage left by Turner's plundering. "His masters had let him walk all over the county to share his visions. Even the white folks called him the Prophet. Understand, Master George, back then he wasn't preaching about killing, only about black folks being one with Jesus, the same as whites."

"We're all God's creatures," I agreed.

"When Nat's army got to our place, he was angry that all of you had left. I told him you were good masters, but he didn't care. His own master had been good to him, but Nat said all the white devils must die. I was so happy when we could slip away from them. We're not killers."

"I know it, Sam, I know it."

There were thousands more Negroes than whites in that part of Virginia, and only a handful had given in to Turner's temptation. Most were as righteous as Sam. If it had been in my power, I would have set Sam and our other servants free that day for their goodness and wisdom. Tragically, Sam didn't live long enough to witness the end of slavery.

Soon after Turner's rebellion, Virginia lawmakers considered emancipation. But the power of money and property won the day, and instead, harsher laws were enacted in many Southern states concerning the treatment of Negroes, both slave and free. One law would have made me guilty of the crime of teaching them to read.

Did I think the Negro the equal of the white man? No, not then. Do I think so now? As I said, my opinions are evolving. Had the Negroes in Africa been the first in the world to create gunpowder and the sextant, mankind's history might be very different. But they didn't, and this is the history we must endure.

As a callow youth, was I in favor of liberating all the South's slaves, not merely Sam and his peers on our farm? No, I was many years away from favoring full emancipation, yet I began to dimly perceive that someday far in the future not just Sam but all the other Negroes in the South, the good and the Turners, would have to be set free. For the terror that Turner fostered across the South had put white people in bondage to their fears. I did not want to be this kind of slave.

Such lessons offered by Turner's carnage were lost on my family, especially my sisters. They were like too many Southern women, so dependent on their servants that they pushed their menfolk into war rather than give up the peculiar institution. Yet if I would have them forgive me, I must forgive them. Their scorn toward me cuts deeply because I remember the many happy times we had in our youth.

I was born in 1816. Our father was of Welsh descent; our mother, Elizabeth Rochelle, had Huguenot forebears. My full name is George Henry Thomas. I was one of nine children; seven of us survived infancy.

We had a good farm and lived comfortably, at least until my father died. There was a fine white house shaded by a large oak tree. Southampton County in Virginia's South Side was fertile land close to the North Carolina border, full of apple orchards and fields of corn, tobacco, and cotton. The Tidewater region had many forests and wetlands, fine places for exploring or hunting wildcats and deer. We were also close to the Great Dismal Swamp, three hundred square miles of lagoon wilderness. Some escaped slaves made a home in this quagmire, preferring it to servitude. Our servants never felt the need to flee there.

My father's untimely death ended my easy youth. I was already well-formed, solid, and nearly six feet tall. I was big enough to take on the responsibilities of a man. I kept my own counsel, finding no reason to buy a cabinet or a saddle when I could learn to make my own. My independence did not always please my mother; still I am sure my father would have approved of my bearing. What he would have thought of my giving up farming, I fear to speculate.

I was curious to know many things, and I had mastered most of what the farm and the local academy had to offer. Suspecting there was more education to be had in a law office, at age eighteen I entered the service of an uncle in Jerusalem. My suspicions were not greatly fulfilled—I was able to handle documents in an acceptable manner, but I was restless to gather more fruit from the tree of learning.

Despite my appetite for enlightenment, I might well have returned to run the farm with others of my family when a congressman gave me the chance to find my destiny.

John Young Mason, our district's representative, appeared at my uncle's office with the news that he had an appointment available to the United States Military Academy at West Point.

This intrigued me, despite the fact that the profession of arms never held great interest for me as a child. The roles I play-acted with my siblings had more to do with being a wilderness scout than a cavalier.

As much as we Americans revered George Washington, we didn't love the idea of armies in those days. Our elders held vivid recollections of the outrages the British army had inflicted on us in two wars. Still, West Point lured me with a new world of knowledge that I could not get in Southampton County. Here was a chance I must take.

Mr. Mason told me that no one from the district had ever persevered enough to graduate from the Academy and that he was gambling on me only because he had heard kind words said on my behalf. I agreed to the examination, pleasing him enough that he wrote a letter of recommendation. I have seen that document, and I was glad to know that the congressman described me as "seventeen or eighteen years of age, of fine size and excellent talent, with a good preparatory education."

I hope Mr. Mason was truthful about my other qualities because he was in error about my age. I was nearly twenty, two years older than the average first-year plebe cadet. Perhaps he gilded the lily in order to ensure my acceptance. If so, he was successful because Old Hickory himself, President Andrew Jackson, gave his approval. I wish I could have met the old gentleman to give him my respects. President Jackson was the first general since Washington to be truly loved by the masses of the nation. He was another wilderness scout, closer to Daniel Boone than Napoleon. Supposedly our seventh president had been informed of my small role in alerting my Virginia neighbors of Nat Turner's uprising, and he thought my actions augured that I would make a good Army officer.

God bless Andrew Jackson. Like most of our past presidents, he owned slaves, but the Tennessean always stood firm for the Union.

When South Carolina talked of seceding during his presidency, he made that traitorous state back down.

I traveled to Washington to thank Mr. Mason for his help. He was not warmhearted to me. Mindful of the past failures of cadets from his district, he fulminated: "If you should fail to graduate, I never want to see your face again."

This was the first time in my life that my qualities had ever been seriously doubted. I have been undervalued often since then, and I have always resented it, but never more than that first time. I take comfort in the fact that I have always proved my doubters wrong.

"You will see me again, Mr. Mason, and you will be proud of me."

"I'm glad to hear that, young Mr. Thomas, but many a fine-looking horse can't finish the race. In four years, either have a degree or begone from my sight."

At the end of that four-year span, I made a point of meeting with the congressman so I could receive his congratulations. "When I first expressed doubts about you, Mr. Thomas, it was only because I've found that scorn makes a man work harder than praise," he told me. Perhaps he was right, at least with me, though I've found that such disrespect can turn many men bitter and sullen.

Mr. Mason had a distinguished career as a statesman, holding many government posts before becoming U.S. Minister to France. He died in Paris in 1859. Would he have joined the rebellion in 1861? I do not know.

My mother was saddened when I left for West Point, knowing she would seldom see me again on this earth. Though her passing in 1856 was grievous to me, at least she was spared the "disgrace" brought upon her family by my loyalty to the Union five years later. She died in a field accident while I was stationed in Texas. Farming is a difficult endeavor, but it ought not to be so dangerous, and I rue the bitter irony that my parents died in pastoral tasks while I have survived a lifetime as a soldier. My mother was a fine woman who, though she was not the farmer my father was, should be commended for keeping our bodies and souls together after his death.

My sisters and brothers were also unhappy about my departure, knowing that they would miss the skills I had for managing the farm. I do not write their names upon this paper, not wishing to "shame" them further, not even in my own study.

Well now, recounting the events of my life is helping me become clear in what I must say to Grant and Schofield in my Tribune letter. I will continue writing of my past. Reaching back for these memories has its rewards as well as its pains.

My wife, Frances, has read these pages and encourages me to continue. She also says she will help me edit my writing as needed. Though she already has heard most of these tales of my early existence, she is glad I am putting them down on paper for her own private reading. I do so to please her.

CHAPTER 2

IN WHICH I BECOME FRIENDS WITH SHERMAN

William Tecumseh Sherman seldom let a moment pass in silence. A more talkative individual never existed, yet for all his chatter he seldom wearied the listener, for he always had something of interest to say. If you had pressing thoughts on your mind, he would not demand your undivided attention. No, he would let you think to yourself while he continued to think aloud. Being reticent by nature, I grew to know his voice very well.

"Cump" Sherman is now the most hated man in the South, more despised than Lincoln or Grant. I am merely an imp of the devil, but Sherman is considered Satan himself. He was only a nervous, wiry, redheaded boy when he became my roommate.

"You're a plebe?" Sherman asked after we introduced ourselves. "Good Lord, I thought you were an upperclassman. How old are you anyway?"

"I am only twenty, not a Methuselah," I replied. "And you would be, say...twelve?"

"Sixteen, by God, and I'm old enough for anything. And where in the South are you from?"

"Southampton County, Virginia. And you?"

"Ohio, by God. The West. And we Westerners are starting to

drive the wagon now that Andy Jackson's in the White House. You Virginians have held the whip hand too long."

"That may be. I would have voted for Jackson had I been old enough. I only hope Ohio will bring forth a George Washington or a Thomas Jefferson in our future."

"I know it will. I'm glad you like Jackson. We'll get along."

Cump came from a prominent family, which I'm sure helped him gain entry to West Point at such an early age. His nickname came from his middle name, Tecumseh, the great Shawnee Indian chief. Sherman's family connections would help him several more times in his life, especially early during the South's rebellion.

I had already been at the Academy for several weeks when Sherman arrived. I went there before the start of classes with the congressman's admonition in my ears. I wanted to prepare myself for a rigorous academic ordeal and instead found that a young man's entrance to the Point demanded little more than simple reading and arithmetic. No matter, my education had already begun on my journey through the North.

Except for when the trails of wild animals led me into North Carolina, I had never been out of Virginia and barely out of Southampton County. I knew my home state was the cultural and historic heart of the nation, yet the wonders of Virginia's western mountains were unknown to me, and Richmond to the north was only a place of legend. When I first passed through the state's capital city, I was suitably impressed by a metropolis of sixteen thousand people, so teeming compared with Jerusalem's few hundred souls. I was less entranced by our nation's capital, larger than Richmond but far dirtier and smellier. I was glad to leave Washington after my visit with Mr. Mason.

The North, though, how the North dazzled me. That part of the United States was becoming industrialized, with bigger cities and factories undreamed of in the South. It was exhilarating to witness such progress, to sense that we might no longer have to depend on the whims of nature but instead force the Earth to do our bidding.

Most Southerners saw only the evil in Northern cities, the

squalor and crime in the slums where the laborers lived, so many of them foreigners, Irish and whatnot. My response is that those Irish were better off jostling in American cities than starving back in their rural homeland. Too many Southerners, like the English lords they emulated, saw only the beauty in their bucolic life, ignoring the burden it placed on the serfs, be they Negroes or poor whites. The latter, condemned as mudsills or white trash, often yearned to buy slaves themselves and rise beyond their station. Though Jefferson spoke of the virtues of the small yeoman farmer, even middling men like my father felt scorned by larger plantation owners such as our third president. And did the peculiar institution ensure prosperity? Northern farms without slaves seemed more flourishing than many I passed in Virginia on the way to West Point.

No, my journey North did not turn me against my home state. I still loved Virginia, as I do now, and felt homesick for the familiar sights of my boyhood. As beautiful as the upper Hudson River could be, it was still populated by strangers who spoke a language with strange accents compared with the pleasant speech of Southampton County. But I was so grateful to go beyond its borders. The Army gave me the chance to truly know the United States and the North American continent. My military travels eventually would take me from ocean to ocean, from Central America to Alaska. This lifelong pilgrimage began with my journey to the U.S. Military Academy.

There was little unity in the United States in the year 1836, and our path even then was veering toward Fort Sumter. The divisions were between East and West as well as North and South. Except for the pioneers pushing westward, few Americans were widely traveled, and we looked at people from outside our own regions with suspicion.

Thank goodness Sherman and I had a common respect for Old Hickory. Ohio was still part of the Western frontier in those days while Virginia was proud of its longtime leading role among the states. We both looked with dismay at our third roommate, Stewart

Van Vliet, a Yankee from Vermont. Southerners and Westerners were united in their distrust of those sharp-dealing Easterners, especially someone from oh-so-clever New England.

"Stewart, loan me half a dollar," Sherman might say.

"When will you pay me back?" Van Vliet would reply.

"The same as ever. When my family sends me money."

"That makes $10 you owe me. Don't they teach you thrift out there in Ohio?"

"Damn it, Stew, just 'cause you have money doesn't mean you have to act so superior."

"I'm from New England, Billy. I don't act superior to you rustics, I *am* superior!"

"Are you going to let that stand, George?" Sherman asked me.

"I heard no insult," I'd say. "Virginia has no rustics, and even so, we're superior to New England puritans."

"Those of us at Plymouth Rock did better than you ne'er-do-wells at Jamestown," Van Vliet replied.

"Hush up, both of you," Sherman interrupted. "Give me the half-dollar, Stew, or neither of you will get any of my Ohio hash."

"Oh, very well, here it is, Billy. Now feed George. He looks ravenous."

Van Vliet was actually quite generous and usually forgot about Sherman's debts. Would that the national tensions had melted away as quickly as ours did in that West Point room. We three became lifelong friends—and the Point helped create many other friendships that crossed the Mason-Dixon Line and the peaks of the Appalachians.

What united us in our early Academy days was the hazing from the upperclassmen. Too often they treated plebes as if they were sulking mules in need of a whip. We would not put up with it in our room.

Once an upperclassman paraded in without our leave and attempted to give us orders after the school day was done. Sherman was stronger than he looked, and Van Vliet was also sturdy. Knowing they were there to reinforce me, I was emboldened to stand up to this arrogant cadet. I told him that if he did not leave at once, he would depart through the window. Dreading defenestration, he backed away, and the three of us were never bothered again by upperclassmen.

Let me be clear—as an officer, I have always been firm in my discipline with those who do not obey my orders as quickly as I give them. But I have never tried to inspire fear in my troops, the kind of fear upperclassmen delighted in. If my troops are to hate someone, let them hate the enemy, not me. Nearly all men make good soldiers if you treat them like men.

With the hazers at bay, I found life tolerable at the Point. The constant drilling was a necessary method to build military spirit. Order and neatness are good qualities to possess, and we learned their value. I must make allowances for Sherman. Cump was never as well-groomed as Van Vliet, whose record and uniform were always spotless. Stewart's neatness helped make him the best supply officer in the Union Army during the Southern rebellion.

Billy, on the other hand, often had grease spots on his uniform from making his famous hash, which cost him many demerits but filled many a stomach. Meal time during daylight hours always seemed scanty, made worse by upperclassmen who often ordered us from the table before we could do justice to our plates. It is a wonderment I filled out as well as I did during my cadet years.

As far as classical studies were concerned, an education at West Point was superb, the equal of William & Mary or Harvard. I preferred the study of nature, and I found the subjects of geology, astronomy, and botany quite rewarding. During free time on Sunday afternoons, one could often find me wandering around the Hudson collecting specimens.

On military matters, surprising as this may be, West Point's offerings all too often proved inadequate in the forge of war. I would make many changes if I were on the faculty again. Though we were taught the basic knowledge of infantry tactics, artillery, and fortification, there was little said about the practical problems of leadership in peacetime or under fire.

The greatest emphasis was on engineering, a vital subject to be sure, especially in fortifications. There was still anxiety in the 1830s that the British might again attack the United States, so stronger forts were desired to hold off the Redcoats. Yet I maintain that the Point in those days cared more for engineering than it did for soldiering. When we graduated, we knew how to build a bulwark but next to nothing about shepherding a division, a corps, or an army of the size we would lead starting in 1861.

The weapons of that rebellion were far advanced from our training with short-range muskets. No matter how the South lagged in modern industry, when it came to the mechanics of killing, the rebels drew nearly even with the North in Yankee ingenuity. But many generals (scores of them Southern) were slow to adjust to the greater range of modern killing devices. There are more than a half a million dead men from the North and South to prove it.

It was a different war than those fought by Napoleon, yet too many generals were tardy in fathoming this and still revered the Corsican's methods. Why emulate Napoleon at all, unless you wish to end your days in humiliating exile on Saint Helena?

It is humbling to realize that an untutored rebel like Nathan Bedford Forrest, a slave trader who received little schooling in his Mississippi youth, learned the science of war far better than nearly anyone who graduated from West Point. If not for his record of cruelty to black Union soldiers and his leadership of the Ku Klux Klan, I would nominate this former cavalryman for the faculty today. His astounding success is worthy of several new chapters in books about original tactics and strategy.

Of the three roommates, I brought up the rear in academics. Sherman was sixth among the forty-two graduates in the class of 1840, ahead of the dapper Van Vliet in ninth place and myself in twelfth. Without all those demerits for grease stains, Cump might have ranked first. Paul Hebert, who stood at the top of our class, was more noted as a governor of Louisiana than for his military service. He joined the rebellion in 1861, winning no plaudits as a grayclad general.

I remember the denunciations some in Congress made against the Academy when I was there, that it was soft and aristocratic. Those were false accusations, for the school was strenuous both physically and academically, and there were young men from all ranks and sections of the American democracy. Sherman may have come from a leading family, but Van Vliet and I had more humble beginnings. As much as I have just written in criticism of West Point, I must defend it. Incomplete as the school's military education proved to be outside of the classroom, my mind still had been trained to absorb everything I could learn in the field.

The friendships I made at West Point provided great solace for the spartan conditions of an Army career. Sherman and Van Vliet of course. There was William Rosecrans, who was kind enough to say I looked like Gilbert Stuart's painting of Washington, which provoked Sherman to respond that "we should fit Thomas with a powdered wig." So "Washington" was among my nicknames. "Old Tom" was another, since I was older than other plebes, as Cump was always quick to remind my classmates.

There were many other names I knew from my years at the Point. Too many of them later wore the gray of rebellion, a color they appropriated from the honorable uniform of the Corps of Cadets. Richard Ewell, Bushrod Johnson, Daniel Hill, and William Hardee became generals for the rebels. So did Braxton Bragg, a handsome man in his Academy days, now uglier than Beelzebub. No, that is unworthy of me. I will write more of Bragg later.

There was James Longstreet, for whom I later came to have the greatest military respect, notwithstanding his wearing of gray. Like me, he had an exaggerated reputation for being ponderous. His corps was one of the hardest-hitting in the Southern army, and I'm told that his defensive theories might have saved many Southern lives, if Lee had listened to him. I wish Longstreet had come North with me—I would have listened to him intently.

Don Carlos Buell and Joe Hooker, future Union generals, were also at the Point when I drilled there. Good men, but the war was not kind to them, not as kind as it was to Grant.

Yes, I knew Ulysses "Sam" Grant as a cadet. He was three years behind me and left little impression on my memories of those days, save that he was a widely respected horseman. Certainly he did not then have a reputation for intemperance. I do not mean to belittle him here, only to state that he was not among my circle of close friends. Upperclassmen rarely became chums with plebes. Was I cruel to him then in some thoughtless manner? I think not. Whatever resentments he had (and still has) against me stem from the decisions of 1862 and 1863.

I knew that many of my schoolmates had the potential for military glory. Despite all the sectional tensions that were rising everywhere, I did not dream that so much of my friends' glory would come from the opposite side of the battlefield. These men would want me dead, and I would not greatly mourn their passing, only their treason.

But in 1840 we were united as brothers in arms, not contemplating how the foolishness of politics, commerce, and race would drive us apart. We wanted glory, a war to fight, for what good are young officers unless you can send them into battle?

During my final months as a cadet I read about the Florida Territory, a former Spanish possession that remained an unconquered part of the American nation. Call it an early appearance of prescience in my career. My interests, as always, were more geared toward nature, the animals, plants, and waterways of an exotic region. There were also descriptions of Indian life. These Indians were raiding settlements, killing whites, freeing blacks. All of us young graduates hoped for assignment there, to dip our swords in first blood. Yes, there were those of us who uttered such grandiose expressions in our daily language. Sherman, no doubt.

I received my diploma, a commission as second lieutenant, and a furlough. I went home to Virginia. Before I left the Point, I also took an oath of loyalty to the United States.

CHAPTER 3
IN WHICH I SEE THE ELEPHANT

As Cump put it, "War is all hell, you cannot refine it." Sherman's Civil War eloquence notwithstanding, Florida was one of the places I served in my youth that was a hell in and of itself, even without the dogs of war.

Bragg told me of that Hades when I reported to an artillery company at Governors Island in New York. He had already seen service in Florida and witnessed the savages launching their raids from the devil's own jungles. In November of 1840, we sailed toward my first test of arms.

I was assigned to Fort Lauderdale, a primitive little settlement of tame Indians. Most of the fighting savages, a loose confederation of tribes called the Seminoles, were inland. Closer to my camp were panthers and alligators, though I would rate the greater danger as coming from the malaria, the mosquitoes, and the fleas that were ever present.

There was compensation in the plentiful seafood, and I was given the job of feeding the troops with tasty fish and turtles. The soldiers grew tired of the ocean's bounty, however, and I was obliged to hunt for deer and turkeys, a skill I had acquired as a boy. I did my job well, which in the Army tradition meant that I then

received more jobs as the reward for my proven competence—
quartermaster and ordnance officer, for example.

For a year I was thus occupied, experiencing no combat.
Looking back on my Florida service, I realize that the government
made many mistakes in its war against the Seminoles. We were far
too piecemeal in our activity, allowing the savages to find sanctuary
in their swampland. One giant offensive might have finished them,
but we never had enough arms and men for such a drive. The
Seminoles, who first fought against Americans in 1817, were not
completely vanquished until 1858.

Well, even if I could have conjured a grand offensive when I was
a young officer, I would not have been listened to by any elder in
command. So I awaited my turn for action and pondered how I
would conduct myself when I "saw the elephant," the droll expression I learned from old soldiers about encountering for the first
time something as monumental and fearsome as war. I took
comfort from my inner assurance that the Seminoles could be no
worse than Nat Turner's horde. Indeed, some of the tribesmen were
said to be escaped slaves or their half-Indian offspring.

My curiosity was quenched in November of 1841 when I was
made second in command of a detachment of sixty men. Led by
Captain Richard Wade, we paddled a river in a dozen canoes. Our
orders were to ransack the savages' villages. That we did, killing
eight warriors (two of them boys), capturing nearly sixty natives,
and destroying their homes and food. None of our force was slain. I
acquitted myself well and won a brevet promotion for gallantry and
good conduct to first lieutenant on Captain Wade's recommendation.*

The sight of dead bodies did not upset me. I had seen worse in
the Turner uprising. Through all of 1841 I had heard tales of the
ways Seminoles tortured their white captives, so I was glad to help
ensure the Indians received retribution.

---

* Editor's note: A brevet rank was a temporary promotion for outstanding service
in times of need. It usually did not mean more pay or authority.

That gladness did not mean I loved my first taste of combat as a drunkard loves ale, only that I was beginning to learn that I was good at war. The object of any battle is to win it and survive to enjoy the victory. I observed that it is easier to achieve these objectives by remaining calm and allowing one's logic to guide one's actions.

One could argue that the only logical action in battle is to flee it with all possible speed. Such flight is merely animal panic. Logic, the human instinct that is one of God's gifts to us, allows us to use reason to conquer our obstacles. If we stifle that first attack of panic, our logical instincts will guide us even when danger is rushing toward us. I would have much to learn in the next thirty years of soldiering, but it was reassuring to discover on that Florida riverbank that my instinct was to remain calm and not to panic.

Mrs. Thomas asks me if I was fearless. No, Frances, I have never been without fear. Fear is not the same as panic. It is fear that makes us careful, that leads us to instinctively reconnoiter our surroundings to make them familiar and to devise systematic provisions for dangerous circumstances. If you use your rational fear to logically prepare for peril, you can calmly overcome the irrational panic that leads to defeat.

But I must admit that my calmness on my first day of combat was supported by the fact that I was commanding Army veterans, men who had volunteered for the service and were not intimidated by the smell of gunpowder and blood. Their steadiness was a blessing for a young officer.

The success of this expedition seemed to convince the Indians to move farther inland, giving some security to the settlers in east Florida. This was reasonable, since a barbarous people should always bow to a civilized race. The sad irony was that the "civilized" race of Anglo-Saxons brought their peculiar institution with them, and the Army's action helped smooth the way for Florida's entry into the Union as a slave state. (Perhaps Florida should be set aside as a homeland for former slaves. It is only sparsely settled by whites. I shall mention that to President Grant if he ever seeks my advice, unlikely as that may be.)

These perturbations were not in my thoughts during my Florida sojourn. Early the next year I was allowed to tour more of the South. Our company was sent to New Orleans to refit. It amazed me that such a pleasure-loving French city could exist in the same country as traditional Richmond and business-driven New York. We are lucky that the United States only broke in two during the rebellion and not into a shifting mosaic such as the one that plagues Europe.

It was enlightening to see the city that Andrew Jackson saved from the British. He and his forces displayed laudable grit during that 1815 engagement, but a study of it convinced me that if the British had prepared properly, they would have won the Battle of New Orleans in a rout. Thankfully for my country, the British were not commanded by a soldier of high distinction such as the Duke of Wellington, who in 1815 still had Napoleon to keep him occupied in Europe.

An Army officer never has a fixed abode. This constant move-ment was congenial when I was a young buck. I attended an opera in New Orleans and dined on food that my palate remembers with pleasure. From New Orleans I was sent to Charleston, a city just as charming in its way, despite the secessionist temper in South Carolina. We officers were warned not to talk politics with the fire-eaters, those quick-to-anger supporters of slavery who considered any stance against bondage to be an affront to their honor. With that understood, we often accepted the fine offerings from their tables. My West Point roommates were there, as were Bragg and other friends such as Robert Anderson. The latter, a former instructor of mine at the Academy, would valiantly resist the evil side of Charleston nineteen years in the future when he would command Fort Sumter.

After my first two years of duty, I earned leave to be reunited with my family in Virginia. The sight of my loved ones and home was never so precious to me. Virginia is still my home, regardless of what Virginia may say.

The only sadness during my visit was the state of the family farm, which was not as well run as during my father's life. Had I had stayed home, I might have kept it more prosperous. My mother and siblings could only do as much as their abilities allowed them. They worked hard, almost as hard as their slaves. At least they were not mistreating Sam and the other servants, who were delighted to greet me.

Was I tempted to resign from the Army and restore my family's fortunes? No, my duty and my friendships kept me cheerfully tethered to my military calling. I enjoyed visiting other regions of the nation, seeing how much of the world was beyond the South Side of Virginia. Only the chance of marriage might have kept me in the Old Dominion, and no likely Virginia belle emerged during my visit.

From my home I was posted to Baltimore, another charming Southern city that in 1861 nearly joined Charleston and New Orleans in rebellion. The memories of Florida's hazards faded in the social circles of Maryland that I could enter as a decorated officer and gentleman. Some ladies there almost won my heart. Luckily nothing came of it, and I preserved my worthiness for the future Mrs. Thomas a decade hence. No, Frances, I will not tell you more about those ladies. I have never inquired about your former beaus—of whom I'm sure there were many.

Following my not onerous duties in Maryland, I was sent back to Charleston to seek recruits. A full-fledged war was approaching.

CHAPTER 4

IN WHICH WE WAGE WAR AGAINST MEXICO

Some tiff in Texas turned into a war with Mexico. In the short run it gave satisfaction to us young West Pointers, but in the long run it gave more fuel to the Southern fire-eaters and Northern abolitionists. Bringing Texas, a slave state, into the Union only sped up the process that led to the Southern rebellion.

Sherman differed.

"Had we let Texas stay independent, it would have blocked us from the Pacific," Cump insisted. "Hell, the British had their eyes on Texas back then. So did the French. We couldn't let the Redcoats or the frogs take it."

I remember Sherman making this point during a meeting we held after Atlanta's surrender in 1864. I doubt that I introduced the topic of foreign politics into the conversation, but that never kept Sherman from advancing his opinions.

"That slavery existed in Texas was a bad piece of gristle to swallow, I admit," he said. "It was still a chance we had to take, whether the South had rebelled or not. I mean, would you have preferred that Mexico have California? America was meant to span all the land between the oceans. We were meant to be the colossus of North America. Hell, the Union has a couple of million men under arms right now—after we finish whipping the rebs, we ought to head north and take Canada away from the British."

"You must have been dazzled by all that Manifest Destiny nonsense the newspapers used to blare about," I replied. "It's good to have California's gold, but all Texas means to me is a Comanche arrow in the chest."

"Slow Trot, you were just too slow to dodge that arrow."

"Go to blazes, Cump. You never fought the Comanches—and you hardly fought the Mexicans, either. You were stationed out in California where they surrendered without any fuss."

"Well, there was some bloodshed, but not where I was."

"Well, bless your luck. Then you left the Army to go into that banking foolishness."

"Banking isn't foolish except when I do it," Sherman grinned. "But I still say that when we put ol' Jeff Davis in irons, we should cross the St. Lawrence and make Canada our next state. John Bull could never stop us."

"I must differ with you there. To beat the British would cost us more blood than a dozen Kennesaw Mountains, and we don't have that much to spare."

Sherman's grin dissolved into a frown. He didn't want to hear the word "Kennesaw," at least from me. He changed the subject, probably to something like Roman centurions or Mongol horsemen.

Had Sherman pressed me further on Mexico, I would have admitted that yes, sooner or later, the United States would need to fight the former Spanish colony. Like the Indians, the Mexicans simply had to bow to the stronger civilization.

Young soldiers need no justification for war. We would have been just as happy to fight Britain over the possession of Oregon, the other international dust-up of the 1840s. President James Polk settled the Oregon crisis successfully, so we fought Mexico instead.

In mid-1845, I was in artillery Company E, commanded by Bragg, as we made our way south by stages, first New Orleans, then the port of Corpus Christi on the disputed Texas border. The closer we got to the Rio Grande, the more the United States and Mexico squabbled over where the border would be.

Company E drilled as we waited for General Zachary Taylor and several infantry companies to appear. After Taylor arrived, we passed most of the winter preparing for the commencement of hostilities. In February 1846 Taylor received orders to advance to the Rio Grande, about a hundred miles south.

Despite being nicknamed "Old Rough and Ready," Taylor was actually a friendly sort—a Kentucky Indian fighter still vigorous at age sixty. This plainspoken frontiersman had many strongpoints as a leader, but he certainly wasn't ready for this campaign, a failing that made a great impression on me. We had to wait several weeks for more wagons and mules before our force of four thousand men could move. Hurriedly building a fort on the north bank of the river, we watched as the Mexicans just as quickly fortified themselves on the south.

The beginning of the war was not auspicious for the American forces. Many of our dragoons were defeated or captured, and our supply of munitions and food was inadequate. By late April Taylor went back to Port Isabel, twenty-five miles north, trying to establish supply lines. Major Jacob Brown commanded the forces that were left behind. He was dead by early May, struck by a Mexican shell. The fort and the future town were named for him.

The enemy crossfire that killed Brown rarely let up in the first days of May. We grew weary and sick from lack of sleep. About fifteen more of our men died from the shelling. I was niggardly with our artillery response, preferring not to waste our few shells on the strong Mexican position.

Insults in Spanish assaulted our fort as often as the enemy artillery fire. The Mexicans even demanded our surrender. We never considered accepting the demand. All Americans remembered the fate of the Texas defenders of the Alamo and Goliad in 1836, so we knew we could expect no Mexican mercy.

Almost as deadly as the Mexican shelling were the insects and reptiles that invaded our confines, and the limited supply of water. The heat and the crowded conditions kept many men off their feet.

Taylor, with plenty of wagons filled with supplies, appeared the second week of May and relieved us by pummeling the Mexican forces at Resaca de la Palma. I was especially happy to shell the defeated enemy as they retreated south.

I give great credit to Taylor for his determination and coolness under fire, but it was only his good fortune and God's blessing that the defenders of Fort Brown were not annihilated while he was away seeking supplies.

I never forgot the lessons I received in the Mexican War, more valuable than any military strategy class I sat through at West Point. One must be completely prepared before initiating a major advance, with secure supply bases and lines of communications to the rear. This philosophy gave me a reputation for caution, even slowness. It also kept me from ever losing a battle when I was entirely in command.

Grant and Sherman developed a different philosophy, successful in the end but with weaknesses that needlessly cost Union lives. I will write more of this later, for now I only remember the relief of knowing the enemy was gone from the banks of the Rio Grande.

After a short respite we crossed the river and headed for Reynosa. The only action we had during this advance was trying to convince the Texas Rangers, the state's irregular military police unit, to stop slaughtering Mexican civilians. The Rangers claimed it was just vengeance for the Alamo.

I was given command of two twelve-inch field pieces before we marched on from Reynosa, a pleasant place with high elevation and ripe watermelons, then to the hot and disease-ridden village of Camargo, which did have excellent fried peaches. A soldier on campaign remembers good meals on the rare occasions he finds them. While we marched on toward the major northern city of Monterrey, I enjoyed oranges, grapes, and other fruits in abundance. I estimate I weighed two hundred pounds in those days, proof of a healthy appetite even in war.

Monterrey was a stronghold in the heights, a beautiful place to mar with battle. Cathedrals towered over stout fortifications of adobe. After the horror of being besieged at Fort Brown, it improved our spirits to be the besiegers.

Our guns began firing in September of 1846 but made little initial impression on the thick walls. Street fighting followed, vicious at times as bullets rained on our artillery. The Mexicans had ten thousand men against our 6,600. I say men, but at least one charge of Mexican lancers was led by a woman in a captain's uniform. I don't know if she survived our volley. Valor was common on both sides of the war.

On September 23 we took the city. While the main plaza was still being contested, Taylor and a few members of his staff walked down the street to gauge the situations. Shots were fired at him, and he attempted to enter a store for cover. The door was locked, and even through the din of combat, I could hear the general bickering with the shopkeeper to open it. With the help of an interpreter, Taylor made himself understood and gained shelter. I was gratified to see a commanding general stay close to the fighting, but I was also relieved when he got out of harm's way, because guns under the command of myself and Lieutenant Samuel French were about to open up on the plaza. Our fire helped infantrymen take the position. I became a brevet captain following this action.

Now politics muddled the situation.

Taylor was already being hailed by the Whig Party as a potential candidate for president. Old Rough and Ready was not politically minded, but he was willing to serve as the nation's leader if elected. Polk was a Democrat, and the current president did not want a Whig-favored general becoming so popular that he might gain the White House.*

---

* Editor's note: The Whigs, the forerunners of Abraham Lincoln's Republican Party, were a business-oriented party that favored a stronger Federal government.

Over the next few months, much of our regular force was sent down to Tampico to help in General Winfield Scott's eventual capture of Mexico City. I had great respect for Scott, a fellow Virginian, but we who had served with Taylor resented the political interference that depleted his command. As it happened, Scott was also in the Whig camp, but perhaps Polk thought Taylor the more likely to seek political office.

Polk made another move that was far worse than idling Taylor. He allowed Santa Anna, the villain of the Alamo, to re-enter Mexico from his Cuban exile. Apparently, Polk thought Santa Anna would help make peace. Instead, the Mexican leader had hopes of destroying the commands of both American generals. A courier from Scott had been slain, and Santa Anna learned from the captured message how Taylor had been weakened. He thought to defeat Taylor first, then turn his attentions to Scott.

Bragg, French, and I remained part of Taylor's command, still near Monterrey in February of 1847. Santa Anna was on his way to meet us, doubtless smarter than he'd been a decade before when Sam Houston's Texans routed him at the San Jacinto River.

I was thirty years of age, and even I, a man who took pride in remaining imperturbable during times of tension, found myself wondering if my span of years might be nearing its end. We had 4,650 men; the Mexicans claimed to muster twenty thousand.

Taylor found a good site to make a stand, an area called the Narrows near the hacienda of Buena Vista. It was a rough country of gorges and gullies in the mountains, but Taylor's position had a thin passage at one end that was very defensible.

The next morning was a scenic one to behold. Our bands played stirring music like "Hail, Columbia" as we watched the Mexican army, dressed in uniforms of many colors, take the field. We Americans wore our tattered blue.

The Democrats in those days were more agricultural and working class, and wanted the states to have the greater power. Most Democrats favored Negro slavery, as did many but not most Whigs. Those Whigs who opposed slavery would eventually break away to form the Republican Party.

Santa Anna sent a message insisting on our surrender, which Taylor ignored. There was only minor fighting that day, and we spent another cold night sleeping beside our weapons before the battle began in earnest the next day, February 23. I commanded a field gun, which we fired as rapidly as possible. It was on one side of the Second Illinois Volunteers, with French's gun on the other.

Our artillery tore into the enemy. There is no glory in death by cannon ball, only the indecency of mutilation. Today I can admire the Mexicans for their gallantry in continually advancing in the face of our fire, but at the time I was irritated by their persistence. They forced a retreat by a company on our left. The Illinois fighters stood firm, however, and French and I continued fighting.

Bragg was timely with his reinforcements, as was Colonel Jefferson Davis with his Mississippi Rifles. I was deeply grateful to have such worthy men on my side.

We might have won the battle then and there if the Mexicans had not sent a flag of truce. Our artillery halted firing, yet the Mexican guns kept thundering, allowing their soldiers trapped against a mountainside to instigate a new charge with Santa Anna's reserves. Our forces suffered heavy losses and began to give way.

I looked around and found myself almost alone with my cannon, surrounded by fallen soldiers and dying mules and horses. The Mexicans continued advancing as my few surviving men and I kept firing our gun. With each shot, we let the recoil move the gun back a few feet so that we would give ground only grudgingly.

Some fellow officers later seemed to imply that I should have halted firing and dashed to the rear, that I was too deliberate in my actions. I responded that my men and I saved my section of Bragg's artillery unit by being "a little slow." Others lauded my disinclination to retreat and gave me a nickname that pleased my pride, "Old Reliable."

Nevertheless, as we fired I looked around again and found that French and I were no longer forsaken. Bragg returned to the line, as did Davis and others.

"You look lonely, Captain Thomas," Bragg said as he appeared. "Let us give you some company."

"Thank you, Captain Bragg. It's good to see you again."

"You and French are like Horatius at the Bridge."

"May we have a better fate."

(Frances asks me if Samuel French survived. Yes, he did, but like so many of my comrades in the Old Army, he went South during the rebellion and became a general—one of no distinction. A strange case, French. Though he was from New Jersey, he allowed his Southern-born wife to induce him to become a traitor. Thank the Lord I was more fortunate in matrimony.)

Bragg and I were still resisting the Mexican advance when Taylor rode up on a white horse. He shouted to "double shot your guns and give them hell, Bragg." We did so. That command was later bowdlerized for more delicate ears to become one of Taylor's more popular presidential campaign slogans, "A little more grape, Captain Bragg." Whatever the wording, I was glad it gave deserved recognition to my friend Bragg.

Our combined artillery sent the Mexicans into retreat and won the battle. Our casualties were nearly seven hundred; the Mexicans lost almost two thousand.

By four in the afternoon, after ten hours under fire, I could let my gun rest.

CHAPTER 5

IN WHICH I FIND THE LOVE OF MY LIFE

The war with Mexico went on without me. Others got another chance at glory, and I did not begrudge them this. Buena Vista had slaked my young thirst for honors. My actions there won me my third advance in brevet rank, to major.

My finest honor came from Southampton County. When the citizens there learned of my war record, they passed resolutions praising me. Though I was proud of the respect my former neighbors showed me, I dreaded the fanfare and embarrassment of the public ceremony that would greet me when I returned.

Besides their thanks, I would also receive a splendid sword with a scabbard of silver and a pommel of gold. On its grip was the image of the legendary elephant that soldiers see in battle. My sisters have that blade yet, hidden away somewhere on the farm. I would love to see it again if those ladies would give their consent.

When I received word of the honor in Mexico, I sent Southampton my reply, which said in part: "Next to the consciousness of having done his duty, the sympathy of friends is the highest reward of the soldier."

After our victory at Buena Vista in February of 1847, General Taylor settled into camp near the battlefield, and we anxiously

awaited word from General Scott's column south of us. All communications were cut off until spring, when we learned that Scott had
taken Vera Cruz. Then, in September of 1847, he conquered Mexico
City with the help of officers such as Robert E. Lee, George Meade,
George McClellan, Sam Grant, Tom Jackson, James Longstreet,
George Pickett and many others who would be fighting each other
within fifteen years' time. From all I've been told of this offensive, I
would rank it with the most impressive military accomplishments
in recorded history.

Santa Anna lost yet again. What would become the new American Southwest was taken from him; indeed he was nearly relieved
of an entire country to rule. Some in Washington wanted to annex
all of Mexico. That would have been indigestible—all those half-
Indian, Spanish-speaking Catholics would have been difficult to
incorporate into our already turbulent United States.

Yet as I write this, I see some ironic good that could have come
from it. Instead of Americans slaughtering each other from
Virginia to Kansas in the 1860s, we would have been obliged in the
1840s and beyond to fight guerrillas in Mexico much as Napoleon's
armies did in Spain earlier this century. Lee, Bragg, and my other
fellow Southerners would have continued to be my comrades, not
my enemies.

No, let me put such speculation aside, even in jest. I see no good
in taking Mexico. Jefferson Davis and the other plantation masters
would then have attempted to expand slavery throughout the continent. There still would have been an eventual reckoning over the
peculiar institution.

Mexico and the United States made peace in February of 1848,
but the American northern army stayed in place. Taylor already
had returned to his Louisiana home, awaiting a political campaign
that would win him the White House that year despite the maneuverings of James Polk, who did not seek re-election.

Illness killed President Taylor after sixteen months in office,
leaving it to Millard Fillmore to approve the Compromise of 1850
that delayed war for a decade by limiting the extension of bondage

into the new lands. I suspect it was the stress over slavery that brought on Taylor's final ailment, killing Old Rough and Ready where Mexican bullets could not. Though Taylor was a slaveholder, I believe he would have remained loyal to the Union had he lived to see Lincoln's election. Sadly, his son Richard became a competent rebel general. Even more sadly for the Union, Zachary Taylor's son-in-law was Jefferson Davis.

Enough about the Taylor family. Still in Mexico, I yearned to see the Thomas family. Not until August of 1848 would I return to American soil, two and a half years after leaving it. Another six months would pass before I could go home to see my mother and thank my Virginia neighbors personally for their sword.

It was to be my last happy time in the Old Dominion, and that happiness was lessened by foreboding. My mother loathed the North's abolitionists. The idea of any kind of change to the South's culture and economy was as insulting as a slander against our family's virtue. I stayed mum as best I could and passed much of the time gazing at the land of my father.

(My wife asks me if I believe my father and mother would have sided with the rebellion. I'm sorry, Frances, but I will not speculate on what my parents would have done or said of me if they had still been alive while I fought against the rebels. I can withstand a great deal of pain, but I decline such conjecture. Forgive me if I seem churlish.)

I had been away from my family's farm for nearly six years, and it was still in decline. It had a worn look, as if unfertile. Our valued overseer, Sam, had passed away, and much of his farming knowledge had died with him. I remembered the loyalty Sam had shown us when Nat Turner came to our door, and I remembered my sentiment that Sam should have been manumitted as a reward. I still regret that he never had his freedom.

The rest of the servants needed new clothes and shoes, which I purchased for them. My thoughts on slavery then had not yet advanced to total abolition, but I remembered from my travels how the Northern farms flourished without bondage. Virginia was a proud place that needed to be humble enough to learn from the North.

My other siblings had scattered to various endeavors, and my two spinster sisters were leading lonely lives. My mother was becoming elderly beyond her years. They seemed resentful of me for staying in the Army instead of resigning my commission and returning to run their farm. Perhaps such a future might have appealed to me if they had done what I had requested them to do —find a suitable Virginia lady for me to marry. No such enchantress emerged in the six months I stayed with my family—a regret at the time, but one I was grateful for two years hence.

My Virginia interlude ended when my regiment was sent in September 1849 to Florida, where the Seminoles were again threatening settlers. Seeing this state again brought me no joy. Its worst feature was that it contained the person of General David Twiggs, the most wicked scoundrel I have ever known.

I should explain that while I have no love for Grant or Schofield, they are redeemed a bit because they wore blue. And yes, my opinion of Bragg is not charitable, but as I related earlier, he helped save my life at Buena Vista. Twiggs had no honor, and he would have taken pleasure in sending me to the devil—in fact he would eventually send me to a place that was a purgatory on earth.

Twiggs was one of those generals who thought his stars gave him a divine right not enjoyed since Louis XIV. His enmity toward me dated to the aftermath of the Battle of Monterrey, when I refused his request to give him a team of my artillery mules for his personal use. My refusal was justified because he only wanted the mules in order to squire an amorous Mexican lady, if a lady she truly was. Such conduct was unbecoming for an aged officer from Georgia. Twiggs' rebuffed gallantry rankled him, especially after I appealed to higher authority to keep my mules from his clutches. He never forgave me.

Thankfully, I managed to stay out of Twiggs' sight during most of my term in Florida. I traveled with George Meade, the future victor at Gettysburg, as he surveyed land for a series of forts while I supplied and garrisoned each new outpost. I also renewed my practice of collecting minerals and flowers, a hobby that would not have pleased Twiggs.

This time it took only a nominal show of force to settle down the Seminoles. I then gratefully accepted the Army's transfer to Boston, though the process of going there nearly killed me. The ship I was aboard ran into a storm off North Carolina, a situation not helped by a drunken captain. I was compelled to order him away from the helm so that the first officer could guide us out of the gale. Our woes were not over. Cholera killed nine soldiers under my command, plus two sailors. I gave a prayer of thanks for my health when I stepped onto dry land. The voyage made me grateful I chose West Point instead of Annapolis.

Within a couple of years, I was even more beholden to providence for my choice in military education. I was recommended for the artillery instructor's post at West Point by William Rosecrans, and I won the appointment. The light of my life was waiting for me.

Early in 1852 I returned to the Academy for the first time in over a decade. The superintendent for part of my stay was a man whose friendship I prized, Lee. Under his leadership, I used my Mexican War experiences, and a few French textbooks, to train a new generation of officers destined to use their military education upon each other. These young men were comparable to my peers when I was a student. Many showed the potential for brilliance, but their true worth could rarely be predicted infallibly.

Many would wear blue, praise the Lord, including David Stanley, Oliver Otis Howard, Phil Sheridan, even John Schofield. Others would wear gray. Jeb Stuart was one. Likewise, John Bell Hood, a Texan who was not gifted in academics but was blessed with a fierce determination to be a good soldier. In a dozen years, he would be the victim of my greatest examination in strategy and tactics.

Schofield would try to steal the credit for Hood's last lesson in warfare. Was that revenge for what happened at West Point?

Schofield had nearly been dismissed for hazing plebes, a practice I've hated since I was a first-year student myself.

Up until this incident, I had nothing against Schofield. He had neither impressed nor dissatisfied me as a cadet. But his hazing offenses against the plebes were most objectionable and coarse, the kind of disgusting behavior I will not describe in detail to my wife.* This gave me no confidence that he would make a skilled and honorable officer. During his court-martial, I sat on the panel in judgment of him. I voted to expel him. The majority decided he deserved a second chance.

I have never been a martinet during my Army career. I dare say I am noted for fairness, even restraint, during disciplinary matters. I still defend my vote against young Schofield. Did he ever learn of my decision? It was not something a cadet should ever know. I wonder. Despite my vote, he became a West Point graduate. Enough of that cur. I shall not let him trouble my memories of my favorite years at the Point.

In addition to my duties as artillery instructor, I taught cavalry. I loved this branch of the service best, though I was becoming a bit stout for some of the mounts. I tried not to overexert a horse, even when jumping hurdles and leading charges, enjoyable experiences when no one is shooting at you. When I conducted such exercises, the cadets would be too eager to gallop, tiring their horses too quickly. I would keep my young charges under control by calling for a "slow trot."

Thus, a nickname was born, my least favorite of the many I've received. During the rebellion, "Slow Trot" would be used derisively against me at times, often by Grant, as if speed were always a virtue. Speed is not of the essence; victory is.

On the other hand, when true love appeared, I did not tarry.

Frances Kellogg came to West Point to visit a cousin. When we

---

* Editor's note: Cadet Schofield, while serving as a teaching assistant as an upper-classman, was accused of allowing others in his mathematics classroom to make sexual drawings and jokes on a blackboard.

were introduced, she gave me a warm look of friendship and understanding, a look I had been waiting for all my life.

There was nothing coquettish about Frances, who was tall enough to look directly in my eyes. A mature woman of 31 years, she had the beauty and vigor of a girl a decade younger. When she spoke, she expressed herself with such kindness and intelligence that I was smitten. She made me tremble as Santa Anna and the Seminoles never could. Reading these words I've just written, Frances informs me that when I first addressed her, I was blushing beneath my beard. As I am blushing now.

On that day nearly 20 years ago, Frances was accompanied by her younger sister, Julia, and her mother, Abigail, the widow of a successful hardware merchant in Troy, a Hudson River community a hundred miles upstream from West Point. It is said that mothers with unmarried daughters would travel to the Academy in hopes of snaring a groom. If so, I thank Mrs. Kellogg for her excellent use of strategy.

Frances, reading these words, assures me that her mother had no such calculation. Nevertheless, my wife won me that day as decisively as Napoleon conquered at Austerlitz.

Until my thirty-sixth year, romance played little part in my life (except for that brief time in Baltimore, Frances reminds me). Otherwise, I lived a monkish existence as an officer who did not have time for a family. Rarely did I meet suitable women in my isolated outposts, and I would have no association with unsuitable ones. One can understand my disappointment when my family could not help me find a bride when I was in Virginia. I soon found that my heart's desire was in Troy, New York.

Now the best part of my life began. As an officer and a gentleman, I courted Frances, even reading poetry to her and eagerly listening to her recite verse back to me. She was known to her family and close friends as "Fanny," and I was thrilled when she allowed me the intimacy of addressing her in this manner. We met in the spring of 1852, and on November 17, we were married at the home of her uncle in Troy.

For the first and only time, I wore the sword given me by my friends in Southampton County. The blade was true steel, its silver scabbard engraved with the names of the battles I had fought in Mexico. Without hesitation, I would have handed over this object of great value to my new Yankee relatives if they had asked. Such was my gratitude to this family for giving me Frances. Better it gather dust in upstate New York than in Virginia.

No matter, Fanny's love has more than made up for the things I do not have, even that we were not blessed with children. My only regret in our marriage is that duty kept us apart for so long.

We honeymooned in New York City, returning to the Point in January of 1853. During that time, I received my peacetime promotion to captain, long overdue. All was bliss for a few months. Then the Army transferred me from my happy home, over Lee's objections. Twiggs, who I learned was responsible for the delay in my promotion, performed another act of knavery. He had me sent to Fort Yuma.

CHAPTER 6

IN WHICH I BECOME CLOSE FRIENDS WITH LEE

T he legend is that a soldier stationed at Fort Yuma died and went to Hell. Before he made his journey to the underworld, he requested some blankets, knowing full well that after being in Yuma, anyplace else would seem chilly.

Mrs. Thomas was willing to accompany me to Yuma, but no decent husband would want a woman to undergo such an ordeal. Sadly, I left Frances with her mother and sister in Troy and departed on May 1, 1853.

Getting to Yuma, an isolated way station on the Colorado River that served California-bound immigrants, was hellish enough. A sea journey took me and four artillery companies to Panama for a fifty-mile march across the isthmus. Reaching the Pacific, we sailed to San Francisco, many men falling ill by the time we arrived.

At least I had the compensation of seeing Cump Sherman again. As I related earlier in this account, he had been stationed in California during the war with Mexico, and his only excitement had been sending word to Washington of the discovery of gold. Sherman then retired from military service and became a banker in the ensuing gold rush. He congratulated me on my marriage, and I congratulated him on his new profession. He said he regretted missing all the fun in Mexico, and I assured him that there was no fun to be had. We had pleasant dinners and conversations for two weeks.

I remember that brief time in 1853 warmly as I write these lines today in 1870 in San Francisco, where I am even happier now that Mrs. Thomas is here with me.

The purgatory of 1853 resumed when my command arrived in San Diego following a voyage in a coast steamer. The Army had little understanding of the situation in Yuma, ordering us to march there in July, the hottest time of the year. Temperatures reached 130 degrees during the day, and we were able to reach our destination only by traveling at night.

During my exile in the Arizona desert, I collected plants and minerals and sent an intriguing species of bat to the Smithsonian Institution. With little else to do, I made a study of the language of the local Yuma Indian tribe.

The most noteworthy occurrence of my years in Yuma was my small role in helping gain freedom for Olive Oatman, a teen-age Mormon girl captured by Indians in 1851 after her parents and most of her siblings had been slain. The killers were probably from a band of the Apache or Yavapai tribe, who sold her to the Mohaves. She lived with them about four years, becoming a member of the tribe and bearing the facial tattoos of the other Mohaves.

In the meantime, her surviving brother kept searching for her and eventually found his way to Fort Yuma, where I encouraged him in his endeavor. When we soldiers at Fort Yuma learned she was with the Mohave band, we sent word that the Indians were to bring her in. They were a peaceful tribe and after some hesitation, did as they were instructed.

At first she was not happy being among whites, as she considered herself a Mohave in all but blood. A reunion with her brother and some white childhood friends, however, made her more receptive to us.

Though she might have had what to her was a tolerable existence among the friendly Mohaves, I had no doubt that she was much better off among her own kind. The ways of the Indians will soon die out across the nation. I was glad to hear that in 1865, Miss Oatman married a wealthy cattleman in Texas and was reported to be happy.

Little of a soldier's life resembles the chivalrous world that dwells in the novels of Sir Walter Scott, an author of little interest to me but one who inspired too many of my Southern peers with his tales of romantic warfare. At least in the case of Olive Oatman, we in the Army were able to play a small role in the freeing of an innocent, something a knight errant would salute with a tip of his lance.

Jefferson Davis rescued me from Yuma, an act of chivalry he regrets today. The gallant soldier of Buena Vista had become secretary of war, and he was organizing elite cavalry regiments based on merit rather than seniority. Unfortunately for the Union, being Southern-born was the best kind of "merit." Nearly all the officers Davis selected were from below the Mason-Dixon Line, and I now believe that in 1855 he was already preparing for the rebellion of 1861.

Only because of Bragg did I become a member of the Second Cavalry. He turned down Davis' offer, recommending me in his stead. Bragg had little respect for Davis, a disregard that Davis did not return, considering how many chances the future rebel president gave him to prove his incompetence as a commanding general.

Sherman once showed me a kind letter that Bragg wrote about me in 1855: "Not brilliant but he is a solid, sound man, an honest, high-toned gentleman, above all deception and guile, and I know him to be an excellent and gallant soldier." It is tragic to read this and know that in those days my feelings for Bragg were mutual. I lament the loss of our comradeship as much as I condemn his treason.

I accepted a commission as major in the Second Cavalry and departed Yuma in July 1855, crossing the same inferno that greeted me two years before. I sailed from San Diego to New Orleans, then took a steamship up the Mississippi to St. Louis where I joined my new unit before we would eventually set off for Texas.

Davis made sure we got only the best in horses, saddles, and

firearms. Our uniforms were out of another novelist's fevered imag-
ination—Alexandre Dumas perhaps. We wore silken sashes and
yellow trim. Our hats had ostrich plumes, the kind of cavalier
folderol that Jeb Stuart took to extremes when he wore rebel gray.
Stuart was in the First Cavalry, an excellent body of men led by Joe
Johnston. The Second was Davis' special interest, however. Sidney
Johnston led it at first, and Robert E. Lee was second in command.
Among my fellow officers were William Hardee, Earl Van Dorn,
Kirby Smith, and John Bell Hood—Southerners all.

Early in 1856, I was ordered to New York for recruiting duty. My
most important recruit was Mrs. Thomas, who was pleased to go to
Texas with me. Three years out of my sight had made her only
more beautiful to me. When I took command of Fort Mason in May
of that year, she made it a bastion of domestic comfort.

Fort Mason was part of a string of forts occupied by the Second
Cavalry from San Antonio to Brownsville. Texas was (and is) an
untamed frontier. Comanches and Kiowas were cruel and brutal
warriors who gave no quarter, though we Americans could be
grateful to them for keeping the ancient Spanish conquistadors
cowering south of San Antonio.

The state's police force, the Texas Rangers, did what they could
to stop the Indian outrages, but Texans were grateful to have men
in Federal blue uniforms in the 1850s. Without Federal cavalry to
man the forts during the Southern rebellion, the Indians took the
offensive, nearly driving the whites out of all but the most settled
areas of Texas.

I saw much service with Colonel Lee, and our friendship that
began when we were on the West Point faculty became even
stronger in Texas. Always a handsome man, Lee in those days had
dark hair and a mustache, not the gray beard that became famous
during the 1860s.

We journeyed through much of Texas conducting court-
martials, one of the more disagreeable duties of military life, but
his company made it most amicable. We spoke often of our varied

lives in the service. Mrs. Thomas was honored when he dined with us.

Lee came from one of the more famous families in the Old Dominion, yet he did not put on aristocratic airs around a fellow Virginian from more modest circumstances. His father was Henry "Light Horse Harry" Lee, one of George Washington's best generals in the Revolutionary War. His wife was Mary Anna Randolph Custis, a step-great-granddaughter of Washington.

Lee was as loyal to the Union then as I was, and he saw the evil in slavery and the difficulty in ridding the nation of the practice. I remember a snatch of a conversation we had in 1856:

"I know you are from Southampton County. I've heard tell that you were in danger from Nat Turner's uprising," Lee mentioned after we enjoyed one of Frances' fine meals of roast turkey and plum pudding.

"Indeed I was. My family had to flee from them."

"It is said that you rode to warn your neighbors in the manner of Paul Revere. I salute you."

"You're too kind. Most of what I did was delivering messages as the militia was forming. A man named Gurley gave the first warnings of the revolt. I was just a frightened boy wanting to help."

"Still, I warrant it was a worthy deed. Did your servants join the uprising?"

"No, they fled from Turner as soon as they could. They were loyal and honorable, thank the Lord."

"God bless them. I believe my family's servants would have been loyal, too, had they heard of Turner. Yet I cannot be sure."

"Yes, I know our servants wished to be free, but they resisted bloodshed. And they still deserve freedom, though my family says our farm would wither without them."

"Yes," Lee said. "Some of my family's servants deserve freedom too. But many of them are not intelligent or responsible enough for that gift. I own few slaves myself, but my father-in-law has hundreds. He prides himself on being the step-grandson of our first president, so I hope he'll follow Washington's example and manumit his servants. Yet so much of his wealth is counted in the value of his slaves that he may be loath to let them go."

"We're in a trap we cannot extract ourselves from," I replied. "I'm no abolitionist, but eventually we must free ourselves from slavery or we will have dozens of Turner revolts yearly."

"I pray to God to help us find a solution," Lee answered. "It may be for future generations to find it, perhaps in a thousand years. For now, we must trust to honor but remain on guard. So many of the Africans in our country would turn the South into Santo Domingo if they could."

"I pray you are wrong and that God shows us a solution."

"Amen," Lee answered. "I wish the North shared our civilization. They are growing so quickly up there, not in a good way. I fear instead of a City of God, they are building a Tower of Mammon."

"The North's economy is much more varied than our King Cotton. If money is power, they will soon have more of it than the South."

"God forbid that happens. They would treat the South as Britain once treated us."

Many have asked if Lee ever gave a hint to me that he would not maintain his loyalty to the Union. I was then unaware of such an inclination. Perhaps Lee himself did not know which path he would take or that I would not follow his lead. We had a flimsy faith that such a decision was not in our future. Military men often do not think deeply on the hated subject of politics, preferring to concentrate on our immediate duties rather than dwell on issues over which we have no control.*

---

* Editor's note: Lee was soon entangled in the complications of slavery much more than he could have foreseen. In 1857, his father-in-law died, leaving many debts but promising in his will to emancipate his servants within five years. Lee, as executor of the will, obtained leave from the Army. He wanted to pay off those debts and he tried to do so by hiring out his father-in-law's slaves to other masters. Desiring freedom and understandably dismayed at its delay, the slaves became unruly and caused Lee many difficulties. In the midst of this personal turmoil, Lee was called back to Federal service in 1859 to lead the forces that captured the abolitionist John Brown at Harpers Ferry and put an end to his attempted slave revolt.

As much as I grew to esteem Lee, an enemy came to Texas for whom my loathing knew no limits. The details of yet another spat with David Twiggs are unimportant. Only know that he came on the scene as a commander of the Department of Texas, we scuffled over a ruling in a minor court-martial, and he was angry when I was upheld. Twiggs tried to interfere in my command. I alerted my superiors in Washington of this, and the War Department quickly told him not to trifle with Second Cavalry officers. In a few years, Twiggs would play me false once more, only this time it would be treason instead of some petty act of military effrontery.

Texas was losing its charm for me in the late 1850s. After three years of Texas frontier life, Mrs. Thomas yearned to see her mother and sister again in the safety of upstate New York. Frances returned East. Our love could survive long distances, but my days were less bright without her presence.

And my mother had died. Duty kept me from going home for her funeral. I began to consider life outside the Army.

In 1859, Lee asked me to take command of Camp Cooper, where tensions were rising between Texas settlers and some peaceful Comanches. This tribe is so rarely peaceful that I could understand the settlers' hatred, but in this case those Indians living on the military reservation near Camp Cooper were blameless. Raiding parties from other branches of the tribe were stealing horses and taking shelter in the reservation, making all the Indians there guilty in the eyes of the whites. A battle that broke out between settlers and Comanches left nine men dead.

I called for reinforcements from Van Dorn's command, and we halted the clashes. Politics then played its hand, and the peaceful Comanches were ordered from the reservation. I and my command sadly escorted them to Indian Territory north of the Red River. The only good of the expedition was seeing more of the varied landscapes of Texas, exploring the sources of some of its rivers and collecting additional specimens from nature.

Indian activity renewed in 1860. Lee was unable to offer much help or advice since he was engaged in chasing off Mexican raiders along the Rio Grande. That July I led nearly 100 men on a patrol in search of the hostile Indians. The Comanches, alerted by our relatively large numbers, stayed out of sight. After four weeks in the field, two of the units under my command were detached and sent back to their home forts, and I continued on with thirty men and three friendly Indian guides.

We found a fresh trail. Up ahead we saw eleven mounted Comanches leading a herd of thirty stolen horses. We took up the pursuit, but our mounts were exhausted by the time we got within shooting distance.

Ten of the hostiles escaped, mostly due to the courage of an elder Indian who dismounted in our path and challenged us all. He must have been ritually sacrificing himself so his younger compatriots could escape. The Indian loosed many arrows, one of which glanced off my chin and came to a halt in my chest. I pulled the arrow from my body, gratified that the injury was not serious, though I still carry the scar. Three other cavalrymen were wounded.

I told my interpreter to advise the warrior to surrender, promising that we would let him live if he did. His reply was, "Surrender? Never! Come on, Longknives!"

It took at least twenty shots to put an end to this intrepid savage.

The surgeon dressed my wound and those of the other soldiers, and we carried on.

The Indian was buried. Despite the pain I felt from his arrow, I hoped this worthy foe was in the Happy Hunting Ground or wherever his tribesmen believe they go in the hereafter. In a lifetime spent fighting Seminoles, Mexicans, and Southern rebels, I have been wounded only once, by this Comanche warrior in Texas.

CHAPTER 7

IN WHICH I CHOOSE HONOR, NOT REBELLION

I n November 1860, shortly after Abraham Lincoln was elected president of the United States, I departed Texas on leave to see my wife in New York. My happiness at our approaching reunion was repressed by the knowledge that the nation was dissolving like sugar in scalding coffee.

The events of the year had forced me to pay heed to politics. For president I backed John Bell, a Tennessean committed to preserving the Union even as he endorsed slavery. He won the support of many south of the Mason-Dixon line but had no chance against Lincoln's Northern Republican onslaught. Like too many in the South who claimed they loved the Union, Bell eventually sided with the rebels. I now regret voting for him, although he was a better man than Stephen A. Douglas or John Breckinridge, the other candidates in the bitterly divided race. Should I have voted for Lincoln? Yes, but good heavens, the deluge that came with him! What would we have done in 1860 had we known all that would happen by 1865?

Though Lincoln opposed slavery, as president he was initially willing to tolerate it as long as it was limited to the South—because in 1861, his priority was holding the Union together, not freeing the

Negroes. But too many Southerners thought any limit on slavery was an unbearable affront.

Despite my distaste for the peculiar institution, I found Northern abolitionists as reprehensible as the Southern fire-eaters. The Yankees' self-righteousness galled me. They had no appreciation of the fear that John Brown's raid had put in Southerners such as my sisters. They were terrified that a new wave of armed Nat Turners would ravish and kill them without mercy.

There was also the Southern tradition of racial superiority that whites held tightly. Though never cruel to their slaves, my sisters could not comprehend the notion that Negroes were fully human beings—to them the servants were little better than horses or oxen. Making them our equals was as repugnant an idea as living in a pigsty, an attitude shared by most Southern yeomen who owned no slaves. I cannot justify their convictions, only point out that such beliefs were nearly as common among Northern whites.

And then there was the loss of wealth that would strike Southerners if servants were abruptly freed without compensation to their owners. Much of the South's fortune was based on the value of slaves. Abolitionists would hoot at this point, jeering that such impoverishment would be just what slaveholders merited. To such holier than thou Northerners, I would say that my sense of justice is not that harsh. I did not want my sisters to be poor. Whatever their failings and misjudgments, they were good women who didn't deserve poverty.

On the other hand, I disdained the eagerness of the Southern fire-eaters for secession and war. They prattled about "states' rights," a phrase that is merely the insolent belief that you can allow an outrage in your state that would be a crime within the borders of your more civilized neighbors.

The fire-eaters' arrogance about proclaiming the questionable virtues of slavery shamed me, and their presumption of Southern superiority in the fields of courage peeved me. They claimed that one Southerner was worth a dozen Yankees in a fight. I had already witnessed enough valor by my Northern comrades to know that was a lie.

And most of the fire-eaters, as well as the abolitionists, had never seen the elephant.

My own experiences with slavery made for discomfort. I brought back from Texas my body servant and a cook, whose presence was inconvenient for me in the East. I could not in good conscience sell them, and giving them their liberty was out of the question since they were not yet ready for that responsibility and in fact did not desire to be set free. I could only make sure they were well cared for when I left them at my family's Virginia home.

I am well aware that I can be accused of being a sanctimonious humbug for disapproving slavery while still owning slaves. My frail defense is one I've alluded to earlier in this account—that slavery is a trap that is onerous to break free from. I needed these servants after Mrs. Thomas returned East.

Frances, I know you disapproved of their purchase, but I was unable to find freedmen for the jobs. You predicted that buying and selling human beings would be troubling to my soul, and you were correct—I never had to conduct such business as a youth, and the reality of it greatly distressed me as a grown man. Eventually these two slaves would be emancipated, and I would send them and their children to Mississippi to be the fairly paid servants of one of my brothers, the only Thomas sibling who accepts me as a blood relation.

Though my arrow wound was fully healed, my journey East would become as hazardous as a Texas cavalry patrol. Once again, I encountered many forms of transport across a wide swath of the disunited states. It was first a stagecoach to the Texas coast, then a steamer to New Orleans, another steamer to Memphis, then the railroad to Chattanooga and on to Virginia. And then in my home state, after all my many rough passages in half-civilized regions of the continent, I suffered my only travel-related injury.

On a November evening in Lynchburg, while the train was taking on water, I stepped down on what I thought to be a road.

The moonlight fooled me, and I plummeted down an embankment and wrenched my spine seriously. The pain made it impossible to travel farther than Norfolk. Mrs. Thomas received my wire in New York and came to me in Virginia, which lightened my heart but did not ease the agony in my back. Not until mid-December was I able to visit my sisters in Southampton, where I left my Army goods and my servants.

Three weeks of rest rendered me fit enough to continue north to Washington. There I washed my hands of the ogre Twiggs, who had mediated treachery with the secessionists in Texas in the event the state tried to leave the Union. I reported him to the proper authorities. Winfield Scott, the Federal general in chief, believed my account of Twiggs' misdeeds and sent orders to recall him. But President Buchanan was lethargic and for too long kept Twiggs in his post, where the old villain was able to surrender troops and Federal property to the Texas Rangers when the state did in fact secede.

Of all the Southern officers in the U.S. Army who decamped for the rebel side, Twiggs was the most perfidious. When the others decided to rebel, most announced it immediately and resigned, keeping at least some of their self-respect if not their honor. Twiggs, on the other hand, said nothing for weeks about his turncoat decision but stayed in his Federal post as long as he could, working to supply the rebels with needed men and supplies. If I had captured Twiggs during the war, I would not have been averse to hanging him, something I would not have been willing to do to any other rebel officer. Twiggs never had to answer for his treason, at least in this life. He died of pneumonia in 1862.

Perfidious in another way was the outgoing president of the United States. In his last few weeks in office before he was replaced by Lincoln in March of 1861, James Buchanan did nothing to stave off the rebellion. Though born in Pennsylvania, Buchanan had long been known for his Southern sympathies and his acquiescence to the slaveholders. His reluctance to act against Twiggs' treason supported that traitorous sympathy. Was it active collusion on his part or the weariness of an aging politician who lacked the imagination or gumption to keep his integrity? When the fifteenth president finally dismissed Twiggs from the Army, the old general threatened to challenge the old politician to a duel. Such a farcical scene would have provided unseemly comedy in the midst of a national tragedy.

Buchanan gave statements of support to the Union during the war, but most in the North thought him little better than such faithless betrayers as Twiggs. Before he died in 1868, Buchanan wrote a memoir defending his presidency. No one believed him. I rank him as the worst president in American history.

Mrs. Thomas and I traveled on to New York, where I sought advanced medical treatment. My back made only partial improvement. Before my injury, I had given thought to leaving the Army so I could be a constant companion to my wife. Now it seemed that my back would leave me no option other than retiring from the military. I wondered what profession I was qualified for that would give Frances the better life she deserved.

My wife found a prospect for me in an advertisement from the Virginia Military Institute, which was seeking a commandant of cadets. Such a post was within my capabilities and would not be so strenuous as the cavalry. In those weeks, I stress, Frances and I were sure that Virginia would remain loyal to the Union. In January of 1861, I made inquiries about the position and was informed the vacancy was filled. But the school's superintendent recommended me to become Virginia's chief of ordnance. Though tempting, this prospect was not enough to make me leave the Army.

On March 12, I wrote Governor John Letcher: "I have the honor to state, after expressing my most sincere thanks for your very kind offer, that it is not my wish to leave the service of the United States as long as it is honorable for me to remain in it, and therefore as long as my native State remains in the Union it is my purpose to remain in the Army, unless required to perform duties alike repulsive to honor and humanity."

My critics in the South have used that letter against me on

many occasions, seeing hesitation and opprobrium in my decision to remain with the Union. I see nothing in that letter to apologize for. If my war record in service to the United States is not enough proof of my honor and humanity, I will now try to explain my reasons:

I received a superior education at West Point, something that would have been beyond my means if not for the Federal government. Upon my graduation, I took an oath to defend the United States against all enemies, foreign and domestic. Breaking such an oath is dishonorable, regardless of the example of Lee and some other Southerners whom I still respect. Redeeming such an oath seems to be justification enough for my Union loyalty, but I will offer more words if anyone in the South has the capacity to understand them.

On April 13, 1861, as soon as I knew of the attack on Fort Sumter, I wired my wife and my sisters that I would fight against the rebellion. I see no "hesitation" there. I certainly "hesitated" for a shorter time than the sainted Lee, who used words similar to the ones I wrote to Letcher as my friend made his decision to go South. Because I sought employment in Virginia during the first three months of the year, some have slandered my good name.

Here I plead guilty only to believing in the winter of 1861 that Virginia would resist the siren call of the Deep South states. It seemed incredible to me then (and now) that the Old Dominion would follow in the wake of the uncouth fire-eaters.

Virginia was a noble state, the home of Washington, Jefferson, Madison, and Monroe. How could such a birthplace of American greatness not try to find some sort of compromise and maintain the Union? Was I the only Virginian who thought there must be a way to gradually emancipate the most intelligent slaves, compensate their owners and ship the less advanced of the Africans back to their homeland or some uninhabited frontier? I truly believed that Virginia would fight against South Carolina, not for it.

In fact, many of my fellow Virginians, and citizens of other Southern states, were opposed to leaving the Union, at least until

Lincoln called for a massive army to put down the revolt in South Carolina after Fort Sumter. That threat of force was blamed for pushing Virginia and the bulk of the Upper South into secession. Yet even then, I still believe at least half the whites in the eleven seceded states wanted to stay in the Union but were bullied into rebellion by the fire-eaters and leading plantation owners. Most Southern yeomen didn't own slaves, and while they opposed Negro equality, they felt no compunction to defend the property of rich men who had little respect for less wealthy whites.

Was Lincoln's call to arms a tragic error? The Illinois lawyer made many mistakes as president, yet I cannot condemn him for this. In hindsight, I know that South Carolina and the rest of the Deep South were so obstinate and haughty that only the cannon and the bayonet would bring those states back into the fold. If Lincoln had not quickly taken decisive military action, the Union would soon have fallen apart like a moth-eaten blanket. I had presumed that my home state would show wisdom and greatness in this crisis. I will forever regret that I was entirely mistaken on this point. Though I love Virginia, I love the Union and the Constitution more.

Despite my own experience as a slaveowner, I believe that the peculiar institution is immoral in God's eyes. While my peers in the South have claimed they were only defending their homes, not slavery, it is clear that every battle they won was a victory for wrongful bondage. Although I am aware of the suffering that whites endure in the factories and slums of the North, I still consider a civilization of free men better than one based on slavery. And for more than two centuries, poor Southern whites without slaves paid a high price for Negro bondage—because the worth of their white toil was diminished by putting Africans in chains. As much as I cherish Virginia, for me to fight to preserve its slavery would have been "repulsive to honor and humanity," to quote my letter to Letcher.

If at the end of my life the Almighty asks me what I did to end injustice, I shall be proud of my answer.

Another slander against me is the accusation that I was a mugwump, trying to position myself to take the best offer, North or South. These critics say I was vainly waiting for the South to give me a general's stars because I was disappointed at my slow progress in the Federal service.

This is nonsense. My oath was more important than any disappointments over my sluggish advances in rank. And even had I had been sitting on the fence, why would I hope for the rebels to make any special entreaties? I knew or suspected that most of my fellow Southern-born officers were flocking to the traitors' banner. Many of them had outranked me in the Regular Army or had more notable reputations. Since the rebels easily attracted a surfeit of such men, there was no reason for me to anticipate any extraordinary effort to lure one more officer, one who had attained only a major's rank.

And with so many of my peers from south of the Mason-Dixon line joining the rebellion, I expected the Federal government would be wary of giving another Southerner any quick promotions in the Union Army, at least until my loyalty was assured.

I would never have reported Twiggs' treason to Federal authorities had I been contemplating the same kind of betrayal. It occurs to me now that had I joined the revolt, I might have been put under Twiggs' command. Such an insult I could not have borne.

Others have claimed that Frances Kellogg Thomas, my Northern-born wife, was responsible for my retaining my blue uniform. My wife is very intelligent, far too wise to think she can wheedle me into doing something I do not want to do. Her opinions are highly valued by me, but she does not presume to compel them on my thinking without my leave. We talked of many matters in those weeks, but not once about which side I would serve. My loyalty was understood.

What if I had been clouded in my thinking and wanted to wear gray? There was never any chance of that, but my wife's marital loyalty was also understood. If she had been willing to put up with the rigors of a Texas fort in Comanche territory, she would have been willing to go to Virginia for my sake. For her sake, I'm glad there was never any possibility that she would need to do so.

Frances, having just read this account, reaffirms my words and says she would have followed me South, for better or worse. She quotes from the Bible and the story of Ruth. "Where you go I will go, and where you stay I will stay. Your people will be my people."

My reply to her is that besides my wedding vows, I took a vow to the American people. All the Americans were my people, not just Virginians.

And I was not the only Virginian, or Southerner for that matter, who rejected the rebellion. Thousands and thousands in the border states stayed with the Union, and there were pockets of loyalty in most of the seceded states. In fact, a cavalry unit from Alabama would perform admirably for the Union during the conquest of Georgia. Even Robert E. Lee's family was divided on secession. I know of a Lee sister, as well as a cousin and a nephew, who remained loyal to the Union.

Also, there were scores of high-ranking Southern-born officers in the Federal forces who remained true to their oath, including Admiral David Farragut, a Tennessee native who captured New Orleans and Mobile for the Union Navy. From my home state most prominently was Winfield Scott, but he was not alone. Three of every ten Virginia-born officers in the Regular Army refused to join in the treason, including Jeb Stuart's father-in-law, General Philip St. George Cooke. "I owe Virginia little, my country much," Cooke said.

Yet I seemed to attract the majority of the traitors' ire during the conflict and in its aftermath. I doubt Stuart would have sent the father of his wife to the gallows, a place to which he would have consigned me.

There is a simple reason why I waited until Fort Sumter to finally announce to the nation and my family which side I would choose. I knew that once I proclaimed my decision, I would be cut off from my sisters and brothers, their love forfeit. I would no longer be welcome in the land of my father and mother, and neighbors and comrades who once befriended me would sneer at my name. Infamy, even when undeserved, is a status that most of us want to avoid for as long as possible.

When a man must hurdle an abyss to reach a place of honor on the other side, it is only natural that he pause to gather himself before making the leap. He may even be tempted to peer at the perils below. I regret that Lee and so many others jumped directly into rebellion.

CHAPTER 8

IN WHICH I BECOME A GENERAL

Frances, I have gotten ahead of myself, so please bear with me as I backtrack.

On April 10, 1861, three days before Fort Sumter, I returned to duty, my back steady enough for what had to be done. The pain never left me during the war (it plagues me even as I write this), but compared to the crippling and disfiguring wounds that thousands of others endured, a sore back is a negligible ailment.

I was ordered to take command of more than 500 loyal Federal soldiers arriving in New York's harbor after being sent away from Texas. Stepping ashore after their voyage, these troops had nothing good to say of Twiggs, calling him "Judas" and other curses with which I agreed.

I got on well with these men in New York, and I led my remnants of the Second Cavalry to barracks near the capital of Pennsylvania, Harrisburg. There, on April 13, I heard of Robert Anderson's heroism before the surrender of Fort Sumter. My telegrams to my wife and sisters I have already described, but to make sure everyone knew my stand, I went before a local magistrate and again pledged by loyalty to the Stars and Stripes.

A week later I was ordered to take some two hundred men to Washington to protect public buildings. We marched twenty miles to the train station in York, Pennsylvania. There some of the junior officers, the ones from border states, seemed hesitant about boarding. One asked me what to do. Apparently, my second oath of allegiance had not settled his doubts. I was not gentle in my reply: "We are ordered to go to Washington, and there we will go. There'll be time enough after getting there for you to decide what to do."

Shamefully, we did not get to the capital that day. Baltimore, at that time a rebel-leaning city, stood between us and Washington. Baltimore police had destroyed railroad bridges, blocking our way. I received a dispatch from the secretary of war, telling me that President Lincoln had ordered us back to York to prevent bloodshed.

One could argue that this was the only defeat ever suffered by any force entirely under my command.

When we returned to camp, I was cruelly disappointed to learn that Virginia had seceded on April 17. To finally know for certain that the place of your birth had become enemy territory gave me the kind of agony I would have felt had a leg been amputated.

What made the torment greater was being informed that my friend Lee had made the greatest mistake of his noble life by following Virginia into folly. His rank of lieutenant colonel fell to me. I had expected no quick promotions if I stayed loyal to the Union, and I felt no pleasure in being wrong.

Loyalty to his state rather than his nation played a part in Lee's decision, though I suspect he also feared that if he didn't side with Virginia's rebels, they would have seized his estate in Arlington, leaving his ailing wife homeless. In a sad irony, Lee's treason did nothing to protect her. The Arlington house would be occupied by Federal forces soon after Lee joined the rebellion, and the farmland would eventually become a Union cemetery. Mrs. Lee had to move to Richmond.

How I wish my friend had joined me on the Union side. Lincoln had even offered Lee the command of the Federal forces defending Washington.

Ten days later, another painful promotion came my way when I became a full colonel to replace the departing Sidney Johnston, another capable man who, with a faulty sense of honor, had become a traitor. Each advance in rank meant I was required to again renew my oath. A fellow officer asked me if I minded this repetition. "I don't care a snap of my fingers about it," I replied. "If they want me to take the oath before each meal, I am ready to comply."

Oaths of loyalty I had in abundance; what I needed was more good men. Too many were literally lacking in good horse sense, some even plunging from the mildest mounts. This was not a weakness in the rebel forces, as Stuart and others would soon demonstrate. On the Northern side of the Mason-Dixon Line, I was forced to ask each would-be cavalryman the most basic question: "Can you ride?" By the end of the war, I am proud to say, most Union cavalry could ride like Virginians.

In those green days of 1861, I tried to give the raw volunteers firm but encouraging leadership. Yet it was sometimes necessary to let the new officers learn the art of discipline for themselves. Lt. Thomas Anderson, nephew of the defender of Sumter, came to me complaining of a noncommissioned officer who was having a fit and vowing to shoot anyone who approached him.

"What am I to do with him?" Anderson implored.

"In the last resort, death," I replied in the same detached manner that my superiors used with me when I was a shave-tail lieutenant.

Like a good junior officer, Anderson solved the problem peacefully without involving his superiors. That's the reason the good Lord made lieutenants. Not long afterward, Anderson solved another problem, the commerce of whiskey in the ranks. I asked him how he had ended this illicit trade.

"I knocked in the head of the barrel," Anderson said, "and emptied it into the street."

"Well," I replied. "I am glad you did not come to ask me this time what you should do."

Later that spring, I dined with some senior officers, one of them Abner Doubleday, a worthy soldier of my generation who had fired back at the rebels attacking Fort Sumter. After dinner, a half-dozen of us theorized on the prospects of a short war. Most of the group thought that only one major battle would settle the issue, or at least lead to a compromise and peace. Doubleday disagreed, insisting it would be one of the bloodiest wars in man's existence. When he left, the others derided him as a spiritualist not entirely right in the head. Alas, Doubleday knew the temper of fully roused plantation owners and deluded Southern yeomen as well as I did. I said little to support him in the discussion, thinking it best as a Virginian to be circumspect in such instances.

My own unit was still not fully united. When one captain expressed his dislike of abolitionists, a lieutenant told him he was fighting on the wrong side. That nearly led to a duel, and I had to tell my command to halt any such talk. It would almost be a relief to start fighting the rebels instead of ourselves.

On June 18, I invaded my home state. My cavalry waded across the Potomac at Williamsport, Maryland. As my horse's hooves found dry land on the south bank, I felt both grief and pride in taking part in such a sad and necessary undertaking. I remembered what I had told a Northern officer a few weeks before when he asked me what I would do if Virginia seceded. "I will help to whip her back again," I replied. My stay in the Old Dominion was a short one, however, since I was almost immediately ordered back across the river.

My cavalry was part of the Army of Pennsylvania, commanded by General Robert Patterson, a sixty-eight-year-old veteran of the Mexican War and the War of 1812. I was forty-four at this time, and I had private concerns that Patterson might be too old for the rigors of another conflict. Some aged men did give exemplary service in this war, but in Patterson's case, his best days were not ahead of him.

Patterson had first been ordered to hold back a rebel force northwest of Washington led by Joe Johnston, while another Union army led by Irwin McDowell ventured from the capital to confront the main enemy force of Pierre Beauregard.

Before we could strike Johnston, Patterson was ordered to send some of his forces to reinforce McDowell and protect the capital. Though my cavalry was ordered to be part of the reinforcement, Patterson preferred to keep my regular soldiers close by because he did not trust the volunteers who made up the bulk of his twelve-thousand-man army. Their three-month enlistments would be over in a month.

I was dismayed by our withdrawal. "If the deed must be done, let it be done quickly," I thought then. Yes, "Slow Trot" was in a hurry in 1861, so much so that I was recalling the flavor, if not the exact words, from "Macbeth." Let me remember a play with more honorable characters—let me be one of the happy few, a band of brothers who go once more unto the breach. What little I know of Shakespeare, I prefer him to the rebels' Walter Scott.

Once more, one of my band of brothers appeared. William Sherman, now a fellow colonel, came by on an inspection tour, perhaps to inspect this Virginia Yankee. He had another reason to come to our outpost. His brother John, a senator in his peacetime endeavors, was Patterson's chief of staff.

It had been years since Cump and I had spoken. I assured him of my loyalty. We had dinner at an inn, then placed a large map on the floor and forecast the conflict. We knew at a glance that Chattanooga, Vicksburg and Nashville in the West would be prizes in the coming battles, as important as Richmond in the East. Sherman could see as clearly as Doubleday, and like him, his right-mindedness would be questioned. A prophet is often not honored in his own army. I will say more of this later.

Two weeks after our withdrawal, we re-crossed the Potomac. Joe Johnston's nine thousand rebel troops were forty miles away in Winchester. My unit undertook a flanking movement on Southern troops commanded by Tom Jackson (not yet known as "Stonewall") and Jeb Stuart—the only time I would share a battlefield with these two notable rebels. Since they were outnumbered, the Southern forces retreated without offering much in the way of a fight. Perhaps the mortar was still drying in the "Stonewall," and Stuart was not yet inspired to play the role of a dashing cavalier. Did they know that another Virginian was so close to them in the opposing army?

I wanted to press the attack and drive the rebels out of Winchester, but Patterson stayed my hand, still suspicious of his volunteers.

Winfield Scott, another aged veteran of Mexico and the 1812 war, was still general-in-chief at this time. One of American history's greatest soldiers, at age seventy-five he could no longer command troops in the field. But even from his desk in Washington, Scott knew it was vital to keep Johnston bottled up in Winchester, and he told Patterson in July to do so, though his orders were not as explicit as they could have been. Regardless, Patterson was not aggressive enough in carrying them out. He failed to block a railroad line that Johnston used to escape from Winchester, enabling the rebels to swiftly ride to Bull Run and reinforce Beauregard.

And so Joe Johnston helped the South win the first major battle of the war, on July 21, 1861.

I despise certain subordinates who, after the engagement has been decided, insist that if only the commanding general had followed his advice, the result might have been a triumph. Still that is something I will have to do several times as I recount my experiences in this war, beginning with Patterson. I saw Johnston's forces heading for the train, and I begged Patterson to let me attack them. He told me Johnston would be too late to help Beauregard. Because of my respect for the chain of command, I did not criticize Patterson publicly, but he was soon mustered out of the Army. Patterson may have been the first Union general to make a grievous error—he would not be the last.

Sherman fought in the first Battle of Bull Run, and he assured me that the Union almost crushed the rebels and that even the strong showing by Tom Jackson's forces might well have been too little for the Southerners.

"It was one of the Union's best-planned battles of the war, but one of the worst-fought," Cump told me. "We had no cohesion, no real discipline, no respect for authority, and no real knowledge of war. The South was nearly as bad off. Had they followed us closely when we retreated, the rebels might have had something to boast of."

Would a Union victory on this day have shortened the war? No, I believe it would only have shortened the time it took the Union to capture Richmond, but the rebels would have kept resisting just as obstinately from whatever new capital they would have retreated to in the Deep South.

My friend Lee, then an adviser to rebel President Jefferson Davis, was not at the first Bull Run. He would soon be sent to far western Virginia, where despite his skills, he was unable to keep that Unionist region from seceding from the rebel regime to become the free state of West Virginia. The irony of the Old Dominion being hoist by its own petard might be amusing to non-Virginians, but I find no humor in it. I still lament that so many beautiful mountains are no longer a part of my home state.

Would the result of the first Bull Run have been different had Lee been the Union commander, as Lincoln wished? Lee obviously was a better general than McDowell, but in those ignorant, chaotic early days of the Union Army, it is fruitless to speculate excessively on what one man could have done in the bedlam that was the first Bull Run.

Yet even if Lee had not been able to show his greatness in a Union uniform, at least he would not have been wearing gray, soon to thwart George McClellan at the gates of Richmond, hoodwink John Pope at the second Battle of Bull Run, hold McClellan to a draw at Antietam, throw back Ambrose Burnside from Fredericksburg, send Tom Jackson around Joe Hooker's flank at Chancellorsville, nearly prevail over George Meade at Gettysburg, and give Sam Grant stubborn resistance from the Wilderness to Petersburg.

That is enough speculation for now. What is factual is that after the first Bull Run, Patterson and McDowell lost their jobs and George McClellan became commander of Union forces in the East.

McClellan, proclaimed the "Young Napoleon" by overly optimistic journalists, was adroit at organizing an army but inept at leading it in warfare. Some suspect he had Copperhead sympathies, with no dislike of slavery and no overriding desire to keep the Union together. Thank the Lord I never had to deal with him.

Besides McClellan's advancement, thirty-eight new brigadier generals were named, including Sherman. At first my name was not on that list, not until General Robert Anderson (with his nephew's recommendation) spoke for me. Also, Sherman told me he went to Lincoln himself to press my case. I was gratified to be a general, the dream of every officer, but I was disappointed that many men junior to me were placed ahead of me on the brigadier list.

I am told that when he was choosing these new brigadiers, Lincoln expressed concern that I still might bolt South—this despite his knowledge that I had already crossed my Rubicon and led Union forces against Virginians on the soil of my home state. There was no going back for me now, even had I been so tempted. How little respect Lincoln had for my honor! Lee's betrayal left the president with minimal belief in another soldier from south of the Potomac.

I never met Lincoln, never felt the pull of his personality that made others become worshipful toward him. Some now rank him the equal of Washington. I respected the office more than the man. Great speeches he certainly wrote, and he may well have been an admirable lawyer. But it took him a long time to learn his business as commander in chief, and in my case, it took him even longer to believe in me and my ability. Now a president cannot please every general, no more than a general can please every soldier. Yet Lincoln's lack of trust was, like my poor back, a constant, nagging ache.

That said, I must add that I mourned his death greatly. Lincoln's faith in the Union was as stubborn as mine.

Shortly after his interview with the president, Sherman met with me.

"Tom, you're a brigadier!" Sherman shouted with pride.

I feigned indifference, which was my feeble attempt at humor with an old friend.

"Where are you going?" Sherman asked, now worrying that I was following Lee's path.

"I'm going South," I said as sadly as I could bluff.

"My God, Tom," Cump wailed, "you've put me in an awful position! I've just made myself responsible for your loyalty."

I quickly regretted that my jest had gone astray. I'd been sure he'd laugh, not blubber.

"Give yourself no trouble, Billy," I assured him. "I'm going South at the head of my troops."

He immediately reverted to his standard grin. Knowing Sherman and Anderson were on my side gave me comfort, almost making up for the grief I felt at Lee's decision.

More comfort abided in New Haven, Connecticut, where Mrs. Thomas was waiting to see me. Had I known that our few days together would be our last for three years, my heart would have broken.

Yet when I bid Frances farewell, I was as happy as a soldier in a new war can be. I was a freshly promoted general in a righteous cause.

CHAPTER 9

IN WHICH I COMMAND A VICTORY

One would think that the first Union successes in the war were those of Grant at Forts Henry and Donelson. So Grant's supporters in the Army and Congress would have you believe. As crucial as those triumphs were, I do not think it immodest to remind citizens that the first major Union victory, at least in the West, came at Mill Springs, with troops under my command.

That battle occurred in Kentucky on a cold, rainy day in January 1862. This state was vital to the Union cause, but it was even more precious to the rebels. Unlike the deeper parts of the South, Kentucky was not lashed to King Cotton—it raised food instead, food that must be denied to the rebels. Kentucky's northern border was the Ohio River, and if the grayshirts controlled this waterway, they could threaten Cincinnati and even the Great Lakes. As Lincoln reputedly said, "I hope to have God on my side, but I must have Kentucky."

(I find it repugnant to use the words "Confederates" or "Confederacy" when referring to the rebels. Such terms give them a legitimacy that they did not deserve and certainly did not earn. For that matter, even though I shall often refer to the rebels as "grayshirts" or "grayclads," they wore ill-matched uniforms the color of butternut more often than not.)

Besides its food and northern border, Kentucky had another element worth fighting for—its white men. Many of them, having few or no slaves, had little liking for the rebellion. These men, most of them dwelling in the mountains of the state's eastern counties, leaned toward the Union. Yet nearly as many Kentuckians either favored the South, or the truth be known, wanted only to sit out the war so they could grow their crops, raise their livestock, and enjoy their acclaimed bourbon in peace.

Neutrality is an understandable sentiment, but in a civil war such idlers are in the way and cause nearly as much trouble as the enemy. In the end, we must all choose sides or be trampled. Perhaps a bare majority of Kentuckians chose the Union, and my command was sent there to help sustain that choice.

Before we could defeat the rebels in January of 1862, it was necessary in the fall of 1861 for me to mount a rearguard action against men supposedly on my side. It was a foreshadowing of worse infighting to come.

The esteemed Robert Anderson was commanding the Department of the Cumberland in Louisville. After reporting to him there, I hurried to Lexington with a regiment (about one thousand soldiers) to prevent the state's rebel forces from seizing the state's arsenal in Frankfort, the state capital. With Frankfort's safety assured for the time being, I was sent south to Danville, in the central part of the state, where Camp Dick Robinson had been established.

Named for the land's owner, the camp was a training center for recruits. I arrived there September 15, after taking an indirect route by secret means—Anderson had urged me to take caution due to rumors that disloyal Kentuckians were prepared to waylay me. If so, I never encountered them. A Daniel Boone might have been able to abduct me, but these slave-holding Kentuckians doubtless had lost their wilderness skills.

There were four regiments of loyal Kentuckians and two of

loyal Tennesseans at the camp when I took command. Other than their loyalty, they lacked everything necessary for an army—weapons, uniforms, marching shoes, and wagons. What materiel they did receive was shoddy, and I reported the dishonest contractors to the authorities in order to make an example of them. Greed comes close to bloodshed as the greatest evil of war. It was necessary for me to borrow money from a bank in Lexington to make the purchases. It was yet another practical lesson, this time in finances, that should have been taught at West Point.

Regardless of these difficulties, the men responded well to training, and within a week I was able to report progress to Anderson. Bull Run had shown me the value of drill and discipline. If Lincoln had given McDowell more time to train his forces, he might have won that first battle. My men were serious about their duties because they knew battle could come at any time. A rebel force already occupied part of western Kentucky, troops under Simon Buckner menaced central Kentucky, and another contingent under Felix Zollicoffer imperiled the eastern part. When Buckner's command put Frankfort again under threat, I took a regiment to nearby Lexington to provide protection. Anderson also sent Sherman with a strong unit, and Buckner withdrew without a shot.

I returned to camp to continue building an army. Our Southern-born loyalists were joined by their brethren from the North. Ohio, Indiana, and Minnesota sent men, and by October there were eight thousand soldiers preparing for battle. They were farm boys mostly, stronger than Eastern city dwellers, though illness was still too common. The rebels gave us a lull so I could afford to be patient with the recruits, eager as they were for a fight. As soon as they were ready, I proposed invading east Tennessee, an area of Union sentiment where Zollicoffer had taken control.

Politics nearly unhorsed me at the start. Senator Andrew Johnson, a Union loyalist from east Tennessee, arrived at the camp with a letter from General O.M. Mitchel, who had been ordered to replace me as commander. Mitchel was from Ohio, one of several generals from that state who would do me no good. (I must interject here that Ohio's lower rank officers and enlisted men were as noble as any in the Union Army.) Though a West Point graduate, Mitchel hadn't been in the Army for years, and it seemed that the only reason for him to take my command was that he had not been born in a rebellious state. I saw Lincoln's hand in this.

Of course, being from Virginia, I was essentially a political orphan in the Northern army. The Kentucky-born Anderson had fallen ill and was on his way to New York for treatment. William Sherman had replaced him, and while Sherman was a friend to me, and his senator brother had spoken for me earlier, it remains that they were both from Ohio. In this instance Cump gave me sympathy but no satisfaction. Thus I told Sherman that I would resign on the day Mitchel appeared at camp. I do not consider such a vow unreasonable, though I regret putting my friend under great pressure. Sherman would soon be accused, unfairly, of losing his mind, and my ultimatum surely did not calm his nerves.

Mitchel never arrived. Did my threat work? It must have helped. It also helped that Anderson, ailing as he was in New York, heard of my plight and wrote Washington in protest. And I was no longer an orphan in Washington, for I had made a friend in Andrew Johnson, the man who would succeed Lincoln as president on a mournful day in 1865. Johnson spoke with many of his fellow Tennesseans in camp and knew they supported me. Since there were so many Southerners in this little Northern army, he must have told Lincoln that it would cause dismay in the ranks for a Southern but loyal commander to lose his post in such a way. Johnson also helped by making sure my troops got a shipment of breech-loading Sharps rifles, far more efficient than old muzzle-loaders.

The camp became full of politicians. Johnson lingered along with another east Tennessean, Congressman Horace Maynard, who also became my supporter. Later Sherman arrived, accompanied by a former senator from Kentucky, John Crittenden.

I had great sympathy for Crittenden, whose family was broken by the rebellion as mine was. One of his sons inherited his father's wisdom and followed the Union banner, becoming a general. The other son, called George but whose name should have been Cain, joined the rebellion. I paid my respects to the elder Crittenden, but I wearied of the political dance. After a program of patriotic music by an Army band, the politicians started making speeches. Even Sherman, who could never resist an opportunity to palaver, took a turn.

When Sherman gave his tongue a rest, there were shouts for me to give the encore. My dignity would not allow this. "Damn this speech-making!" I shouted to an aide. "I won't speak! What does a man want to make a speech for?" I went to my office and shut the door, staying there until the next day like Achilles in his tent. It was the only retreat I was glad to make.

(My wife, reading these chapters, asks if it's necessary for me to use profanity in my writing. Forgive me, Frances, but sometimes yes, it is necessary to recall exactly how I expressed myself. Please remember that you would faint if I ever quoted Sherman fully.)

My distaste for public speaking was not the only reason for my being less than frivolous that October. Zollicoffer's men were moving into Kentucky at this time, and I had sent soldiers under General Albin Schoepf, an experienced Austrian officer who had joined the Union Army, to block him until the Camp Dick Robinson recruits were fully prepared for battle. Schoepf's forces did well in a spirited engagement, sending Zollicoffer back to the Cumberland Gap.

When they heard of this success, the east Tennesseans under my command got their blood up, and I decided it was time for them to meet the elephant. In early November, all of us at camp prepared to reinforce Schoepf.

Yet Sherman would not let us go on. Poor Billy was seeing gray ghosts everywhere and wanted all Union troops to fall back and go on the defensive. He was sure there was an overwhelming host of rebels in southern Kentucky under Sidney Johnston that would soon force him to swim across the Ohio to safety. Sherman did not learn until later that Johnston had cunningly planted rumors that his army was far more numerous than its actual strength. The pity is that if Sherman had let us press on, I am sure we would have driven the rebels out of east Tennessee before winter. Yes, a general who would later be labeled "slow" was brought to heel from an "impetuous" advance. And the general who leashed me would later be accused of headlong recklessness.

The strain of departmental command would not for much longer bedevil Sherman, who was heard fretting that it might take the Union thirty years to subdue the rebels. He was replaced by Don Carlos Buell, an officer with a name more fitting for a general in Santa Anna's army. If not for his family connections, Sherman might well have been cashiered from the Army. Instead, Sherman's senator brother made sure Cump was assigned some lighter duties in Missouri to help him recover his poise. He would soon win another chance to prove his fitness for generalship.

Buell had been a year behind me at West Point, and I wondered how he had been promoted ahead of me. Ohio-born, he grew up in Indiana just across the river from Kentucky. Like many Union officers at the time, Buell had no objections to Negro bondage and in fact had once owned slaves through his Georgia-born wife.* He was close friends with McClellan, so presumably the Young Napoleon convinced Lincoln to put Buell in power in the Blue Grass State.

Like Sherman, Buell would not let us advance when I wanted. My east Tennesseans were in despair that they could not reconquer their homeland, and they might well have mutinied and marched on without me but for the assurances of a Tennessee Unionist general, Samuel Carter, that this was only a temporary retreat.

The press was also indisposed toward me. Newspapers in Cincinnati published vile stories that implied that I did not move toward Zollicoffer because my loyalties were to the grayshirts. I chased the war correspondents away from camp. Such vermin would not believe I was following orders like any good Union man.

Zollicoffer, God rest his soul, gave me a chance to prove myself

---

* Editor's note: Buell and his wife freed their slaves after the attack on Fort Sumter. They settled in Kentucky after the war.

that was better than any oath of loyalty. He crossed into Kentucky from the Cumberland Gap in the last month of 1861. He was a journalist before he joined the rebellion (I suspect a better one than those Cincinnati snakes), and I could see his skills in a public proclamation he penned:

"People of Southeastern Kentucky, the brigade I have the honor to command is here for no other purpose but war upon those Northern hordes who with arms in their hands are attempting the subjugation of a sister state."

Like most newspapermen, he had a way with words, though they were lies more often than not.

Buell at last gave me the order to go forward. I departed with nearly eight thousand men on Dec. 31. They marched through snow and freezing rain, carrying fifty pounds of materiel on their backs, including forty rounds of cartridges. The mud nearly swallowed many wagons and mules. Unlike the rebels, we were under orders not to live off the land by "borrowing" food from farmers who may or may not have been loyal to the Stars and Stripes. With only three days' rations available, I believe not all the soldiers were able to follow the orders to the letter. Some pigs and poultry "wandered" into our camps during the advance, and they did their part to fortify us. Fear not, we caused the farmers of Kentucky no serious loss.

After two weeks on the march, we were within ten miles of Zollicoffer's camp. His strategic placement was beyond foolish. He had the rain-swollen Cumberland River to his back and was cut off from any easy retreat. I am told that General George Crittenden, that rebel son of the former senator, went to inspect Zollicoffer's position and beseeched him to withdraw. The former journalist told him that it would be unmanly to do so with the Yankees near at hand. Crittenden accepted the situation, perhaps thinking the grayclads would still have the advantage in numbers.

There were twelve thousand rebels versus fewer than eight thousand Unionists. Initially we did not have the services of Schoepf's brigade (1,500 men), which was cut off from our main force by a rapidly rising body of water called Fishing Creek. I arranged what forces I had at a place called either Logan's Cross-roads or Mill Springs. Thus the coming battle would have three names, but I lean toward the latter.

After resting the men and allowing time for our weapons to dry, I planned to attack the enemy as soon as possible. We had four infantry regiments, a cavalry unit, and an artillery battery, plus Samuel Carter's brigade on an adjacent road. All told, it was a tiny army compared to what would be common a few months hence in the new year of 1862.

The rebels recognized that Schoepf was cut off and tried to launch a surprise attack on my forces early on January 19.

A surprise attack should never actually surprise a competent soldier. No matter what plans you make, you must expect the enemy commander to do the unexpected. There is no reason to panic. Simply move your forces to deal with the threat, knowing that to make this threat, the enemy likely left a weakness elsewhere. Hold fast and wait for the chance to counterattack.

Pickets are the traditional way to blunt the impact of a surprise attack. It's good to post plenty of them, but these dispersed men on foot might be captured before they can sound the alarm about an advancing enemy. So while most of my men were sleeping that Sunday morning, I sent out cavalry, which ran into rebel skir-mishers about 6:30. The horsemen were able to fight a delaying action, then race back to us and warn of a heavy enemy column.

The mud and cold rain that had made our march miserable now became our ally, hindering the rebels' flanking maneuver to our left. I sent for Carter's brigade to reinforce us as the rest of my men rushed from their tents and formed lines. Not the best way to wake upon the Sabbath.

In the first five months I had been a general, I kept wearing the insignia of a colonel. This was not false humility on my part, merely my dislike of pretentious display. Now I deemed it time to show my true rank. With brigadier stars on its shoulders, a new uniform was taken out of my baggage. Tight though it was around my midsection, I was proud to put it on. (It is incomprehensible to me that with short rations, I still gained weight during our winter march.)

In my general's regalia, I gave each regiment some quiet words of encouragement as they filed into position. I had decided to keep their actions as simple as possible. Green troops, no matter how well drilled, shouldn't be asked to do complicated maneuvers their first time under fire.

One colonel, disheveled and overly excited, rose up to report his men were ready. "Damn you, sir, go back to your command," I told him. An officer must remain steady if he doesn't want his men to take fright. The colonel calmed down and fought well that day.

We heard the shots of our pickets, a sound more like a range firing than a battle. Then the pickets came running to us with double columns of men in muddy gray uniforms close behind.

At first we recoiled from the shock of their attack. Quickly we stiffened our resistance. Kentucky and Indiana units withstood the first rebel advances. I rode forward to see the battle more closely and noticed rebels trying to flank us. I ordered an Ohio battery to come up to shell them. My experience in placing artillery, gained in West Point drills and Mexican battles, paid off.

Soldiers from Minnesota and Ohio relieved the front-line troops. They became entwined with the enemy. Rebels and Union forces even stuck their rifles through the same contested fence, shooting and bayoneting each other.

Luck was with us that day. The dampness of the march made many outdated rebel guns impossible to fire. Despite the rain, Schoepf's troops were able to make their way across Fishing Creek to reinforce us. And a regiment of German immigrant soldiers from Cincinnati, led by Major Gustave Kammerling, pushed many of the rebels back with a bayonet charge. Kammerling supposedly bellowed as the charge began, "If it gets too hot for you, shut your eyes my boys—forward!"

In the mist and smoke of daybreak, Zollicoffer made another critical error. Dressed in a white raincoat that made him conspicuous, he ordered one of his regiments to hold its fire, thinking they were shooting at fellow rebels. Zollicoffer rode forward to the supposed rebels, who actually were Union troops from Kentucky commanded by Colonel Speed Fry. Mistaking Fry for one of his officers, Zollicoffer told him, "We must not shoot our own men." Fry was on the verge of backing away when one of Zollicoffer's officers rode up, shouting that Fry was a Union man. Now realizing that the officer in the white raincoat was the enemy, Fry took out his revolver and shot him point-blank.

That took the fight out of the enemy. Seeing their general killed made the rebels cry out the traditional wail of a defeated army— "Betrayed!" The panic of the troops who saw Zollicoffer fall spread to the others, causing a mass retreat. Crittenden, I am told, had already imbibed too much of Kentucky spirits to fight off the January chill, and he was unable to halt the rout.

I had used all reserves to blunt the first waves of the rebels, so we were unable to pursue them as quickly as we should have. There were still some pockets of gray resistance, but Kammerling's bayonets cleared them away. When Carter's troops arrived, we reformed our lines in a cornfield, taking time to replenish our ammunition, though we did not halt for food, famished as we were.

At 8:00 a.m., about ninety minutes after the battle began, we started our pursuit of the defeated foe. Their camp was nearly ten miles away, but by the time we arrived, most of the enemy officers had already retreated across the Cumberland River on a steamboat that the rebels then set afire. Examining the strong fortifications in front of the remaining gray forces, I decided that enough had been won that day. About 750 men died in the battle, five hundred of them rebels. We had captured twelve cannon, one thousand horses and mules, 150 wagons and half a dozen regimental colors. An exemplary day for untested troops.

I must have been as weary as my men, for it never occurred to me to send a demand to the leaderless rebels to surrender. Fry, the man who had done so much to make the enemy leaderless, finally in some exasperation suggested it that night, and I could only reply, "Hang it all, Fry, I never thought of it."

By then there was hardly anyone left to wave a white flag. The disheartened rebels had scattered, crossing the river on small boats, then running or riding away on stolen horses and mules. Many of them deserted, fleeing to their homes and farms. Even had I moved quicker and captured most of them before they could cross, all we could have done at that point was parole them and send them home. I sent a dispatch saying that such a demoralized army can be a very effective deterrent to our enemy. These rebels troubled the Union no longer.

We sent Zollicoffer's body to his home. I always tried to show respect to enemy troops after a battle, expecting the same regard from them.

This first great Union victory spread cheer throughout the North. However, I received no promotion for this success, and indeed my name was not even mentioned in the official order of thanks to "the gallant officers and soldiers who won that victory." Other commanders, Grant for instance, would receive individual honors and recognition for their early victories. Even this triumph apparently did little to convince Lincoln of my worthiness. Maybe he, or whoever had his ear in the White House, didn't want to recognize that the North's first crucial victory of the war had been won by a Virginian. It was even rumored that the president convinced Harper's Weekly not to put my picture on the cover of its issue reporting the battle.

If the president had been wiser, he would have promoted me immediately after Mill Springs to major general. Then I would have outranked Buell and Grant. Forgive my conceit, but I would not have made the mistakes these men would commit later in 1862. Giving me an independent command would have allowed the Union to win the war in the West much faster and with far less bloodshed. This I will believe to my dying day.

When we crossed the Cumberland the next morning, we entered a region even more impassable than the one we had left, with even less in the way of provisions. In the fall we could have taken Knoxville, but in winter I was forced to withdraw. The grayshirts had lost a battle, but thanks to the Union delays during the autumn, they held onto east Tennessee. My soldiers from that part of the state were disconsolate. It was little solace to them that we had saved Kentucky for the Union.

George Crittenden's fate was crueler than Zollicoffer's. The enemy needed a scapegoat for the defeat, and he faced a court of inquiry. Acquitted of treason, he was convicted of intoxication and eventually lost his rank in the gray army. I have no sympathy for a man unfaithful to the United States, yet I see a parallel for Crittenden and myself. Because Crittenden's father and brother were loyal to the Union, he was suspected of being disloyal to the rebels.

Before Mill Springs, many in Washington suspected me of disloyalty to the Union. If I had lost that battle, my fate would have been far worse than Crittenden's. Lincoln would have seen to it. Prison, or the gallows, might have claimed me.

CHAPTER 10

IN WHICH THE UNION NARROWLY
AVOIDS DISASTER AT SHILOH

Enter Grant.

In February 1862, a month after the Battle of Mill Springs, Grant's command captured Forts Henry and Donelson in northwest Tennessee, giving the Union practical control of the Tennessee and Cumberland rivers. The Union now had an open water route deep into the so-called Confederate States of America. This success, coupled with the victory at Mill Springs, forced Sidney Johnston's Southern army in Kentucky to fall back to Nashville, and then farther south.

Grant, with the crucial help of Navy gunboats at Fort Henry, showed great ingenuity in taking the river forts and had the good luck that a winning commander always seems to have. While I did not think of demanding a white flag from the enemy at Mill Springs, Grant was able to bully an "unconditional surrender" from the rebels with relatively little bloodshed. If only the rest of the South had surrendered as quickly and easily as the grayshirts capitulated at Fort Donelson. There was but one rebel commander, Nathan Bedford Forrest, who showed some grit by leading his cavalrymen out of the fort and avoiding Grant's troops.

At the time of Grant's victories, I was cheered by these Union successes that followed mine. Today I confess a touch of envy at how he became so beloved after those first two triumphs while I remained obscure. (Not that I envy Grant's current job. Better a man-to-man saber battle on horseback with Forrest than being a politician in the White House.)

The press played its part in making Grant the hero of the winter of 1862. Sam Grant became better known by his full name of Ulysses Simpson Grant, which the newspapers turned into such nicknames as "United States" Grant, "U.S." Grant and "Unconditional Surrender" Grant. Journalists felt no love for me in those days. I had deservedly booted them out of my camp before the Mill Springs campaign, so these jackals felt little call to praise a Southern-born general for a Northern victory. So Grant was promoted to major general instead of me.

It was also the bad luck of the victors of Mill Springs that we were unable to press our advantage and take east Tennessee. It was Grant's luck, and the Union's, that the way was now clear to strike far into the enemy heartland. Buell recalled me to Louisville, where we would prepare to chase after Sidney Johnston.

The cold rain was relentless that February as my command— the First Division—marched back to the Kentucky port on the Ohio River.* We looked forward to a journey into the southern spring. Since we had already fought and won a battle, my division was rewarded by being assigned to the rear of the advance. More importantly, the men were able to rest a bit as we floated down the Ohio to the Cumberland, then worked our way upstream by flatboats to Nashville, arriving there on a pleasant day in early March. Andrew Johnson was with us as we entered the Tennessee capital, and he became the military governor of that part of the state that had been restored to Federal rule.

Nashville was the first mutinous state capital to be taken by the Union, and it was gratifying to know how dismaying our conquest was to the rebels. Before we arrived, there had been rioting and

----

* Editor's note: Union divisions usually had at least four thousand men, sometimes more.

plundering by the city's residents, who didn't cease until Forrest and his cavalry charged into them with sabers flashing. Now the city was half-empty, many of the citizens trailing Johnston, Forrest, and the other retreating rebels.

We stayed in Nashville three weeks, putting up fortifications and setting up supply lines. When that process was completed, Buell sent us on the road south. Our ultimate target was the city of Corinth in northeast Mississippi, a key railroad crossroads. We would rendezvous north of Corinth with Grant's forces on the Tennessee River at a place called Pittsburg Landing, better known today as Shiloh.

Sherman was leading the advance for Grant's troops, and it was he who chose their campsite near the small church called Shiloh Meeting House. While I am no friend of Grant today, at that time I was pleased with him for giving Cump another chance after his earlier troubles. Some newspapers had questioned Sherman's sanity, yet another crime by the journalists who badgered us.

Still there was justice in the knowledge that Southern newspapers had been nearly as cruel in their treatment of Sidney Johnston for his retreat from Kentucky and Tennessee into Mississippi. His earlier clever suggestions that he had a giant army mighty enough to swallow the Ohio River—the very tall tales that had so vexed Sherman into an agitated state—were now being used against the rebel general. Southern journalists questioned his fitness for command, if not his loyalty to the slaveholders.

We know today how eager Johnston was to prove his doubters wrong. His troops and those of Pierre Beauregard were lurking only twenty miles from Pittsburg Landing. They took Grant's army by surprise early on April 6, 1862. Newspapers later reported that the rebels were on the Union so quickly that many officers were bayoneted as they slept in their tents. (Sherman has always claimed that the papers were lying about the slain slumbering officers, but for once I tend to believe the mongrels of the press.)

If I were instructing a West Point class on the Battle of Shiloh, I would stress the paradox of military history. Thinking Johnston was far away in Mississippi, Grant's troops did not entrench themselves. Even if Grant had known the grayclads were close enough to smell the Union's freshly cooked breakfasts, he would not have ordered entrenchments, the theory then being that it would be bad for morale for green soldiers to take such defensive measures.

Yet in Nashville we had dawdled too long because we were preparing elaborate fortifications that were not needed in that city, at least not in 1862. In retrospect, we know that Buell should have hastened us to Pittsburg Landing where, if the entire Union forces had been together on that first day of battle, we might have completely crushed the gray army and ended then and there all hope for the rebels in the West.

As it was, the forty thousand grayclads nearly pushed Grant's army of thirty-three thousand into the Tennessee River while Buell's five divisions, including mine, were on the opposite shore, unable to lend assistance because of limited transport across the river. All we could do was listen to the shouts, screams, and gunfire and wonder who was winning.

Troops under Sherman were the first to feel the fury of the rebel attack, and they were the first to be put to flight. Yet Sherman is to be congratulated for collecting enough forces to make a stand farther back on the battlefield after the green troops' early panic had worn off.

"So help me, Old Tom," Sherman once told me, "Shiloh was as fierce a fight as I ever saw. I guess I showed those newspapermen that I don't scare easy, not after all that cow flop about me being crazy."

"You're as true as steel, Cump. We all knew it," I replied.

"I thank you for that. That first day, I have to thank three units near me that kept the rebs from overwhelming the rest of us. The Hornets' Nest, that's what the rebs called those Yanks, and that's what they were until many of them finally had to surrender."

"You also did well," I insisted, "and you didn't surrender."

"Well, yes, my forces acquitted ourselves well later in the day after we stopped our skedaddling. I hear that before the battle, ol'

Johnston told his boys they'd water their horses in the Tennessee River that evening. He never knew how close he came to making all of us Billy Yanks drown in that damn river."

A commander's luck, all bad in the South's case, played a decisive role. Sidney Johnston died early in the battle, bleeding to death from a leg wound. Without his unquestioned skills and leadership, the butternuts were unable to finish off the reeling Unionists, far too many of whom were cringing at the river's edge, under a bluff. Grant, who had been at breakfast at a nearby mansion when the battle began, returned in time to help his soldiers (those still acting in a valorous manner) hold the line on the first day of Shiloh. Still, if Johnston's replacement as commander, Beauregard, had not halted the grayshirts' attack as the sun set, it seems likely the North would have been utterly defeated before Buell could arrive.

On the second day, the first of Buell's reinforcements crossed the river (not my division, however), and the Union was able to force the enemy to march back to Mississippi. Perhaps Grant and Sherman could have held on that second day without reinforcements, but I say that Buell's arrival swung the battle to the Union.

As terrible as Shiloh was for the Northern forces, it can still be considered a Union victory. For most in the North, it felt like a defeat. About thirteen thousand Federal soldiers were killed, missing or wounded—the rebel losses totaled eleven thousand. Such an effusion of blood made the first Bull Run or Mill Springs seem like a skirmish. It should be remembered that the mass of blue soldiers had never engaged in battle before. Yes, many initially panicked or malingered, but most eventually recovered their nerve.

There was courage on the Southern side, though I've heard that many rebels were so busy looting the Federal camps that they paid no heed to the unfinished battle. My old friend Bragg was at Shiloh, battling on despite having several horses shot out from under him as he encouraged his men to put down their plunder and attack. He later fumed that the Southern army lacked discipline, blaming it on universal suffrage and whiskey. Generals such as Bragg apparently despised their white yeomen more than their Negro slaves.

Shiloh was the battle in which both sides, including the politicians and civilians safe in their far-away homes, truly saw the elephant. The lists of the dead sobered those behind the lines who thought that the war would be a short and nearly painless adventure. Mourning would become common for too many families, North and South.

Because of the lack of transport vessels, my division was not able to cross the river until two days after the battle was over. The land was still covered by mangled bodies and the suffering wounded. I had seen and smelled the horror of war before but never on such a scale. The true horror was that it had been Americans killing other Americans. After Mill Springs, I had mainly felt satisfaction in a good performance by my soldiers and the weariness of a long day in combat. On looking at Shiloh's bloody ground, I could sense the despair that Sherman had felt the year before. And there was far worse to come.

Of course I did not let these feelings show on my face, nor did I allow them to master my mind. All soldiers, generals especially, must harden themselves to the sights of war and make them only harmless memories that do not intrude on what must be done in the present.

As I said, Shiloh was a victory for Grant, one that nearly ruined him, and one that nearly ruined me, eventually.

The gentlemen of the press turned on Grant, calling him a butcher and demanding he account for what many at first thought was a Union disaster. It was a hard thing for ignorant newspapermen to grasp that when you force your enemy to retreat, it's a triumph, no matter how bloody, or how narrowly you had avoided defeat.

Many politicians also could not grasp this concept. Lincoln apparently was one of the few to support the general, likely because the vagabond Grant had settled in Illinois before the war, and the president wanted to give this home-state voter another chance. "I can't spare this man; he fights," the president said, not realizing there were other generals just as willing.

However, General Henry Halleck arrived and decided he would take command of the combined Federal armies in the West. Sherman tells me that Halleck, known as "Old Brains" for his non-combat mental abilities, feared that Grant had returned to the intemperance that had plagued him in the 1850s. Despite his concern about Grant's past inebriation, Halleck promoted him to second-in-command of the Western armies. Grant, as I know now, saw this as a ploy where he would have no real power. He resented it, Sherman tells me, especially when he saw that Halleck divided the Western forces into three wings commanded by John Pope, Buell, and myself. Sherman would be under me.

I had little contact with Grant at this time. We nodded hello to each other in the aftermath of Shiloh and exchanged some inconsequential but civil remarks. When the change of command was made, I was not aware that he harbored any grudge over his new status.

Now, however, I believe that what first provoked Grant's ire toward me was that my new command, newly designated as the Army of the Tennessee, was formerly his. Grant would have resigned from the Union Army but for the urging of Sherman, who told him that the situation might change. Indeed it did.

Here I must gather my thoughts about the man who is now the eighteenth president of the United States.

Regarding Shiloh, if Grant were to be judged only for the first hours of battle, he would have been deservedly stripped of his rank and dismissed from the Army. The sanguine lack of entrenchment and the haphazard placements of his troops were shameful. The center of the Union line was left empty, waiting for Buell and myself to fill this gap. And Grant had sent out no extended pickets or cavalry to sniff out the enemy. He had no suspicions that Johnston was so close. Grant was rightfully denounced for these failings. He and Sherman would always deny that they were taken by surprise, but no one believed them.

Yet Grant, Sherman and others kept the enemy from devouring the Union forces, and they held on long enough to be reinforced and drive the enemy from the field. A good general learns from his mistakes, and Sherman tells me Grant never made the same mistake twice. I disagree there. Grant made one mistake continually, that of undermining me.

I have also heard that Halleck believed that Grant's success at Forts Henry and Donelson was mostly due to luck and the Navy's gunboats. If Grant was lucky, he had the wisdom to make use of it. As I wrote earlier, good luck often follows good generals. And Grant could be good, despite the many Union lives he wasted later at Cold Harbor and other Virginia battlefields.

As for his alleged intemperance during the war, I have no evidence of it. During our time together in the war, I never saw Grant show any signs of current or recent inebriation. What his conduct was before Shiloh I cannot swear to, but Sherman assures me that Grant did not imbibe.

I submit that Halleck was swayed by slanders spread about Grant by those in the Army who were jealous of his early success in the war. And while I have every reason to dislike Grant, I will not be party to these slanders. I believe that whatever mistakes he made were those of a sober mind. If he didn't get drunk following Shiloh, he surely had mastered his demons as regards liquor. But too often he acted as if he wanted to drive me to drink.

Certainly I did not know I would be ensuring his enmity by taking command of the Army of the Tennessee. I was simply glad to have a command I thought I deserved by dint of my victory at Mill Springs. Not until days later did I learn that Grant was promoted in name only. The political maneuverings of the enlarged wartime Army were seldom clear to me—they were much harder to judge than the tactics and strategy of the rebels.

As I reflect now in these writings, Grant and I had this in common: He was a victim of slanders over his past drinking, and I was a victim of slanders over my Southern birth. We should have forged a friendship over these injustices.

CHAPTER 11

IN WHICH I DO GRANT A GREAT FAVOR

L ittle time must be wasted recounting the Corinth campaign.

After the Battle of Shiloh, the retreating rebels made for that Mississippi railroad town. We did not begin our pursuit until May 7, a month after the battle.

Henry Halleck, so anxious to avoid the incautious mistakes of Grant, was even more mistaken in his timidity. Our huge army of 120,000 men moved ever so slowly, digging our way instead of marching. Yes, Grant should have entrenched before Shiloh, but at least he knew a soldier carries a gun, not merely a spade.

The enemy took advantage of Halleck's bashful advance. It took us a month to go less than twenty miles, and when we were on the edge of the town, we learned that the grayshirts had strengthened their fortifications with wooden "Quaker" cannon and stuffed dummy "gunners" that were convincing when seen from a distance.

The rebels were even more clever during the night. While we gathered our forces to assault Corinth, we could hear trains arriving and the shouts of troops welcoming reinforcements. Actually, the noise was providing cover for the enemy's escape. When we marched into town in the morning, all we could find was an empty town barren of food.

As horrendous as Grant's bloody victory at Shiloh had been, it accomplished far more than what Halleck called the "beautiful" capture of Corinth. Holding a town means little if the enemy is allowed to flee unpunished.

Machinations in Washington again shook the Union forces. Lincoln ordered Buell and his troops to leave Halleck's command and take the offensive in east Tennessee against the cities of Knoxville and Chattanooga, just what I had desired to do after Mill Springs.

Somehow the empty advance into Corinth won a promotion for Halleck—to general in chief. Perhaps Lincoln understood how worthless the Corinth campaign had been and thought Halleck could do less damage from a desk in Washington. Lincoln made so many poor decisions about generals, he was bound to get something right.

However, the impetuous John Pope was also sent East to replace the irresolute George McClellan, a move that would soon prove that Lincoln had more to learn.

The rise of Halleck left me in charge of Corinth's superfluous fortifications. This was an assignment I did not relish, not when the real war was going on in east Tennessee. Also, I was no longer oblivious to Grant's disgruntlement at not being in command. Both of us reticent by nature, we spoke little in Corinth of our unhappiness over our postings, but I could tell by his morose face that he took no pleasure in my company. Because I wanted to fight, not sit, I asked Halleck to put me back under Buell. In truth, I also wanted to escape Grant's dour presence. On June 10, my request was approved.

I saw Grant before I left. Standing only five feet eight inches tall, he coldly looked up at me as I spoke.

"Well, General Grant, I'm on my way back to Buell. You have the Army of the Tennessee again," I told him at his quarters.

"That is well, but that army should never have been taken from me in the first place," Grant muttered.

"That was not my doing, but now it is restored to you."

"It would never have been taken from me if Buell and you had arrived at Pittsburg Landing in time for the battle."

"General Buell and I came with all due dispatch from Nashville. We would have been here even sooner had anyone known how close Johnston was."

Grant growled. Being taken by surprise was a tender spot for him and I should have remembered that before speaking so bluntly about his Shiloh blunder.

"But the battle was still won," I quickly added.

"The damn press doesn't know it, and Halleck doesn't know it. I hope Lincoln does."

"I'm sure the president is well-informed. Good luck to you, general."

He grunted something in reply, possibly "good luck to you." It was difficult to understand him when he was chewing his cigars. I abhor tobacco.

Grant did not smile, thank me, or offer his hand in farewell. We exchanged salutes. Then I mounted my horse and rode away. I would not see him again until well more than a year had passed.

If I had not given Grant this chance at leading an army again, what would have happened to him? More fruitless speculation. Yet without my yielding command to him in 1862, Grant would never have taken Vicksburg in 1863. Maybe he would have been out of the Army by then, returning to his whiskey demons. Maybe I would have displayed the skill, tenacity, and luck it took Grant to conquer that Southern citadel on the Mississippi River. I prefer to think so —that's why I believe I should have outranked him. Still, for the good of the Union, it is perhaps well that Grant was in Vicksburg and I at Chickamauga in 1863.

It occurs to me that while the late Civil War was the greatest calamity to ever afflict the United States, it was a wonderous blessing for Grant. Dismissed from the Army for drunkenness after the Mexican War, he spent most of the 1850s in near poverty, failing at every enterprise he attempted. The South's rebellion meant he could return to the Army and rebuild his life. And now the former wastrel is president.

My mind wanders. Let me return to June of 1862. I left Corinth and marched east with my favorite First Division, one I had trained personally. Following weeks of repairing railroads and guarding them from guerrillas, we joined Buell in Decherd, Tennessee, in August.

Command weighed heavily on Don Carlos Buell. His assigned task was to take the offensive against Braxton Bragg, who now led the Southern army guarding Chattanooga, another key railroad city. Buell, however, was so concerned by other rebel forces in Alabama and raiders like Forrest near Nashville that he dithered, waiting for the inspiration on where and whom to attack. His shillyshallying damaged the morale of his army, which was eager to close with the enemy.

Some have called Buell "the McClellan of the West," a phrase I find is close to the mark. Both generals were so slow and cautious they made me look like a greyhound. Paralysis of this nature comes when a general fears to lose more than he desires to win. Some would confuse my careful preparation with such paralysis, wrongly of course.

Please understand that I am not accusing Buell of cowardice. He was a brave soldier, willing to fight and die for his country. But too often he was not willing to let his men fight and die for the same cause. McClellan also was a brave man, despite his similar procrastination. Grant and Sherman were brave. So was Bragg, traitor that he was. I rarely saw a general who was not brave. Schofield was a mewling exception.

Some of Buell's dithering may also have been caused by his hesitation to wage an all-out war against fellow Americans. He didn't want the South's people to suffer, so he hoped he could gain by demonstrations and maneuvering what could only be won by the clash of arms. I respected his desire to safeguard civilians, but his timorous tactics made him lose sight of our true objective, which was to win the war. Buell's loyalty to the Union, however, was never in doubt, at least to me.

His dawdling was especially frustrating because I had left Corinth expressly to find action and avoid this kind of wavering. But during this time I defended Buell's irresolution as much as I could, especially in the face of civilian interference. It is a point of honor to me that I will stand with a commanding officer as long as I believe there is a chance he can achieve a victory. It is a matter of loyalty to the Army and to West Point, even if such loyalty to seniority might cost me quicker promotions.

This was my thinking when Andrew Johnson, a civilian I respected, told me by letter that he hoped I would replace the "dilatory" Buell.

I replied by telegram that "I most earnestly hope I may not be placed in the position, for several reasons. One particular reason is that we have never yet had a commander of any expedition who has been allowed to work out his own policy, and it is utterly impossible for the most able general in the world to conduct a campaign with success when his hands are tied, as it were, by the constant apprehension that his plans may be interfered with at any moment. ... I can confidently assure you that General Buell's dispositions will eventually free all Tennessee and go very far to crush the rebellion entirely."

I was wrong. Buell did not justify my faith in him. But for me to live without faith in the chain of command would be like asking a pastor to live without faith in the Lord. And God knows that the chain of command has often treated me like the Almighty treated Job.

No, Frances, I do not believe what I just wrote is blasphemy. Please forgive me for my frankness.

Bragg moved north from Chattanooga. Buell sent me to discover the rebels' target and find a suitable place to stop them. I learned from trustworthy spies that Bragg's objective was Kentucky, but Buell refused to believe it or follow my suggestion to protect the

Bluegrass State by concentrating in east Tennessee, where we could block Bragg's path.

Instead, Buell decided the rebels were threatening central Tennessee and so directed Union forces to Murfreesboro, just south of Nashville. Buell dreaded even the thought of allowing the rebels to threaten the Tennessee capital. Bragg then gratefully took his grayclads to Kentucky unmolested. Andrew Johnson was justifiably upset, and he made his feelings known to Buell and myself. Though he didn't say it, Johnson must have fumed inwardly that I hadn't taken command. I cannot blame him.

We pressed northward in pursuit of Bragg, who, to his credit, was making a well-orchestrated advance so far. It was a hot, dry September, made worse by the rebels' habit of leaving dead mules in the springs, spoiling many water holes for our thirsty soldiers. Fortuitously, we found an underground stream near Cave City that even Bragg couldn't foul.

We thought Bragg's specific target was Louisville, Kentucky's major port on the Ohio River. Indeed, we feared that if the rebels captured Louisville, they would jeopardize Cincinnati and other parts of Ohio, even threatening Indiana and Illinois. Those states were sending us thousands of new recruits, and we needed them, for Bragg's army had a few successes in Kentucky, including the capture of six thousand blueclad soldiers near Richmond and the surrender of four thousand more in Munfordville. The rebels even overran Camp Dick Robinson, my division's old training grounds. Earthworks and trenches were being dug rapidly in Louisville and Cincinnati.

At a time when we were on our heels, we were helped by Bragg's refusal to mount a full-scale battle at key points where he would have had the advantages. The more he advanced north, the more Union forces could be gathered for the chase.

We knew we wouldn't receive any assistance from the East. John Pope's short reign had ended with the disaster of the Second Battle of Bull Run, and now Lee was invading Maryland, soon to be involved in the Battle of Antietam against the restored George

McClellan. In the East and West, the rebels hoped to bring two border states, Kentucky and Maryland, into their "Confederacy."

To our great relief, Bragg left Louisville alone and headed for Frankfort, the Kentucky capital. With the rebels thirty miles away, my troops entered Louisville on September 27.

There it seemed the Northern army had as much to fear from itself as it did from the rebels. On September 28, two Union generals, William Nelson and another with the unfashionable name of Jefferson Davis, stupidly got into an argument over their conduct as officers that escalated into violence. Davis killed Nelson with a gunshot to the heart. Though Nelson was a fool to have agitated Davis so, I regarded him as a better soldier than the man who slew him.

Somehow in the greater turmoil of the war, Davis escaped a murder charge and eventually would return to duty, becoming a trusted subordinate to Sherman by the end of the conflict. Davis deserved to hang for the slaying of Nelson, in my opinion, but others of higher rank thought that since we had already lost one experienced general, we couldn't afford to lose a second. This kind of logic mystified me. In fact, Buell wanted to file murder charges, but on September 29 an event forced us to put thoughts of Davis aside. Buell received an order from Halleck that relieved him from command and put me in his place.

I should have accepted the command. Even Buell thought so. But I did not want to do him an injury before he had his chance to prove himself against Bragg. Though Buell's decisions on Kentucky had proved faulty so far, I respected how he had saved Grant from defeat at Shiloh. Buell was one of the few who publicly recognized my contributions at Mill Springs, and he had supported my recent promotion. I owed him my support. I replied to Halleck:

"General Buell's preparations have been completed to move against the enemy, and I respectfully ask that he may be retained in command. My position is very embarrassing, not being as well informed as I should be as the commander of this army and in the assumption of such responsibility."

Such was my telegram. Do not confuse my self-effacement with a lack of self-confidence. I know my ability. In an official report a few weeks later, I would further explain my resistance to this promotion: "I am not as modest as I have been represented to be. I did not request the retention of General Buell's command through modesty but because his removal and my assignment were alike unjust to him and to me. It was unjust to relieve him on the eve of a battle, and unjust to myself to impose upon me the command of an army at such a time. If I had taken command at this late time, I would have been limited to what Buell had already set in motion."

In other words, I prefer a clean slate.

While awaiting Halleck's reply, I took a room in a hotel, my first time in a bed in weeks. I found I could no longer sleep in such comfort, so I had an army cot set up. I then spent a restful night and learned in the morning that Buell had kept his post and I was second in command.

Bolstered by my support, Buell was ready to stop his fretting and start fighting.

CHAPTER 12

IN WHICH LINCOLN AGAIN DOES
ME AN INJUSTICE

Kentucky's membership in the "Confederate States of America" was brief.

On October 4, Braxton Bragg installed a governor in Frankfort under the rebels' flag of treason. As this disreputable puppet commenced what would have been a lengthy and stultifying inauguration speech, Union troops showed what they thought of the ceremony by shelling the town. Bragg and his play-actor of a governor beat a hasty retreat.

During their invasion, the rebels brought wagons loaded with thirty thousand extra rifles in the delusion that any uncommitted Bluegrass citizens would flock to the gray banners. There were few takers. As I related earlier, most Kentuckians supported the Union, while many of those who leaned toward rebellion found it difficult to trade the comforts of their farms for the dangers of battle. Bragg was disgusted by these mugwumps, blaming their hesitation on a love of ease and prosperity. "The people here have too many fat cattle and are too well off to fight," he said, an assessment I cannot gainsay.

The best way to have pushed these reluctant combatants into the rebel army would have been if the Union forces had outraged them by confiscating all their livestock and crops. This kind of "living off the land" was a practice I tried to limit during the Mill Springs campaign, and I was even more determined to head it off now. Once I was approached by a Kentucky farmer whose loyalty to the Union was unquestioned. He complained that a Union officer had taken his only horse.

The farmer pointed out the officer, who was mounted on the horse in question. I demanded to know where he had gotten his mount. This officer, unaware of his peril, replied flippantly that he had "impressed" the animal. Knowing that he lacked this authority, my anger overflowed.

Drawing my sword, I put the point under this officer's shoulder straps signifying his rank, and sliced them off as if I were cutting bacon back at my family's Virginia farm. The officer, never knowing how close he came to having his head removed, now realized the severity of his offense. I made him lead the horse back to the farm and give the farmer compensation. I trust the story of my rage spread throughout the ranks and discouraged other would-be pilferers.

This incident occurred as the Federal force of nearly sixty thousand men went after Bragg, who had perhaps fifty-two thousand. We departed Louisville at the start of the month, divided into three corps. We were led on the right by Thomas Crittenden (brother of the rebel I had bested at Mill Springs), Charles Gilbert in the center, and Alexander McCook on the left. Buell stayed back in the lines because he was nursing a leg injured in a fall from a horse. As second in command of Buell's army, I accompanied Crittenden. The treason of his brother was a subject we tactfully avoided.

When the Union shelling interrupted the October 4 speech in Frankfort, it was actually a feint by two Federal divisions. The rest of our forces were heading toward Bardstown, about fifty miles southwest. Bragg withdrew from Frankfort after a short skirmish, and for the next two days the opposing armies maneuvered south by southeast as each sought better ground for a battle.

We also were seeking water, as the summer's drought had worsened in the autumn, turning the normally lush Kentucky fields into a dry and dusty wasteland. Even worse, when we found any creek beds with a trace of water, we often found more of the rebels' dead mules.

The two armies converged on Perryville, a village where the nearby river and streams still flowed. Bragg's forces occupied the town while Buell's army took positions to the north. The quest for water, and the many hills, had kept the three Union wings from staying abreast. Crittenden's troops, including myself, were moved far to the right to control access to water holes.

About noon on October 8, Bragg attacked, throwing his force against McCook's twelve thousand troops on the Union left. They were pushed back a mile, taking four thousand casualties. McCook's men, though green, fought well and limited their retreat, inflicting 3,400 casualties on the rebels.

The rest of the Northern forces, including Buell, were not aware of McCook's ordeal until late in the day. The hilly terrain and high winds had deadened the sounds of the nearby battle so that we couldn't hear it. I am embarrassed to say that I spent the afternoon awaiting orders from Buell and was not informed a battle had taken place until 6:30 that evening. No blame was placed on me for this, but I wish I had not been so conservative in waiting for Buell's decisions. Buell himself blamed Gilbert for being slow with reinforcements and McCook for positioning his soldiers too far forward of the other wings. I don't know enough about Gilbert's situation to judge him, but I give McCook credit for keeping his retreat from turning into a debacle.

The next day the rest of the Union force was ordered to attack, but by then Bragg had lost heart, knowing he should have had a decisive victory and that he would now be outnumbered. Many of his troops were scattered south of Perryville. He withdrew through the Cumberland Gap to Tennessee, leaving Kentucky back in Union hands, so the Battle of Perryville at least accomplished that.

If the South had routed us there, the rebels might have truly made Kentucky a Confederate state and turned the Ohio River into an impregnable border. So Perryville, like Antietam, was an indecisive battle that was essentially a victory for the Union because the rebels retreated. Perryville was the highwater mark for the rebels in the West.

Yet this battle did not profit Buell, nor me. First let me detail Buell's fate.

Weeks after the battle, a court of inquiry was held on Buell's conduct. You would think that with the war still being fought, there would be better ways to use our time and energy, but politicians and generals must grind their axes. Prosecutors initially attempted to prove Buell was guilty of treason—that he had correspondence with Bragg that indicated the Union general wanted to hand over Kentucky and Tennessee to the rebels. This was false of course, a slander on a good Union man, and the kind of lie that might have been used against me had I ever lost a battle.

The prosecution eventually gave up on this absurd line of inquiry, deciding instead to focus on Buell's judgment in command. Both Buell and the prosecution called me as a witness.

Though Buell put on an active courtroom defense, he was generous to me about my undistinguished role at Perryville, supporting me in my decision to await his orders as the battle was waged elsewhere. Nonetheless, when questioned by either side, I said the simple truth, without animus or bias toward him. I could not hide the fact that Bragg had often outmaneuvered Buell in the weeks before Perryville.

Queried on this by the prosecution, I had to testify that Buell could have kept Bragg out of Kentucky if the Union forces had concentrated at two Tennessee cities I had recommended to him, Sparta and McMinnville. Shaken by my testimony, Buell questioned my veracity.

No one should ever question my veracity.

"Please tell the court, general," Buell said, "whether that opinion has come from a study of the situation since or whether it suggested itself to your mind at the time."

"If you will give me your book of telegrams," I replied, "I believe it will answer better than I can."

When the book was produced in court, I turned pages until I found the telegram that showed I had indeed suggested these cities as the right places to concentrate. Buell read it aloud in court, a humiliation he could have avoided by accepting the truth of my testimony.

He was acquitted of any intentional wrongdoing, I am glad to say. But the inquiry, and my testimony, essentially ended his military career. I was not as close to Buell as I was to some other West Pointers, but I was distressed that while we did not become enemies, we were no longer friends.

As for my fate after Perryville: The only winner in that battle was William Rosecrans.

I have always liked "Rosy," ever since he nicknamed me "George Washington" at West Point. But the way that he, and not I, was given Buell's command made me think that King George III was ruling in Washington instead of Lincoln.

Politics and religion, I am told, won the post for Rosecrans. Though Secretary of War Edwin Stanton, an Ohio man, spoke up for me in a cabinet meeting with the president, it was another Ohioan, Treasury Secretary Salmon Chase, who was adamant for Rosecrans. And where did Rosecrans come from? Ohio, of course. So many blasted Buckeyes in this war.

It was also to Rosecrans' advantage that he was Catholic, indeed that he was the brother of the curate in Cincinnati. Catholics in the North were not as supportive of the war as their Protestant brethren, so it was thought that a Catholic general's promotion might encourage more ardor in Roman breasts. There was also my lack of distinction during the Battle of Perryville. And lastly, my support for Buell before Perryville did nothing to boost my candidacy. It made Lincoln and Halleck believe that I shrank from leadership. They could not fathom my respect for seniority and the chain of command.

"Let the Virginian wait; we will try Rosecrans," the president said. He may not have had malice toward me, but he showed me little charity. Consider this: I was commissioned a general on

August 7, 1861. That would make me senior to Rosecrans, who was commissioned on August 21. Lincoln got around that by changing the date of Rosecrans' commission to March 31.

And they called him "Honest Abe."

In mid-October of 1862, a week after the Battle of Perryville, Rosecrans presented himself to Buell at a Louisville hotel, the same establishment where I had passed a night on a cot. Buell was still recovering from his tumble from a horse, and Rosecrans completed his fall from grace by telling him he was demoted.

When I received the news, I felt as if a horse had thrown me, then trod on my legs. Buell's former army and I were 100 miles south in Bowling Green, where we were chasing after Bragg. Certainly I thought I deserved the command, especially after the honorable way I allowed Buell to have his chance at Perryville. I was in my customary state of ignorance about the politics involved, especially of Lincoln's dishonorable trickery with the commission dates, when I sent my protest to Halleck on October 30.

"On the 29th of last September I received an order … placing me in command of the Department of the Ohio and directing General Buell to turn over his troops to me. This order reached me just as General Buell had by most extraordinary exertions prepared his army to pursue and drive the rebels from Kentucky. Feeling convinced that great injustice would be done him if not permitted to carry out his plans, I requested that he might be retained in command. The order relieving him was suspended, but today I am officially informed that he is relieved by General Rosecrans, my junior. Although I do not claim for myself any superior ability, yet feeling conscious that no just cause exists for overslaughing me by placing me under my junior, I feel deeply mortified and aggrieved at the action taken in this matter."

Halleck's reply was very complimentary of my abilities but gave me no satisfaction: "Rest assured, general, that I fully appreciate your military capacity and will do everything in my power to give you an independent command when opportunity offers."

When Rosecrans, sometime later, informed me of the president's sleight of hand concerning commissions, I could not let this pass unremarked. I again wrote Halleck, who I trust showed this to Lincoln: "I have made my last protest while the war lasts. You may hereafter put a stick over me if you choose to do so. I will take care, however, to so manage my command, whatever it may be, as not to be involved in the mistakes of the stick."

At this point, my feelings toward Halleck and Lincoln were the same that I felt toward the Union officer who had stolen the Kentucky farmer's horse.

CHAPTER 13

IN WHICH WE DEFEND HELL'S HALF ACRE

Except for one fateful day, William Rosecrans performed well as commander of the newly designated Army of the Cumberland. That day was a year hence, and until then he often conferred with me, making me his chief of staff in all but name.

On my recommendation, Rosecrans rid our army of some unworthy officers and made living conditions better for the enlisted men. Since he was a longtime friend, it was not so painful to put aside my pride and help him succeed in a command that by rights should have been mine.

Rosecrans was a six-footer, nearly an inch taller than myself, energetic, sandy-haired, and handsome, save for a large red nose that signified a man who enjoyed liquor. It inspired soldiers to give him the nickname "Old Rosy." Unlike Grant, Rosecrans had never allowed his craving for spirits to get the better of him.

Perhaps his fervent Catholic faith gave him strength in this. He delighted in discussion of religion, not that he was trying to convert any of us to the pope. He simply liked to talk about the Roman church the way Sherman liked to talk about the Roman Empire.

Rosecrans never drew me out on the matter. I preferred to keep my religious feelings to myself and the Almighty, though I cannot understand how a man can be an atheist and remain brave. Belief in God is like confidence in one's general; it holds us to the front. My faith is a simple, personal one, though Frances laughs and tells me she may yet entice me into the folds of her rather elegant Episcopal church in Troy.

When he put aside questions of the hereafter, Rosecrans did well inspecting the here and now. He took an interest in every part of the Army of the Cumberland, from hats to shoes, from bullets to cannon, even encouraging the men to complain to their officers if anything vital was missing. The food and pay improved, as did the mail service. Soldiers fight better when they know their commander keeps their welfare in mind.

That does not mean a general must be beloved by his men to be effective. Give me respect and obedience first. Yet I envied Rosecrans' outgoing nature. He could be angrily profane one minute, jovial the next. After lights out, he would walk through the camp, looking to see if a lamp still burned in a tent. If he noticed one, he'd beat on the canvas with the flat of his sword. When the offending soldiers emerged from the tent ready for fisticuffs, they'd immediately become shamefaced at the sight of their commanding general. They'd apologize, and Rosecrans would kindly forgive them, even joking with them as they returned to their tent.

I could never be so familiar with the enlisted men or the officers. My senses of reserve and dignity have been with me always. Only my wife and a few close friends know the better angels of my nature, if I may borrow another phrase used so well by the Illinois lawyer. Somehow the soldiers knew I was not always stern and exacting.

They never called me "Slow Trot," the nickname that never amused me. The Cumberland men knew me as "Old Pap" and "Uncle George," names which I hoped were signs of high regard, though they may only have been comments on the growing gray in my whiskers.

I was less guarded with animals. Horses and mules were favorites of mine, and woe to any teamster who mistreated them.

These beasts were cruelly fated to die at a horrific rate in the war, and I did not want them to suffer more than was necessary. I always made sure my favorite horse, Billy, was well cared for. Yes, Billy was named for Sherman. The beast was a big bay, strong enough to carry my bulk for many hours.

Smaller animals also won my affection. A stray cat followed me around, purring because it knew it would eat tidbits from my table rather than needing to hunt field mice. For a while there was also a goose that claimed my protection after I rescued it from orderlies who wanted to feast on it. This goose liked to settle at my feet at camp, knowing I would keep it out of the cooking pots.

Like Rosecrans, I often made inspections to make sure the regimental hospitals were treating the wounded men properly. When I found a drunken orderly delinquent in his duties, I used a penknife to rip off the miscreant's shoulder straps (much like the method I used against the horse thief in Kentucky). I told him, "Go home, sir, by the next train. You may do to feed cattle; you shall not feed my soldiers." Rosecrans applauded when he heard of my anger.

Another of the reasons I liked Rosecrans was that, despite his mercurial temperament, he was not rash with his army, at least not in the fall of 1862. Don Carlos Buell had felt constant stress from Lincoln and Halleck because they thought him torpid. Rosecrans was under the same pressure to speedily drive the rebels out of the rest of Tennessee, but the new commander would not be rushed. He wanted his army fully prepared so we would not have "to stop and tinker" on the road. Such intelligent caution had gotten him on the wrong side of Grant in Mississippi earlier in the year, despite Rosecrans' winning a couple of minor battles for his fellow Ohioan. Our mutual antagonism with Grant and Halleck was another reason I was ready to give Rosecrans the benefit of the doubt.

International politics were a bigger mystery to me than our machinations in Washington, but as I write this in 1870, I know more of what was driving Lincoln in 1862. England and France were on the brink of giving official diplomatic recognition, along with military and economic aid, to the so-called Confederate government in Richmond. With these Europeans in the war, it would have been impossible for the Union to put down the rebellion.

Lee's retreat after Antietam in September of 1862, a month before Bragg's retreat from Perryville, stayed the hand of the Europeans, for the moment. Antietam also gave Lincoln a strong enough political position to declare the Emancipation Proclamation. This partial ending of slavery put the Union on the side of the angels and made it more politically risky for Europe to come in on the side of Jefferson Davis and his plantation masters.

Regardless, it would take more Union victories, and greater Union advances into rebel-held territory, to ensure that the English and French would stay completely out of an American conflict. Lee remained powerful in the East, so powerful that Lincoln again removed the ineffectual George McClellan from command, replacing him with the untried Ambrose Burnside. McClellan would go into politics and become a rival to Lincoln. It was up to Rosecrans to show Europe that the Union would prevail deep within the American continent.

By November the Army of the Cumberland was well-established in Nashville. That was all well and good, but Bragg's army was just twenty-five miles down the road in Murfreesboro, blocking our way to Chattanooga. Conquer that railroad city and we'd cripple the South's transportation of food and other vital goods. Rosecrans bided his time, building good lines of communication, making sure there was plenty of materiel for when we took out after Bragg. This preparation did not impress Lincoln and Halleck, who were clamoring for a quick victory, especially as November turned into December and Lee defeated Burnside at Fredericksburg. The news was just as bad in Mississippi, where Sherman, under Grant's command, was badly thrashed at Chickasaw Bluffs near Vicksburg. Sherman seemed more embarrassed about this defeat than he was of the earlier rumors suggesting he was insane.

I counseled Rosecrans to wait until he was ready. Of the seventy thousand troops in our force, many had to be left behind to guard against rebel raiders. Nathan Bedford Forrest was causing havoc in western Tennessee, and John Hunt Morgan was doing likewise in Kentucky. In a way this was encouraging, since these dangerous men would not be pestering us on our advance to Murfreesboro. However, we would attack Bragg with only forty-four thousand men. The odds were still in our favor, as the rebel army stood at not quite forty thousand, and Bragg was expecting us to wait until spring to launch an offensive. We heard he was holding a series of holiday parties, with plenty of feasting on food confiscated from nearby farms.

On the day after Christmas, Rosecrans gave the order to advance. We set out in good spirits. Our force was divided into three wings. I commanded one, Alexander McCook (who had so much trouble at Perryville) led another, and Thomas Crittenden had charge of the third. McCook was young for a general, barely over thirty, yet he never lacked confidence. Unfortunately, he lacked skill and luck. At least all in his family were on the right side. I believe his father and at least seven of his brothers fought for the Union, and several were killed in battle. Crittenden was more to my liking. We had gotten to know each other well enough in Nashville that we could console each other about the heartbreaks of seeing our siblings give their loyalty to the rebellion.

I must credit Bragg with quickly rousing himself from his post-Christmas rest once he learned we were on the move. Morgan and Forrest may have been far away, but other grayclad cavalry under Joe Wheeler gave us grief. His horsemen destroyed at least three hundred of our wagons loaded with supplies. Most of them belonged to McCook, whose battle luck hadn't changed. Our cavalry was overmatched, mainly because a fool in the War Office (Halleck, I'm sure) limited the Cumberland army to only three thousand mounted men, far fewer than the enemy.

On the twenty-ninth and thirtieth, the Union forces made camp three miles from Murfreesboro, close to the Stones River, which was easily fordable despite the constant rain that soaked our advance. The rebels were close by; we could hear their bugle calls quite clearly. After both sides shelled each other on the evening of the thirtieth, the bands began their musical assaults. One side would play "Yankee Doodle," the other "Dixie," then "Hail, Columbia" followed by "The Bonnie Blue Flag." Ultimately, one band started to play "Home Sweet Home," and the other side joined in. Eventually thousands of men in blue and gray sang along in unison.

The sound gave me pause as I made preparations for the battle that would come the next day. I gave a thought to Southampton, Virginia, but mostly I dwelled on my memories of Frances, for my real home is wherever she may be. I could afford little time to indulge in better days. If I failed to make the proper placements of my men, many more of them than necessary would not live to see their homes again.

Rosecrans' plan, of which I approved, was to advance on the left and strike the enemy's right. Bragg apparently had the same idea, and both armies might have circled each other like dancers at a Baltimore soiree if we had started at the same time on the morning of 1862's final day. Again, reluctantly, I must credit Bragg. He called for a dawn assault while Rosecrans told us to wait until breakfast was completed before we moved forward.

Crittenden's wing was on the left, accompanied by Rosecrans, who was there to encourage the assault. My wing was in the center, and McCook had the right wing, which the rebels hit with fury. Two of McCook's three divisions were swamped, and some of the men didn't stop retreating until they reached Nashville. The third division, led by Phil Sheridan, was more stubborn. Yet Sheridan and the remnants of McCook's other divisions were thrown back on the center—my two divisions, led by Lovell Rousseau and James Negley. We were also giving ground, and Negley's command was nearly surrounded in thick woods. One of his aides ran to me to report they were trapped. "Cut your way out," I told him, and they did so. Sheridan asked for help, but I had to await orders from Rosecrans before I could send over two brigades. It was now mid-morning, and the Union force had been driven back three miles.

Most of my men had withdrawn in good order, and despite the

initial rout among some of McCook's units, I saw few skulkers. Sometimes when I was glancing at how our men were conducting themselves, I could tell if one was considering slipping away to the rear, but a severe look from me was often enough to remind him and his peers of their duty to hold fast.

One soldier particularly impressed me with his valor. I rode up to a sergeant, who was left in command of two artillery pieces after some accurate rebel shelling had killed or wounded his officers. Understandably, he was anxious to retreat with the other enlisted men. "I want you to save those pieces, my good fellow," I shouted at him. That stiffened his resolve. When next I saw him that evening, he reported to me that "the guns were right where I saw them, only I shoved 'em round."

The good fellow did not think he had accomplished anything extraordinary, for when I made him a lieutenant, he hesitated about accepting—as he preferred remaining with "the boys." But he took the promotion on the expectation that it would soon enable him to go on leave and see his wife.

Rosecrans, being far on the left, did not know for some time the danger to the right. When he did, he stopped Crittenden's advance and sent some of that force to shore up the other side of his command.

Rolled up as we were, I found we actually became stronger as we became more compressed near a bend of the Stones River. The rebels had pushed us into a woody knoll there that the locals called the Round Forest but which our men would call Hell's Half Acre. After we established a new line and dug in, it was a suitable defensive position that would have dismayed Lucifer. It didn't deter Bragg. He ordered attack after attack on the forest.

Union men under the command of Colonel William Hazen were particularly stout defenders. Had Bragg sent his forces toward us in one giant wave, we might have been overwhelmed, Hazen's soldiers notwithstanding. Thankfully, the rebels came in only piecemeal, and each surge was pushed back in devastating fashion. The sun went down at 4:30 on a tortured and exhausted battlefield.

I was well-pleased by the splendid resistance we put up in Hell's Half Acre. I would rank the fortitude and stubbornness of the men as the equal of the stand we would make at Chickamauga nine months in the future.

Rosecrans was personally acquainted with the carnage of the day. He was riding to join us when a cannon ball nearly hit him, and instead tore off the head of his aide riding beside him. The man's brains and blood covered Rosecrans' uniform, and those who saw the general at first assumed he had been gravely wounded.

"Brave men die in battle. Let us push on," Rosecrans told them.

Those who had taken part in Shiloh assured me that Stones River was just as terrible. Some of my brigades lost half their strength.

Despite his inability to take Hell's Half Acre, Bragg thought we were defeated and wired Richmond that "God has granted us a happy New Year."

The evening was cold and stormy as the Union generals gathered at a cabin to decide our course for the next day. We were getting the first reports of casualties. By the time the Battle of Stones River would be over, the North would list 1,730 dead, 7,802 wounded and 3,717 captured or missing. The South, we would learn, had similar totals. For Union officers, the casualties were ten colonels, ten lieutenant colonels, six majors and hundreds of line officers. As we walked to the cabin, we saw a tall pile of amputated arms and legs.

It was supposed to be a meeting to exchange opinions, but after the day's events, even loquacious generals were struck dumb. Many were bleeding from minor wounds. I was unmarked. After hours of cannon fire, the quiet made me drowsy. While I was in a state of near-slumber, Rosecrans, still covered in the blood and brains of his aide, broke the silence and asked our opinion—stay or retreat? McCook, a wit in spite of his poor showings of late, replied that "I would like Bragg to pay me back for my two horses lost today."

In my sleepy state, I was barely aware that most of the other generals favored withdrawal. Rosecrans asked the surgeon general if we had enough wagons to transport the wounded back to Nashville. Assured that we did, Rosecrans gently shook me around midnight to ask if I could cover a retreat. I emerged from the Land of Nod long enough to mutter that "this army can't retreat."

At least this was what Rosecrans and most others recalled my saying, never mind that the army already had retreated that day, by three miles. Others have claimed I uttered something more gaudy: "Gentlemen, I know of no better place to die than right here."

I don't know that I could have been that pithy—no Admiral Nelson am I. But whatever I said was apparently enough to inspire eloquence from Rosecrans. The next morning his orders were to "prepare to fight or die."

Blessedly, there was little fighting or dying on a cold and rainy New Year's Day. Because of the destruction of so many wagons, our food supplies were low. We were so hungry that we thought that meat cut from horses killed in battle tasted better than buffalo. Both sides were too exhausted to do little more than skirmish and exchange some artillery fire.

Bragg had expected us to retreat, something he would have done had he been in Rosecrans' position. The insolence of our refusing to admit defeat must have galled him. So he spent the first day of 1863 waiting for us to prove he had achieved a victory. At nightfall, the Cumberlands began to stir. Rosecrans sent a division across the river to occupy some high ground that allowed him to threaten the rebel right.

On January 2, Bragg learned his "happy New Year" had not been attained. Since our right side, ultimately, had held on December 31, the rebel general decided the left side would be vulnerable, even with the Union's new position on the high ground. The left was now our strongest side, as John Breckinridge knew. He was the general chosen by Bragg to lead the assault, and the former vice president of the United States went on record as saying it would be a rebel disaster.

It was, though it was nearly a rebel success. Breckinridge hit the Union hard. H.P. Van Cleve's division took the brunt of it and was nearly overrun. Negley asked for volunteers "to save the left" and the 19th Illinois responded, wading through the Stones River to plug the gaps. With the help of our artillery and our small cavalry, led by David Stanley, Breckinridge was shoved back into Bragg's ungrateful arms.

That was enough for Bragg's other generals. They wrote a letter to him advising withdrawal. The next day he took their advice and went south. As at Perryville, he proclaimed victory, then retreated.

Lincoln and Halleck were just as ready to proclaim Stones River a Union victory, sending Rosecrans congratulations that contrasted with the harping complaints they had sent him before we departed from Nashville. The issue of Rosecrans versus myself caused a new round of disagreements in the president's cabinet, according to Stanton, the secretary of war, who related this conversation to me after the rebellion was finally extinguished.

Chase, the Treasury secretary, said our victory proved that Rosecrans was the right choice to lead the Army of the Cumberland. Stanton insisted that I had saved the Cumberlands with our stand in Hell's Half Acre.

"If you knew as much about Stones River as I do," Stanton told Chase, "you would not feel so cocksure of your friend. But for George H. Thomas, the man I wanted to head that army, Stones River, instead of being a victory, would have been a defeat."

"Come now, Stanton, be just," Chase replied. "We selected Rosecrans, and Rosecrans had the sagacity to select Thomas. Then, you know, nothing is so successful as success."

All this debate was unknown to Rosy and myself that January, but if the cabinet had asked me who had won the battle, I would have told them that the Union soldiers were the victors, not an individual general.

Stanton would continue to be one of my strongest supporters in Washington. Unfortunately, he would waver at a crucial time nearly two years in the future.

The Battle of Stones River further ensured that Kentucky would remain firmly bound to the Union and that the rebels would have no chance of regaining control of the Tennessee and Cumberland rivers.

Following Lee's overwhelming victory at Fredericksburg, Lincoln had feared that "the nation could hardly have lived over" another setback. The year just ended had been a bitter one for the Unionists. There were only a few victories for the men in blue, and several disheartening defeats. And some of the technical victories, such as Shiloh, Antietam, and Perryville, had the stink of stalemates. Stones River, as near as we came to defeat, gave the Union a bit of cheer in the beginning of 1863.

It was also a reminder to Europe of the Emancipation Proclamation. Without our victory at Murfreesboro, England and France might have ignored the issue of slavery and given recognition to the rebels' government, thus insuring the establishment of a permanent Confederate States of America.

A few days before the battle, the rebels' Jefferson Davis visited Murfreesboro, encouraging the soldiers and the town's residents in their revolt. Soon after the traitors' president departed, the city was back in the hands of its rightful government.

CHAPTER 14

IN WHICH WE CONDUCT THE
GRANDEST CAMPAIGN

Once during the fall of 1863, Sherman taunted me about how we each had fought the war during the first half of that bloody year.

"While you and Rosy were cavorting in Tennessee," Cump said smugly, "Grant and I were doing what a soldier's supposed to do, fighting our way forward. Right to Vicksburg."

"Floundering would be the word for it, not fighting," I replied steadily. "How many times did you try and fail to get to Vicksburg? Even Burnside would have blundered into it about the same time you did."

Teasing me is like baiting a muzzled bear. Even the most patient tame bruin will eventually lose its stupor and slash at his tormentor. Not that that would ever dissuade Sherman.

"Burnside couldn't walk across a hog wallow without getting his whiskers soaked, much less the Mississippi," Cump answered, his face getting as red as his hair. "But at least he tried to advance at Antietam and Fredericksburg instead of squatting around the campfires for six months like you and Rosy did, getting all that food stored up instead of grabbing what there was from the rebel farms. You had to wait until every shoe was shined, every button polished before you ever got out of Murfreesboro. And then you just danced Bragg backwards instead of closing with him."

"We danced him all the way south of Chattanooga with little loss of men or materiel," I countered.

"Ha!" exclaimed Sherman, rushing for the obvious opening. "South of Chattanooga is where Bragg gave the Union Army the worst defeat we've had in the whole war."

"How can somebody who led the Chickasaw Bluffs fiasco say that any other Union defeat was worse?" I asked, smiling as Sherman sputtered. I pressed my advantage before he could respond. "Rosecrans got beat at Chickamauga because he turned reckless. Had he kept dancing at a slow trot, he would have kept his command, and you and Grant might still be in Mississippi trying to catch Forrest. Except that old slave trader would have shot you both right out of your saddles by now."

"Yes, Forrest would bedevil Old Scratch himself," Cump said, grinning again. "But I still say Rosy took far too long to get started after Stones River. Slow and careful works sometimes, for you anyway, even though I wish to heaven you'd hurry more. But damn it all, Rosecrans stayed in Murfreesboro so long he must have thought he was the second coming of McClellan."

"You have a point," I admitted. The only way to silence Sherman is to pretend to agree with him. And there were many who shared his opinion about the lack of motion of the Army of the Cumberland in the winter and spring of 1863.

The first days of that year were the aftermath of Stones River, a Union victory that was nearly a defeat. Rosecrans took our narrow escape as proof that our army must be totally prepared before it ventured out again to face Braxton Bragg's grayclads. It took six months to rebuild the Louisville & Nashville Railroad, which was our main supply line. And we knew the roads south of us would be nearly impassable in the spring rains, another legitimate reason for our delay.

No matter how Lincoln, Halleck, and Stanton urged and even

ordered Rosecrans to take the field, the commander of the Army of the Cumberland would not be hurried.

In this, Rosecrans initially had my support. We needed time to rebuild our forces. Bragg's rebels weren't going anywhere. Like us, they were entrenched for the rest of the winter, healing their wounded and burying their dead.

"Do you know what that fool Halleck is doing now?" Rosecrans asked me. His face could get as red as Sherman's. "That wooden-head is offering the next promotion to major general to the next commander who wins a major battle. What an insult! I don't need such an incentive to do my duty. Maybe Grant does, as bogged down as he is near Vicksburg. Someone who came by a promotion that way is a disgrace."

"I agree, general," I replied. "I see Lincoln's hand in that. It smells of politics, or business. A lawyer's trick."

"I will do my duty as I see fit," the Cumberland commander concluded.

While I applaud Rosecrans' rejection of Halleck's promotion "contest," I fear that he was too harsh in rejecting it, offending Halleck needlessly. This may have put Grant ahead of Rosecrans among Halleck's favorites, which likely hurt the Army of the Cumberland later in the summer when we desperately needed reinforcements.

Rosecrans even threatened to resign in March over the harassment from Washington. I urged him to hold on. As irritating as the wires from Washington could be, the weight we were under was far less than what bore down on Lincoln. I seldom felt so forgiving toward our superiors in Washington, but I knew that the general's resignation at that time would not have improved matters. I doubt I would have gotten Rosecrans' job, anyway. Not at that time.

When spring began, many of our troops, and theirs, received leave to visit loved ones and tend to their farms. I too won a chance to see Frances, but I feared Bragg might attack while I was in New York. So many regrets I had during the war, not least of which is that I gave up an opportunity to enjoy my wife's company because I gave too much respect to Bragg's ambition. He didn't stir.

Not every Union soldier shared my concerns about a possible rebel offensive in early spring. One private, who wasn't fortunate enough to win leave, came to me directly and asked for a furlough. He did not stand on ceremony as he made his request.

"I ain't seen my old woman, general, for four months," the private said as he whittled a stick down to a toothpick.

"And I haven't seen mine for two years," I replied righteously. "If your general can submit to such privation, certainly a private can."

"Don't know about that, general, you see me and my wife ain't made that way," the private responded.

The two of us enjoyed a laugh. I gave him a furlough after all.

At a careful and deliberate pace, the Army of the Cumberland built up an adequate supply of men, horses, mules, food, clothing, arms, and ammunition. As I told a battery commander trying to repair a broken harness, "Keep everything in order. The fate of a battle may turn on a buckle or a linchpin."

Rosecrans' command grew to nearly ninety thousand soldiers. It was divided with the Fourteenth Army Corps in the center, the Twentieth on the right wing, and the Twenty-First on the left. Plus a reserve corps.

I commanded the Fourteenth Corps, and I took special care in its training, as parade-ground marching impressed me less and less. War had caused me to evolve in my thinking. I decided that the best way to prepare soldiers for major battles is to send them out to fight little ones. A man who has fought a lion might not be as frightened the first time he sees an elephant. While we occupied Murfreesboro that spring, I would send out small detachments as skirmishers against Bragg's cavalry or forward units. After short but not too deadly encounters with the enemy, the new Union soldiers would return to camp sprinkled, but not drenched, by a baptism of fire. (My wife tells me my use of metaphors is labored here. She can edit this later.)

In May, we heard of the Battle of Chancellorsville, another

tremendous victory for Lee. My old friend bested another Union commander, Joe Hooker this time, and halted another Union invasion of Virginia. Yet it was a crippling loss for the rebels as well. One of Lee's best generals, Tom Jackson, was killed, accidentally shot by his own men.

Though I did not mourn the death of an enemy, I was saddened as I remembered how earnestly in early 1861 I wanted to command the Virginia Military Institute, where Jackson was considered an unimpressive instructor. Had wisdom prevailed, had Virginia been courageous enough to resist secession and make the fire-eaters stand down, there might have been no war, and I might eventually have been placed in charge of VMI. Then I would have taught Jackson how to be a better teacher.

Now he was a slain hero known as "Stonewall," beloved in the South, feared in the North. Better for him had he stayed a simple classroom instructor, obscure but alive to be with his family. That is all the sympathy I could spare for a traitor.

Hooker's loss at Chancellorsville made Lincoln even more anxious for Rosecrans to take the field. May passed, however, and Rosecrans remained in Murfreesboro. June was running out, and still Rosecrans waited. The telegrams from Lincoln and Halleck grew ever more exasperated. It was the kind of pressure I myself would encounter eighteen months hence, but in June of 1863, even someone as deliberate as I could appreciate Lincoln's impatience.

However, Rosecrans had devised a brilliant strategy, one he kept secret for a long time, and one that I, when informed of it at last, did not like. Its results are not to be gainsaid, however.

The main part of Bragg's army was about twenty miles south of us, well entrenched. Between us and the enemy was a long mountainous ridge, a barrier that could have been an obstacle to us, but one that Rosecrans turned into a screen that shielded our movement from rebel eyes.

There were four gaps in that ridge, two of which were the quickest, most direct way to get at the butternuts. Rosecrans rejected such a frontal assault. Instead he employed what he called a double feint. One part of the Army of the Cumberland moved far to the west, another far to the east. Plus he sent just enough units toward the center to make the enemy think the main Union attack might also come there. But Rosecrans planned for the primary force, led by my 14th Corps and McCook's 21st Corps, to go southeast through Hoover's Gap. If we could get through this gap before Bragg knew what was happening, we could force him out of his entrenchments into the open, or better yet, make him retreat and trap him against the unfordable Tennessee River.

As I said, a brilliant plan, if it worked. What appears feasible on a map often doesn't exist in the reality of battle. I remember expressing my doubts to Rosecrans.

"General, I wonder if this maneuver is too much even for experienced troops to handle."

"Explain your reasoning, Old Tom."

"It's so intricate that I'm concerned some unknown element may throw us off and cost us the element of surprise. Bragg is not always a fool."

"Yes, I realize the double feint is a risk, but I trust your troops will be quick to the mark."

"Quick yes, but it's almost a triple feint you've conjured up."

"It will work, Tom, it will work. Even if Bragg is not a fool, he'll be as helpless as a motherless calf."

"Very well, we'll be ready as soon as you give the word. But we must also trust to luck."

"I believe that our Savior will give us luck."

"I envy your faith. Mine is that we must be prepared for whatever the Redeemer plans for us, good luck or bad."

"With my luck and your skill, we can steal a march on Bragg and avoid another Stones River. And Tom, as an added inducement, if we pull this off, it will silence Halleck's insults for a while."

"You have admirable goals, general. We shall do our best."

Early on the morning of June 24 came the order to strike tents. After nearly six months in camp, it was good to leave Murfreesboro behind. Seemingly the heavens did not agree, for there came rain, not a sprinkling shower but a drenching downpour for days.

Yet before the deluge turned most roads into rivers of mud, the Union achieved a fast success. A mounted infantry brigade led by Colonel John Wilder, armed with seven-shot Spencer carbines paid for by Wilder and his men themselves, captured the whole three miles of Hoover's Gap, holding it until relieved. Their daring opened the way for my corps to advance around the rebel flank and strike them in the rear. I shook Wilder's hand and told him that "you have saved the lives of a thousand men by your gallant conduct today. I didn't expect to get this gap for three days."

Bragg reportedly was suffering from boils when he heard that my command and McCook's were through the gap. Now he had something more painful to plague him. By June 27, we were at the town of Manchester, ten or so miles from Bragg's eastern flank. If our forces in the far eastern feint, under Crittenden, had not been delayed two days by the mud in their path, we would have cut off Bragg's way to retreat. The rebels saw their peril and quickly pulled back to the town of Tullohoma. Three days later, seeing us threatening the railroad bridges that led back to Chattanooga, Bragg gave the order to retreat again. After a year in which he nearly conquered most of Kentucky and Tennessee, Bragg and his boils were back in Chattanooga, close to the Georgia line where he began.

It was a happy time for the Army of the Cumberland. It even stopped raining. When I met Rosecrans at Tullohoma, I told him that his army's efforts were "the grandest campaign of your life." It cost us only 570 lives, an effusion of blood to be sure, but a series of pitched battles would have been much more murderous.

Hearing of the Union victories at Vicksburg and Gettysburg made us even happier that July. Sam Grant and George Meade had done well. I let myself briefly hope that I might see Frances soon.

I was so happy I even made a speech, a short one. When some of my men serenaded me with the Fourteenth Corps band, I came out of my tent to acknowledge their cheers. I raised my hand and nearly shouted: "Soldiers, when I saw the gallant charges and assaults you made that drove the enemy out of Hoover's Gap, I felt proud of my corps."

Their cheers must have been heard in Chattanooga.

But ofttimes victory is a prelude to defeat. A general becomes overconfident, too sure he has the enemy on the run, and he becomes a bit less prudent in his strategy and tactics. That was Rosecrans' hubris.

At least he realized that the campaign would become more difficult after Tullohoma. The enemy was retreating but not routed. Rosecrans wanted to take Chattanooga by outflanking Bragg, again by dividing our army in three. Only now the mountain passes we would advance through were so far apart that each third of the Army of the Cumberland would be cut off from any support from the other two corps. If Bragg smelled out this strategy, he could defeat each corps at his leisure.

I suggested going much farther south for the flanking maneuver, where we would present a united front. Today I will not insist that my suggestion would have been a success, only that we might have avoided the disaster that lay ahead.

When the corn in the fields was ripe enough to provide feed for our mules and horses, we knew it was time to go. We gathered food and ammunition for a twenty-day march and finished building a bridge over the Tennessee at the aptly named Bridgeport. On August 16, we renewed our hunt for Bragg.

It was hard going. There were rivers to ford, mountains to avoid and roads to be made where there were none. Still there was satisfaction, even comfort, in being a member of an advancing army. Being on the move keeps soldiers healthier and happier than being bivouacked in one place too long where disease can flourish. When the food and water are plentiful, the weather pleasant and each night's position secure, there is a prideful pleasure in looking out upon a well-organized campsite, smelling the cooking fires, tasting the coffee and hearing the soldiers talk, laugh, and sing. Before I knew the joys of married life with Mrs. Thomas, I would have said such a campsite was better than any place I had ever lived, better even than the farm in Southampton County when my father lived.

As Frances, with an attractive smile, reads this latter sentence, she asks me if the enlisted men and low-ranking officers would have shared my opinion of now happy army life could be. She is thinking of the whittler who asked me for a furlough. Well, I reply to her, that private surely would snort in derision if he had the chance to read that preceding paragraph. Even if this soldier had all the creature comforts of the camp that were my due as a general, he might still have nothing but regret for ever being apart from his "old woman." And yes, Fanny, I know that regret all too well.

Most soldiers, however, would nod in acknowledgment at the sense of comradery and purpose that a safe campsite, decent shoes, and a full stomach will give you. You find contentment where you can, even as you yearn for home and family. Such good memories give one strength to withstand the hellish ones.

As August turned into September, McCook took his third of the Cumberlands far around the right end to the town of Alpine, and Crittenden took the direct course to Chattanooga. My command was in the center, pushing toward Lookout Mountain, 2,200 feet above us, overlooking the Valley of the Tennessee and our objective. On September 8, advance troops reported dust clouds floating south of the city. Bragg must be retreating again, I thought. Crittenden's advance, and the other flanking movements, forced the rebels out. Rosecrans' strategy had worked so far. A United States flag flew again over the vital railroad city on September 9.

Yet the Union forces were still scattered over a sixty-mile front. Rosecrans ordered us to keep after Bragg. I sent him a message suggesting consolidating our troops in Chattanooga before setting another trap for the rebels. We could secure our supply lines back to Nashville and make the newest Union city a citadel.

Rosecrans was in too much haste to ponder my advice. He could taste victory and thought Bragg's army was whipped. If only Rosecrans hadn't strayed from his clever strategy that had taken us so far. Also weighing on his mind must have been the vituperation that Meade received from Lincoln and others when he failed to destroy Lee's beaten army in the aftermath of Gettysburg. So the Cumberlands' commander told me to advance toward the Georgia town of Lafayette, helping McCook threaten Bragg's flank.

Rosecrans might well have succeeded if he could have gotten reinforcements from Knoxville, the east Tennessee city that Ambrose Burnside's Union forces had just captured. Burnside, who had been thoroughly thrashed by Lee at Fredericksburg, had been transferred west after this 1862 defeat and given command of the Army of the Ohio. Why he received such a prestigious command I cannot say, but politics would be my guess. To be fair, Burnside did better than one might expect. His army set out from Cincinnati in mid-August of 1863 and captured Knoxville virtually unopposed in early September, mainly because nearly all the rebels defending that town had been sent 100 miles south to defend the more militarily important city of Chattanooga from Rosecrans' advance.

Once he was settled in Knoxville, Burnside ignored all requests to leave the city to reinforce Rosecrans. Likely he was all too aware of his inadequacies, and thus refused to risk another defeat like Fredericksburg by taking the field.

It also might have helped us if Halleck had immediately ordered Grant to send us reinforcements from his troops, who were idle after the fall of Vicksburg in July. Apparently, Halleck wasn't impressed by the relatively easy advance we had made toward Chattanooga, thinking we should have shed as much blood as Grant did in Mississippi. He let Grant rest far too long.

None of us on the Union side was aware of the reinforcements headed Bragg's way. There was desperation in the South after the twin defeats of Gettysburg and Vicksburg. If Bragg were beaten, the road would be open to Atlanta and then the Atlantic, and the end of the war. To stave off such a collapse, the South was sending Bragg troops from Joe Johnston's failed effort to lift the siege of Vicksburg, and Lee was sending James Longstreet's corps from the Army of Northern Virginia.

And the bulk of Bragg's army was headed to Lafayette, where

they could have overwhelmed my smaller command. I began to suspect this when James Negley, commander of one of my advance divisions, reported capturing a rebel officer whose non-cooperative answers during questioning hinted that a major enemy force was waiting for us.

I sent a message to Rosecrans with this information, and he replied by chastising me for slowness. Hang it all, I thought, now Rosecrans is becoming as silly as Halleck. "Old Brains" reportedly had the insane notion that Bragg was sending part of his army to Lee.

Soon Negley's division found out that the major enemy force was no phantom. His troops were able to draw back without being trapped. Rosecrans still believed I was jumping at shadows. It was not until September 12 that he realized how dangerous our position was, calling it "a matter of life and death." He ordered the three parts of his army to unite, which we did by September 17. Bragg had missed his first chance to destroy us. But such a hurried consolidation left us more vulnerable than if we had been united from the start of our march in August. So I believe, even if Rosecrans disagrees.

By September 14, even Halleck could grasp what was happening. He ordered Burnside and Grant to send every soldier they could spare to Chattanooga. His order came far too late to affect the coming battle. The Army of the Cumberland was near the banks of the Chickamauga River.

CHAPTER 15

IN WHICH WE ENDURE THE 'RIVER OF DEATH'

The American people know me chiefly because of a battle that began on September 19, 1863. It gave me a nearly unpronounceable nickname, "the Rock of Chickamauga." I do not glory in this sobriquet, complimentary as it may be, for it was bestowed in the aftermath of the most tragic day ever experienced by the Army of the Cumberland. The bitterness of this defeat is still freshly painful to me.

Some with too fanciful a sense of foreshadowing claim Chickamauga is a Cherokee word meaning "river of death." I care not. Hearing that word only reminds me that the first day of the battle was terrible, and the second was nearly an apocalypse.

It should be remembered that in the midst of this defeat, most Cumberland men did their duty with great skill and bravery, which allowed a beaten army to fight again within weeks. There were thousands of Union troops who stood like a rock against the rebel wave. Together, we made a mountain.

Faulty intelligence work was the bane of Chickamauga. It decided where the battle began, and it eventually decided the victor. A colonel reported to me that there was a single enemy battalion on our side of the Chickamauga and that he had destroyed the only nearby bridge, stranding the rebels on the western shore. I sent part of my command to rout this "isolated" unit.

As you might suspect, it was no small rebel force at all—it was Nathan Bedford Forrest's cavalry, which dealt roughly with the Union attackers. A blueclad general with a ready sense of humor, John Croxton, sent me a message asking which "isolated" brigade I wanted captured of the five or six he had run into. It was the only time in those two days that I laughed. Thus began the Battle of Chickamauga.

Things were piecemeal at first, with fierce clashes in my sector while the rest of Rosecrans' army, though consolidating, was still strung out for nearly seven miles, mostly to the south of me.

Bragg, too, was out of position. He was to have made his main attack to the south, but Croxton's adventure had caused the battle to spread to the north. Forrest's cavalry and rebel infantry nearly overwhelmed us until we received reinforcements.

That was the nature of the first day: A blue or gray formation was threatened and calling for help; other units would scramble to save them, and by twilight both armies were fully involved.

It seemed as if I spent the entire first day on horseback, sending couriers hither and thither, including a nephew I was proud to command, Captain Sanford Kellogg. Mrs. Thomas would have been especially proud of him that day. But when battle is joined, I forget who is related to me. I even forget whom I love. I am only aware of the fighting and what I must do to win the battle or save my command. My apologies, Frances. She understands.

Even dusk gave us no peace that first day. Forces under Pat Cleburne, one of the rebels' best divisional commanders, pushed us back a mile before darkness was full. A hard day was over, and we knew a harder one would follow. The soldiers passed a chilly autumn-like night, most of them shivering because they had thrown away their blankets in the heat of battle. The two armies were camped so close to each other that they could hear the groans and mewlings of the wounded and dying of both sides.

For me, that night was passed in yet another council of war. I rode south to a widow's house where Rosecrans had made his headquarters. The Cumberland commander thought we were greatly outnumbered. Prisoners taken that day came from so many different rebel armies that he believed Jefferson Davis had sent Bragg every spare man in a butternut uniform from Texas to Virginia. Later we learned that the opposing armies were evenly matched, about sixty thousand each.

Not knowing this during the night at the widow's house, Rosecrans didn't want to hear about taking the offensive—defense was his priority. I concurred and told him I was sure that with reinforcement, the troops under me could hold the north side of our position, or the left as it looked on our maps. I suggested that the right and center of our lines be withdrawn to hills behind Lafayette Road (a north-south route) and the eastern part of Missionary Ridge, ensuring our control of the major roads back to Chattanooga.

Was I, the general who once proclaimed that "this army can't retreat," advocating the kind of backward maneuver that Bragg specialized in? No, by thunder, I was thinking of victory as always!

From the defensive position I recommended, we would have been an imposingly rocky shore that would have broken up the gray tide into harmless trickles. Did I express myself in such overwrought imagery? No, I'm afraid I again slept through much of the council, only occasionally bestirring myself to remind the other generals to strengthen the left. "Where are we going to take it from?" Rosecrans would ask each time. I would drift back to sleep without answering him, for the solution was obvious. My reinforcements could be taken from the center and the right.

Rosecrans did not want to relinquish as much ground as I proposed, but he did withdraw the center and right of our army slightly to the west of Lafayette Road in this way: Alexander McCook moved his two divisions to connect with James Negley's division on my right, while Thomas Crittenden pulled his divisions back for close-up support of the center, or to quickly go wherever they were needed, left or right. My five entrenched divisions on the left remained slightly to the east of the road.

Rosecrans was wise to keep three brigades under Gordon Granger covering the Rossville Gap, the best way to travel the ten miles back to Chattanooga. Protecting this passage was why I was so insistent on protecting our left. Of Granger I will have more to say in this narrative.

About midnight, after all was agreed to, Rosecrans served coffee and McCook entertained us by singing a sad ballad called "The Hebrew Maiden." I tried to sleep through this as well.

When I returned to my campfire, I studied a map for a few minutes by its light. I could sense many eyes upon me, soldiers of my corps who had shaken off slumber to see what my temper was, a forecast for the next day's combat. Perhaps they gained reassurance from my countenance, for they shuffled back to their fires silently. Those weary men had already toiled long into the darkness to entrench our position with fallen trees, fence rails and stones.

I felt no foreboding over what awaited us at dawn on this Sunday, merely the expectation of another difficult day. But of one thing I was certain as I gazed at the map—unlike at Perryville, Stones River, and Tullahoma, Bragg would not voluntarily retreat from this place.

It was good I had napped at the council of war, for at 2:00 a.m. I received a message from a divisional commander, Absalom Baird, that his forces could not extend all the way to their assigned position and would be driven back even farther if Cleburne's infantry assailed them as they had that evening. A horseback inspection convinced me that Baird was correct, and I requested that Negley's division on my right move closer to me. Rosecrans sent me a message agreeing to my request, allowing me to rest easy for the remainder of the night under an oak tree, a root serving as my pillow.

I awoke about 6:00 a.m., becoming ill at ease as I was informed that Negley had yet to show. Still I was almost exuberant compared to Rosecrans, who had come north to encourage the men of my command. He looked as if he'd never found time for any kind of repose. Doubtless the strain of our five-week campaign was nearly overwhelming the commander, whose face was as gray as the haze left from the previous day's gunfire. But his words were inspiring. "Fight today as well as you did yesterday, and we shall whip them," Rosecrans shouted to cheers.

Misunderstandings and blunders often decide battles. There were a host of them that Sunday, most of which I didn't learn of until we were licking our wounds in Chattanooga. Negley hadn't moved because his withdrawal would have left a mile-wide gap in the Union's center. Negley was waiting for Thomas Wood's division to relieve him. Wood was waiting for Crittenden's order, and Crittenden was waiting for McCook's order. Rosecrans could not hold his temper as he learned of the inefficient chain of command, and he lit into Wood in the presence of the division leader's staff. I was not witness to this, but others reported to me Rosecrans' exact words.

"What is the meaning of this, sir?" he snarled at Wood, an honorable West Pointer. "You have disobeyed my specific orders. By your damnable negligence you are endangering the safety of the entire army, and by God I will not tolerate it! Move your division at once, as I have instructed, or the consequences will not be pleasant for yourself."

Wood, who was not truly at fault for his delay, kept his composure during this upbraiding, as a West Pointer should. He did as his commander ordered and would not tarry again over any order from him. Had I been in Rosecrans' position, I might well have been tempted to be as severe in scolding Wood, though I would not have done it in the presence of his staff. But I often resist using a verbal whip on a man, just as I resist using a leather whip on a horse. In either case, the whip can scar the user as well as the target.

Rosecrans might not have castigated Wood so fiercely had he known that Bragg was having just as many problems getting his generals to move. One of them, the Episcopal Bishop Leonidas Polk, was still at breakfast long after Bragg expected him to initiate the rebel attack. Polk's delay put Bragg in an even blacker mood than usual, I am told. The grayshirts did not strike us until nearly ten in the morning, at least four hours past the time Bragg wanted the belligerence to commence. He wrote after the war that if the attack had started on time, "our independence might have been won."

When the rebels began their artillery assault, I sat on horseback just behind the Union lines. An enemy shell passed between me and one of my staff. We smiled at each other, sharing the humor that sometimes accompanies danger. Then a second shell also passed between us, and neither of us smiled. "I think we had better retire a little," I told the aide. We went back a few yards into the woods momentarily.

My five divisions were commanded by Absalom Baird, John Palmer, Richard Johnson, Joseph Reynolds, and John Brannan. Good men all, especially on this day. All five were under assault as soon as the tardy butternuts began to advance. I needed Negley to shore up our position, but he was even more tardy than Bragg's generals. Parts of Negley's command would arrive in haphazard fashion, and I would promptly send them wherever the need was most dire.

Then came the decisive blunder. One of my observers, whom I shall not shame by writing his name even in this private correspondence, was riding along the line when he noticed what he took to be a gap.* It was between the forces of Brannan and Wood, the latter being the general so recently humiliated by Rosecrans. This observer neglected to reconnoiter the situation fully. Had he done so, he would have found that Brannan had merely withdrawn a short distance into the woods to meet a flank attack.

The observer jumped to the conclusion that this was a dangerous gap that threatened another of my divisions, the one commanded by Reynolds. I was informed of this non-existent crisis, and, not having the opportunity to make my own observation

---

* Editor's note: The blundering observer may have been Sanford Kellogg, the nephew of Frances Thomas. If in fact Mrs. Thomas was writing down the general's narration at this time, he may have shown the better part of valor by not naming him in her presence.

and believing the situation required a speedy response, I sent an aide to apprise Rosecrans of the apparent emergency. Rosecrans, to his credit, quickly sent an order to Wood to reinforce Reynolds, the next man over. To Rosecrans' discredit, the order was unclear.

It read: "The general commanding directs that you close up on Reynolds as fast as possible and support him."

Had I received this order, I would have wondered if Rosecrans wanted me to close up on the side or from the rear. During the recriminations in the days ahead, Rosecrans insisted that he meant for Wood to close up to the side of Reynolds, plugging the supposed gap. Wood, however, took it to mean that he should move up "in support" of Reynolds, meaning to the rear. Had I been in Wood's place, I would have asked for a clarification, but Wood, having been so mortified by Rosecrans earlier that morning for sluggishness, was not going to hesitate now. Thus Wood speedily shifted his division rearward so he could march completely around Brannan to find Reynolds. The apparent gap was now an actual one.

One might defend the vagueness of Rosecrans' order because of his lack of sleep and his overall exhaustion from the previous day. That is an excuse that cannot be accepted, no matter how much respect I have for Rosecrans. Everyone in the Army of the Cumberland was fatigued. It is the responsibility of a commanding general to shake off exhaustion during battle and be clear-headed.

Should I have mistrusted the observer's report and gone myself to see if his supposed gap existed? Until this instance, the observer had always been accurate in his reports, so I feel no guilt for having trusted him again. I could not be everywhere at once, though I was in the saddle constantly that morning. No blame ever fell on me over the mistaken gap, yet I wish I'd had the premonition to ride even farther and see where Brannan actually was situated.

The Union blunder was compounded by one of Bragg's rare strokes of good fortune. As the Union gap appeared, so did several rebel brigades. They were part of James Longstreet's forces, who only two months before had failed to break the final blue line at

Gettysburg. At this fateful moment at Chickamauga, there was no blue line to stop them.

A third of the Union army melted like lard on a hot griddle. Rosecrans, who was seen making the sign of the cross as the battle reached him, discovered that he was not God's favorite on this day. The good Catholic retreated along with many more of other faiths. McCook and Crittenden took flight, as did Sheridan and too many other generals. They were not cowards; they simply lost control of their soldiers. McCook and Crittenden told me later that they had no idea I hadn't joined them in their abandonment. Rosecrans also thought that the entire line had collapsed and we would have to make a last stand in Chattanooga.

All this happened before noon on what I remember as the longest day of my life. At this time I was unsure of the extent of the disaster. Had I been fully informed, and had I the leisure to consider the irony, it would have struck me that the left side of Rosecrans' army, what I considered the weakest part of it, was now *all* that remained of it.

We made our stand on two small hills that would loom large in the lore of the Army of the Cumberland. Horseshoe Ridge and Snodgrass Hill were the very part of Missionary Ridge that I had wanted the whole army to occupy. Now this piece of land would have to serve as our Thermopylae, the place where a few hundred Spartans held off thousands of Persians more than two thousand years ago. As desperate as our situation was, at least we were not as badly outnumbered as the Spartans. Nearly forty thousand men in blue so far had refused to give way to the sixty thousand rebels.

Brannan's division held our right side, almost perpendicular to the rest of my forces I placed on our left. I rode my big bay Billy among the soldiers, helping distribute ammunition and bolstering their resolution, for I knew the temptation to run for Chattanooga would seem quite sensible now. Not for me. This Southern-born Union man knew he had to stand fast. Once during the fiercest part of the fight, two officers felt the need to retire and ran straight into me. "Gentlemen" I told them, "your regiment is there, or ought to be there, and you will join your commands instantly!" They did so.

Most other officers never wavered. I told Colonel Charles Harker that "this hill must be held, and I trust you to do it." He answered, "We will hold it or die here." I made a similar request to Colonel Emerson Opdyke, who gave an even more poetic reply, "We will hold this ground or go to heaven from it." Their soldiers nodded at these words, then strengthened their barricades that were as strong as the brave sentiments of their officers.

Soon the rebels were hammering at our left. Thrice they surged up the slope, and thrice they were forced to retreat. As heartening as this was, my concern grew for our right. Negley, the tardy Negley, finally arrived on the far right but was immediately thrown back. The general then decided to head for Chattanooga and, to add to his day's accomplishments, took our ammunition train with him. The men on Horseshoe Ridge and Snodgrass Hill became so low on cartridges that they had to search the bodies of the dead and wounded. This was not the worst that the casualties had to suffer. Some of the woods caught fire from flaming shells, burning many men on both sides who either couldn't move or would never move again.

Had Bragg sent all his forces in one giant systematic wave, it might have gone ill for us. Thankfully for the Union, he could never get his generals to work in concert.

And then another crisis emerged, a dust cloud in our rear. Was it friend or foe? God forbid, was it Forrest? I could not tell which flag the advancing column bore. If they were the enemy, I feared the Cumberlands' heroism would be in vain. I am known for remaining calm when all about me are in an uproar, but in those moments I was fidgety in my saddle and pulling on my graying beard. Then a war correspondent, William Shanks, told me he was certain he saw a United States flag.

"Do you think so, do you think so?" I asked, for the first time in the war glad to have a member of the press along. Then I myself could make out the Union banners of Gordon Granger's brigades, and I knew we might yet survive this day. "Damn the enemy! Bragg is fighting without any system," I shouted with relief.

Without Granger and his men, we might have suffered an annihilation as total as that suffered by Napoleon's Old Guard at Waterloo. Yet Granger's timely appearance was against orders. His reserves, 3,500 men, had been guarding the Rossville Gap as a possible path of retreat. About 11:00 a.m., the time Longstreet made his advance that sent Rosecrans on his way to Chattanooga, Granger climbed a haystack to find out what was transpiring to his south. Seeing the smoke and hearing the gunfire, he became convinced that my position was in mortal peril.

"I'm going to Thomas, orders or no orders!" he exclaimed. Granger left one brigade to guard the road, then set off in search of me with two brigades led by General James Steedman. They had to fight their way through to reach me.

Now the whole of military discipline depends on the assumption that an order will be obeyed. But in combat, situations change rapidly, and an officer must be wise enough to know when an order no longer has meaning, and indeed, that following that order to the letter could lead to catastrophe. This was the case for Granger, and if, on another day, he had chosen the wrong course, his action could have meant a court-martial and the end of his military career. I salute the wisdom and courage of Granger in making the correct decision.

When he arrived about 1:00 p.m., I greeted him with a smile and a handshake. "I'm very glad to see you, general," I told him.

My Union soldiers were holding on the left, but the right was near to being overwhelmed by the butternuts. Granger saw this at once, telling me that "those men must be driven back."

"Can you do it?" I asked.

"Yes," Granger replied. "My men are fresh, and they are just the fellows for that work. They are raw troops, and they don't know any better than to charge up there."

If soldiers' mothers and sweethearts were to read that last quotation, they might condemn Granger as a ruthless ghoul. No, no, ladies, in the heat of battle, Granger's frankness was most welcome, as were the ten thousand rounds of ammunition he brought with him.

When Steedman arrived, I greeted him as happily as I did Granger.

"General Steedman, I have always been glad to see you, but never so glad as now."

I then pointed to the right and said, "Take that ridge."

He did not hesitate but got his men ready immediately. Just before Steedman departed, he heard me give instructions to an aide to relay to Harker.

"Where will I find you when I return?" the aide asked.

"Here!" I bellowed.

The aide saluted and did his duty. I wanted no one within hearing range to think I had any plans for retreating. I wrote earlier in this chapter that I try to resist using a verbal whip. Sometimes I do not resist.

Steedman grinned at my outburst, told a staff officer to make sure his name was spelled right in the obituaries and led those "raw troops" into one of the most important charges of the war. When a few of them hesitated, he took hold of some regimental colors and shouted, "Go back boys, go back, but the flag can't go with you!" Though his horse was shot out from under him, he and his men persevered through some of the most ghastly close combat I have ever seen. Steedman halted the enemy's advance at the cost of half of his men being killed or wounded. But his own obituary, at least, was not needed on that awful day.

I must mention another general who came to our rescue, Ferdinand Van Derveer, who like Granger and Steedman, moved his brigade toward our position without orders at the sound of the guns. There were others I could name, and in fact I did name them all in my official report weeks later. So many wise and brave soldiers.

About 4:00 p.m., Rosecrans' top aide, James Garfield, made his way to me and told me all of what happened to the rest of the Army of the Cumberland.* He advised me to retreat as soon as possible. I replied it would ruin us to pull back in broad daylight. Garfield looked about, saw how we had withstood everything the enemy sent against us, and rode back to Rosecrans, telling him that the Union could still win this battle if I were reinforced.

Garfield also wired the War Department that night, saying, "Thomas standing like a rock. ... General Thomas has fought a most terrific battle and has damaged the enemy badly. ... Longstreet's Virginians have got their bellies full. ... I believe we can now crown the whole battle with victory."

Regretfully, Rosecrans also had his belly full, and he sent me an order to retreat. In truth, I can't predict what might have happened if Rosecrans could have convinced the retreating part of his army to reverse course and join us on Snodgrass Hill and Horseshoe Ridge.

After sunset, I sent for Steedman, who had done so much to keep us from being totally conquered. When he reached me, I was sitting on a log, picking off pieces of bark, biting them and throwing them away. If I hadn't been doing that, I would have been grinding my teeth.

"General Steedman, you know we must obey orders in war," I told him. "I have received orders to fall back on Rossville."

"General, you should protest this!" he replied. "We can hold out all night here. The rebels are spent—we can beat them in the morning. We can make Bragg run all the way to Atlanta."

"Lord knows you may be right, but this order must be followed because Rosecrans and the others aren't coming back. Please help me plan how it should be done."

The retreat was a difficult maneuver, and a galling one, to pull back so quickly in the face of the enemy and hear the rebels' ugly screeches in their triumph. Most of our divisions did well in maintaining control in a situation that easily could have been a repeat of

---

* Editor's note: James Garfield was elected U.S. president in 1880. His daring journey to Thomas' position was often mentioned in his presidential campaign, and "Garfield's Ride" was credited with helping convince voters that he deserved the White House.

that morning's rout. Reynolds' division, especially, conducted a splendid counterattack that kept the way open for other divisions to retire.

I was so moved by the troops' courage in this that after I saw a regiment fire its last cartridges and beat back a charge at bayonet point, I went to one of the soldiers to shake his hand and thank him for his gallantry. I could have shaken the hands of forty thousand other soldiers, for all of them did credit to the United States flag.

Of the 60,000 Union men who took the field that Sunday, 1,700 died, 10,000 were wounded and 4,700 were missing or captured. It was a sad day for the rebels as well, even in their victory, with 2,300 dead, 14,000 wounded and 1,400 captured or missing. One of the South's wounded was General John Hood, who lost a leg. He had already lost use of an arm at Gettysburg.

Among the South's dead was another general, Benjamin Hardin Helm, the Kentucky-born brother-in-law of Abraham Lincoln.

As I related at the beginning of this chapter, the recognition I received after this battle was more bitter than sweet. Better to be hailed for helping assure a victory than being the rearguard in a defeat. But years later, I learned that Chickamauga had at least raised me in the estimation of the president, who I'm told mourned greatly for his brother-in-law.

Three days after the battle, a political hack from New York sent the president a telegram that questioned my patriotism and competence. Lincoln wrote a reply, saying, in part, that "nothing could be more ungracious than to indulge any suspicions towards General Thomas. It is doubtful whether his heroism and skill exhibited last Sunday afternoon has ever been surpassed in the world."

Then the president decided not to telegraph these words, thinking it was beneath the dignity of his office to reply to such a political scoundrel. "I will pay no attention to the crazy fellow," he told the cipher clerk on duty that night at the War Department.

But the clerk saved Lincoln's reply. This man, Charles Tinker, met me in Washington in 1867, two years after the end of the war, and gave me his copy of the president's words, a gift for which I was most grateful. Had I had known of Lincoln's sentiments after this battle, I might have been more charitable in my feelings toward him.

Riding to Rossville late on September 20, 1863, I had never been so drained. Sheridan, from whom I had expected reinforcements earlier in the day, came up in the darkness to cover our retreat. One of those swept along by the disaster that morning, Sheridan looked more exhausted than I did. He would eventually receive great accolades in this war, but not for anything he did this day.

We shared a sip of brandy from my saddlebag, neither of us yet ready to confront all we had to do to take back what we had just lost.

CHAPTER 16

IN WHICH I INADVERTENTLY INSULT GRANT

As horrendous as our defeat had been at Chickamauga, the Union was still in control of Chattanooga, and as long as we held this vital city, Bragg's victory was an empty one.

If the butternuts had stayed on the offensive and tried to take the city immediately after Chickamauga, I dread to say what the Union's fate would have been. Those Union men who had run from the rebels were still shuddering, and those of us who had resisted the onslaught were worn beyond measure. Yet Bragg hesitated, apparently cowed by the bloody cost of his triumph, and was content to watch us from the heights overlooking the city.

We soon heard rumors that this inaction infuriated Forrest, who insulted Bragg to his face, calling him a scoundrel and coward, and left his command. I'm surprised a duel did not occur, or that Forrest didn't simply shoot Bragg like a rabid hound.

Other generals made their disdain known in a more polite fashion, and their unrest forced Jefferson Davis to come down from Richmond to shore up this friendless general. Now Bragg is a scoundrel if ever there was one, but I must be fair to him. He is no coward. Nonetheless, his dithering made him so ineffective he might as well have been a poltroon.

So much for the victors. This rebel infighting might have cheered us had we known more details of it. We the vanquished had our own bitter aftermath. When the recriminations and demotions were over, some might have said I won more in defeat than Bragg won in victory. Grant, still idling in Vicksburg, won much more.

When I rode into Chattanooga, Rosecrans greeted me. He was shaken, knowing his once sterling reputation was tarnished.

"Thank you, general, for saving us from an even worse defeat than what we suffered this day," he told me.

"Well, there are many men to thank. My division commanders were superb, as were their troops."

"But I was sure you'd been overwhelmed, like the rest of us."

"Thank the Lord for Granger and his command. They arrived just when we needed them."

"I should have been with you, George, I should have been with you. When the right side collapsed, there was nothing I could do to stop the rout. I tried to get to you, but I was cut off. What happened —why was there such a gap?"

"We'll answer those questions in due time," I replied. "I'm sorry you couldn't be with us. Now we must prepare to defend this city."

"Was Garfield right?" Rosecrans asked. "Could we still have won the battle?"

"I don't know, general, I don't know. We would have needed every man who retreated to come back."

Some have asked me if Rosecrans had been drinking heavily before or during the battle. I think not. Even had he been so inclined, he wouldn't have had the time to drink.

The next day, Rosecrans wisely concentrated our forces in Chattanooga. Unwisely, he also withdrew from Lookout Mountain and Missionary Ridge, giving the rebels the high ground as well as two ferries over the Tennessee River that were crucial to our supplies. The grayclads took over these excellent defensive positions, putting us in a state of siege. In the Middle Ages, a besieged army was usually safe in a fortified castle. In 1863, we were in an exposed valley and the only castles were the highlands from where Bragg could see our every move.

Rosecrans' order to withdraw from the heights was followed despite protests from myself and several other generals. We told him he should not concentrate to such an extreme, to no avail. He considered the highlands too vulnerable.

Before the war, I would have been heartened by the beauty of Chattanooga, set as it is in the bend of the Tennessee, surrounded by green hills. Now the war had consumed it, and I only saw the city as a trap we must escape. Most of the city's six thousand citizens had already fled and so did not have to witness our troops taking food and other necessities from their homes, burning their trees and fences for fuel, and grazing our horses and mules wherever they could find anything edible. There were only about a thousand mournful white townspeople and perhaps the same number of hopeful Negroes left. They would all be as hungry as our soldiers.

Expecting a rebel attack that never came, we made the city ugly as we dug in. Our barricades would be all for naught if our supply lines were not renewed. Without food in Chattanooga, the enemy would not have to come within bullet range, because Bragg could simply wait for hunger to do its work.

I remember a proverb, whose origin escapes me, that victory has a thousand fathers, but defeat is an orphan.

Not Chickamauga—there were many generals blamed for its conception. Rosecrans of course. Negley most assuredly. Crittenden, McCook, and Sheridan deserved criticism, as well as poor Wood. Because of the thousands of gallant men who made their stand with me on Horseshoe Ridge, I was immune to the vituperation. I refused to join in the berating of my peers, thinking it was more important to set up lines of supply and defense.

As I've indicated previously in this narrative, Halleck and the War Department deserve part of the blame for our defeat for not reinforcing us quickly with troops from Grant and Burnside. But I did not express myself openly on this until much later. Even after the battle was over, I still had hopes that Rosecrans could rally us, and I did not want to undermine a commanding general for whom I had a personal and professional regard.

The most effective person at undermining Rosecrans was Charles Dana, the assistant secretary of war. Dana had been on an official visit to our army when it was caught up in the Chickamauga debacle. He was napping behind the lines when Longstreet's forces made their breakthrough, and he kept close to Rosecrans during the panicked retreat.

I have conflicting opinions about Dana. He had been a New York newspaper editor before the war, and you know my aversion to the press. Yet I've recently become aware that he praised me extravagantly to Lincoln, even repeating Rosecrans' old observation that I resembled George Washington.

But he also sent Lincoln unwarranted denunciations of Rosecrans, including questioning the general's making the sign of the cross during battle. Such a Catholic gesture gave us no heavenly assistance at Chickamauga, but it didn't signify that Rosecrans was unfit for command. Had I not been so busy during that dreadful day, I too might have sought divine succor.

Dana also had heard of an incident that discomfited both myself and Rosecrans. When the two of us inspected the progress of our barricades, many soldiers dropped their picks and spades and crowded around me in appreciation of our stand at Horseshoe Ridge, ignoring Rosecrans all the while. Their adulation embarrassed me and humiliated the commanding general, who did not deserve this abashment. Thankfully, it did not affect our personal or military friendship.

Three weeks after the battle, the assistant secretary came to my quarters, telling me that his superior in the War Department, Stanton, had long wanted me as commander of the Army of the Cumberland. Dana read me this telegram that Stanton had sent him: "The merits of General Thomas and the debt of gratitude the nation owes to his valor and skill are fully appreciated here, and I wish you to tell him so. It is not my fault that he was not in chief command months ago."

I could not speak for a moment. Who wouldn't enjoy such official praise after years of being ignored for deserved promotions?

"Tell Secretary Stanton I am grateful for his kind words," I finally replied, keeping my expression as solemn as I could manage. "Tell him and President Lincoln that I do indeed wish to command an army, one that I myself might organize with the proper discipline. But I do not want to take over an army where I might be accused of having intrigued to supplant the previous commander. General Rosecrans deserves better than that. So does the Army of the Cumberland, who are brave men despite our unfortunate second day at Chickamauga."

Dana tried to assure me on this point, even as he implied that I might already have been given command of the Cumberlands save for the opposition I still inspired in some Northern politicians. Oh Lord, this lack of respect was something I was used to. Horseshoe Ridge wasn't enough for these Yankees to prove that my Southern birth did not impede my loyalty. Dana insisted that Stanton and Lincoln had always known that I would be true to the Union and my sacred oath.

I thanked Dana and took counsel with myself, and then I warned Rosecrans of his jeopardy. I soon had Garfield tell Dana that I could not take over the Cumberlands, not under these conditions. At the risk of repetition, let me explain my principle on rank. This was a position I wanted and should have had much earlier in the war. But I wanted it in such a way that would not offend my sense of honor nor disrupt the proper chain of command. I know now that I wanted too much.

Our situation in Chattanooga soon put my desires on the wayside. Matters were growing worse for the troops.

Some men were so malnourished they could barely conduct themselves as soldiers. Without the ferries, supplies could only come in by wagon on a treacherous route from Nashville. Thousands of our mules and horses were dying, and those that survived had to be guarded so they wouldn't be butchered for what little meat was left on their bones. Starving bluecoats picked out grains of corn from where the livestock were fed, finding a little sustenance. Others argued over offal and whatever other scraps might be digestible. Some developed a taste for dog. Though we were moving at all speed to solve our supply problems, Dana's wires to Washington berated Rosecrans for dawdling, going so far as to accuse him of "imbecility."

What sealed Rosecrans' fate and ensured my promotion was a report by James Steedman, one of the generals who came to my relief on Horseshoe Ridge. At Lincoln's request, he went to the White House on October 16 to give his honest assessment of the other generals in Chattanooga. Steedman had been a rising politician in Ohio before the war, a Democrat who supported Stephen A. Douglas for president. In spite of that, Lincoln valued his opinion, and I cannot fault a general for telling a politician the truth. Steedman recommended me to lead the Army of the Cumberland. For all my complaints about Ohio generals, Steedman was a worthy man.

On October 19, nearly a month after our defeat at Chickamauga, Rosecrans was relieved and I became the commander of the Cumberlands. He took the news manfully and was not angry at me, knowing I had not undercut him for the command. When I read the orders, Rosecrans told me, "Thomas, don't say anything— there is no misunderstanding that can come between you and me. I know what you want to say, for Garfield told me, but what you have to do is to do it like a soldier."

I replied, "Well, I suppose I must do so, but I don't like it."

Old Rosy smiled, and we got on with the work that a change in command entails.

It seems as if all my promotions lacked joy. When I advanced early in the war, it was because those ahead of me in the chain of command were betraying their oath to the Union. I prefer to rise because of achievement, not because there is no one else available. Other promotions came late or were put off because of political considerations or some superior's personal dislike. This one came at the expense of a friend.

And this latest promotion held a hidden sting. Grant, the victor of Vicksburg, would become overall commander of three armies, including my Cumberlands. Dana and Stanton had implied to me that I would have an independent command, and when I accepted my new promotion, I thought my independence was assured. Not for a few days would I know better. Lincoln again gave me the short stick, feeling he had to appease Northern congressmen by making me answer to the Ohio-born Grant. His former command, the Army of the Tennessee, would go to Sherman, and Burnside would continue as head of the Army of the Ohio. All would be combined under Grant's leadership in something called the Military Department of the Mississippi.

Of the generals whose careers were marred by Chickamauga, Rosecrans was eventually sent to Missouri, a border state where small battles between regular armies were overshadowed by the horrors of guerrilla warfare. McCook, Crittenden, and Negley were court-martialed, and though acquitted, all had to wait more than a year before they were considered for command vacancies. Wood and Sheridan kept their jobs, however, and would soon distinguish themselves. I also appointed two exceptional generals to key Cumberland posts. W.F. "Baldy" Smith became chief engineer, and John Brannan became chief of artillery.

As I reorganized the Cumberlands, some officers complained when they did not rise in rank. I told one of these malcontents my philosophy after thirty years of Army life: "I have taken a great deal of pain to educate myself not to feel." Or to be more accurate, to keep my feelings veiled.

The first order Grant sent us was an insult: "Hold Chattanooga at all hazards." Good heavens, Dana's dispatches must have convinced him we were all craven yellowbellies, eager to disgrace ourselves by decamping back to Nashville. Rosecrans was also indignant, and he heartily approved my reply to Grant: "We will hold the town until we starve."

The Best General in the Civil War 147

At times I feared the situation could become that grim. The "cracker line," our only way to get food into the city, was stretched as thin as our horses' flanks. Yet there was hope. My reorganization seemed to lift the spirits of the soldiers, and my trusted quarter-master, James Donaldson, was getting the supply lines working in good order. Rosecrans had come up with a strong plan to lift the siege—a strategy he shared with Grant. The two met in Stevenson, Alabama — Rosecrans on his way out, Grant on his way in.

Sherman was also coming our way, with his new command. There were other reinforcements on the move. Part of the Army of the Potomac was coming south, led by Joe Hooker, the former chieftain of the entire Potomac command. I would be glad to have Hooker, despite the whipping he took from Lee earlier in the year at Chancellorsville. Burnside, another victim of Lee's generalship, would stay in Knoxville with his army.

Nothing definitive could be done, however, until Grant reached us. The last stage of his journey was a 60-mile ride by horse over Walden's Ridge. It was an arduous experience for him, for he had bruised his leg on horseback recently and would reinjure himself as he approached Chattanooga. Once a splendid equestrian, Grant now needed soldiers to lift him into his saddle, and crutches were required when he was afoot.

Late on the rainy day of October 23, Grant and his aides, including General John Rawlins and Colonel James Wilson, along with Dana, came to my headquarters, a one-story frame house I had made as comfortable as possible. Grant and I greeted each other with professional courtesy, certainly with more warmth than he had shown me during our last meeting in 1862 in Corinth, when he had been resentful over his temporary demotion.

(As an aside, Mrs. Thomas has made an observation as she reads this narrative. Frances maintains that Grant, a man of diminutive stature, was intimidated by my greater height and physique, and was jealous of my honorable record in the ante-bellum Army compared with his expulsion for inebriation. Her feminine insight is usually correct, but in this instance I cannot say yea or nay. Perhaps I should have acted in a more subservient manner to Grant in contrast to my more equitable dealings with Rosecrans and Buell. But such self-degrading behavior is anathema to me.)

Now on a cold night in 1863, Grant and I initially were civil to each other as we sat on opposite sides of the fireplace. He could not resist a dig at my army, however.

"Thomas, I met Rosecrans on my way here, and he said how much he appreciated the way you kept Chickamauga from being a bigger disgrace than it was for the Army of the Cumberland."

"General Grant, I'm glad for what General Rosecrans said. However, with all due respect, I have to say that while Chickamauga was a terrible defeat, I do not consider it a disgrace. Two thirds of the Cumberlands did not retreat."

"Well, too many of the Cumberlands ran. I only hope they won't run again."

"They will not."

"We'll see. At least we have Sherman coming to buck us up."

Grant was drenched from his travels, and I briefly considered offering him some of the brandy I kept hidden away for special or emergency occasions, but with his reputed weakness for whiskey, I thought it best to avoid any form of spirits. He did not indicate that his soaking bothered him and, moreover, seemed eager to talk about the reorganization of our forces. For the first time I realized that I had been humbugged again by Lincoln, this time through his underlings Stanton and Dana. My Army of the Cumberland would not be independent, Grant said. I would be at his beck and call.

Now occurred an incident that I believe colored our relations for the rest of the war and beyond.

I was so preoccupied by the news Grant brought that I forgot he was still wet. As Grant and I discussed the military situation, Rawlins must have fumed, thinking me a cad for prolonging his superior's discomfort. Finally Wilson and Dana, who had been out of the room for a short time, returned to see Grant still dripping in his chair. Wilson interrupted our talk and pointed out that my new commander was soaked, cold and in pain from his riding mishap. Immediately apologetic, I had my aides fetch him dry clothes, a warm supper and medical attention.

Dana avoided looking me in the eye. Later when we were alone, the assistant secretary of war told me the political reasons for Lincoln's favoring Grant. My dismay was obvious.

"With all proper respect, I must say that President Lincoln has consistently undervalued my contributions to the Union," I replied. "I will always instantly follow the president's wishes, but this goes hard with me. I wonder if Grant has enough respect for me and my abilities."

"I understand your disappointment, and let me assure you that President Lincoln has the highest respect for you," Dana answered. "He knows your worth and will eventually promote you to your proper rank. Regardless, the president says he must bow to political reality and place a Northerner in command here. General Grant is a good leader, and I'm sure you will find this to be true."

At that moment I felt more anger toward Dana and his superiors than I felt toward the rebels in the hills above Chattanooga, but I only replied, "A man must obey orders." Dana nodded his head in relief.

At first Grant had not seemed perturbed by my unintentional rudeness at the fireplace, for he had been engrossed by our conversation on strategy. Perhaps he thought I already knew about the new chain of command, and thus didn't recognize my dejection. During dinner, we got along reasonably well, talking about our days at West Point. I tried my best to hide my glumness about the Army of the Cumberland's lack of independence.

After our dinner, I suspect Rawlins told Grant I had deliberately snubbed him by not seeing to his comfort as soon as he arrived. And this I believe reawakened Grant's ill feelings toward me concerning his temporary fall from grace after Shiloh—when I briefly commanded the army that he had once led.

I do not have proof that a few extra minutes in wet clothing turned my fellow Union general into a lifelong enemy; I only know that the next day there was a considerable coolness between us that has turned chillier ever since, even today, five years after the war's end.

It is difficult to accept that such a petty, inadvertent slight could play a part in a war fought over the most overriding issues of freedom and justice. Still, that is my belief. Or perhaps Grant was simply indignant that I didn't offer him my brandy that night.

CHAPTER 17

IN WHICH THE CUMBERLANDS ACHIEVE A 'MIRACLE'

Generals lose battles, but they never really win them. Only their men can do that. Never was this more true than on Missionary Ridge.

Braxton Bragg lost this battle, not so much for what he did that day in November 1863 but for what he failed to do immediately after Chickamauga in September. As I related earlier, he should have smashed us then, while we were spent. During both battles, Bragg played the role of King Canute, a mortal ruler who proved to have no control over whether the tides went in or out. And at Missionary Ridge, Grant was just as powerless.

Still, the tide began to turn in Grant's favor on October 24. Our forces took back two ferries, which allowed Joe Hooker's army to enter the Lookout Valley and guarantee the safety of the cracker line. With pontoon boats in place and with steamboats and a wagon train in constant motion, hunger was no longer a problem for Union troops by October 31.

Politics still plagued us. For some reason, Bragg was more eager to retake Knoxville than to hold Chattanooga, so he sent James Longstreet and eighteen thousand grayclads to attack Ambrose Burnside there. Apparently Burnside, who had plenty of men to deal with this threat, feared that Longstreet and his Virginians might manhandle him as they did at Fredericksburg. He wired Washington for help. Lincoln, who still fretted about his fellow Republicans who resided in that part of east Tennessee, shared his concerns with Grant, who on November 7 ordered my Army of the Cumberland to attack Missionary Ridge in the hope that it would lure Longstreet back.

As usual, I was not pleased with Lincoln, but I was more disappointed in Grant for giving this order without full knowledge of the situation. My Cumberlands were just recovering our strength, and we were still short of rifles as well as feed for the surviving horses and mules who would carry our artillery.

After reading Grant's order, I sent for "Baldy" Smith, who agreed with me that it meant "total disaster" for us at this time. Bragg was entrenched on the ridge and could send everything he had at us. Smith concurred that it would be better to wait for Sherman's army to arrive so we could have another wing in the attack. At Smith's suggestion, the two of us rode toward the northern end of the ridge and verified our concerns.

We went to Grant and told him that such an attack, before Sherman entered the city, would leave Chattanooga vulnerable to a counterattack. Grant agreed to countermand his order, but my report seemed to add to the disdain he held for me. He resurrected my old West Point nickname, "Slow Trot," as a slur against me, though never to my face. As it happened, Burnside acquitted himself well against Longstreet.

Sherman came to town a week later, mourning for his oldest son, Willie, who had died of typhoid fever a month earlier. He accepted my condolences for Willie with grace, assuring me he would put his grief aside until after the war. He and his wife, Ellen, had seven other children whose lives were equally precious.

Billy soon was outgoing as ever, telling jokes I won't repeat here. It had been a long time since I'd felt like laughing, and Cump could be amusing when it suited him.

Sherman joined Grant and myself for a look at the enemy lines. We were an ill-matched trio as we rode together, Sherman verbose,

Grant grim, and I taciturn. Grant ignored my presence, addressing himself solely to Sherman as he outlined his strategy. While they discussed the grand scheme, I fixed my eyes on the ridge and the plain in front of it.

"I'll expect your army to strike the main blow, Sherman, and drive the enemy off that position," Grant mumbled.

"That's an imposing sight, no doubt about it, but my boys can do it," Sherman answered. "If we could take Vicksburg, the Gibraltar of the South, we should be able to push our old friend Bragg off this Missionary Ridge. Maybe we'll leave something for your Cumberlands to do. Right, Old Tom?"

"We'll do what we're ordered to do," I replied, keeping my eyes on the ridge.

Grant muttered something, his mouth full of a chewed cigar that obscured his words. A vile weed, tobacco.

Grant's strategy gave Sherman the plum role. His Army of the Tennessee would hide in the hills behind Chattanooga, then re-cross the river and attack the right side of Bragg's line, where the rebels' best division, the one commanded by Pat Cleburne, kept watch. Hooker would try to scale Lookout Mountain, on Bragg's left, while my Cumberlands would feint against the center.

Grant's coolness to me extended to all the troops under my command. He often wondered aloud, though not in my presence, if the Cumberlands had the sand to mount an offense after the terrible defeat at Chickamauga. My soldiers were offended at the gossipy notion that Grant, Sherman and Hooker were "rescuing" them from the trap they had fallen into at Chattanooga. I did not try to stop them from being resentful toward this slander. I wanted them angry about the ridicule and eager to prove to the rest of the Union Army that they were wrong in their dismissal of the Cumberlands.

Indeed, all the Union forces were in a mood to snarl at each other, not a bad way for an army to be if the ill temper could be turned against the enemy. Hooker's troopers, from the Army of the Potomac, were Easterners mostly from the cities, and they looked at their comrades from the West as if they were savages. Admittedly the men of the Army of the Cumberland were ungroomed compared with the prim Potomac paladins. Yet my soldiers were as finely arrayed as parade-ground Zouaves compared with the rustics under Sherman's command. Except for their faded blue coats, Billy's boys could have been mistaken for the vanguard of Attila's hordes.

I was also angry. At Grant, for one, because of his antipathy to me and his contempt for my army. But we were, after all, on the same side, and I knew it best to keep my perturbations to myself.

Sherman was able to see through my mask, and he did his best to humor me, to assure me that Grant had greatness in him and that the tanner's son had respect for me as a general regardless of his hostility toward me personally. Good for you, Cump, I thought, you've become his favorite and will get the choice assignments. If the truth be known, at least in these pages, I was a touch jealous of Sherman, even miffed at him for hitching himself to Grant's wagon.

"Grant stood by me when I was crazy, and I stood by him when he was drunk, and now we stand by each other," Sherman joked with me as we shared rations and studied Missionary Ridge. I grunted in agreement but thought that sober and sane or drunk and crazy, those two should have stood under my command.

So it's logical that my old friendship with Joe Hooker would grow closer during our time in Chattanooga. Both of us subject to Grant's scorn, Hooker and I commiserated together over our hollow status in the Union hierarchy. To others that might seem trifling, two spoiled schoolboys lamenting their losses in childhood games, but it was comforting to confide our mutual bitterness, knowing the other would fully understand.

A handsome soul, Hooker had a reputation as a hard-drinking Lothario among the ladies of Washington, though he had little opportunity for such tipsy gallantry in Chattanooga. He was still smarting from the ignominy of his defeat by Lee and was seeking redemption in Tennessee.

"Dame Fortune has been fickle to me," Hooker complained. "Did you ever hear how I was almost killed at Chancellorsville?"

"Oh yes, that tale has been told," I replied. "Somehow you were struck by a wooden house column that had been hit by a rebel cannonball."

"Knocked me silly for a while, and I was never able to put my plan in operation. I would have beaten Lee had fate been kinder to me."

"Joe, at least fate prevented the cannonball from removing your head."

"Damn, I know a few generals whose heads would be improved by a well-placed cannonball."

"At least one of them is up there on Missionary Ridge."

"Our old friend Bragg, may Satan's flames take him. You should command here, Old Tom, not Sam Grant."

"Indeed. Fate had played me false as well."

"Have you considered resigning over it?"

"No, no, not until this war is over, if then. The rebels must be defeated first. Come, come, let us both husband our anger against Grant and turn it against the enemy."

My greatest anger, the only anger that truly mattered, was toward Bragg and the rest of his butternuts on the ridge. May there be a special place in perdition reserved for that knave.

A letter had just arrived addressed to an officer in his army. I examined it and saw it was harmless to the security of the Union Army, so I had it sent through the enemy line under a flag of truce with a note to Bragg to please deliver it to the officer in question. It was simply a minor matter of military courtesy. Bragg and I had a long friendship. I'll never forget how he helped save my life in the Mexican War. Yet he sent back the letter with this reply: "Respectfully returned to Gen. Thomas. Gen. Bragg declines to have any intercourse with a man who has betrayed his state."

Had Bragg been within my sight, I would have thrown down the gauntlet. No, I would have taken a horsewhip to him. Soon after Sherman arrived, he asked me if I'd had any communications with our former friend. "Damn him, I'll be even with him yet," I replied. A few days later, thanks to the Army of the Cumberland, I got more than even with the North Carolina blackguard. (Mrs. Thomas assures me as she reads this account that my use of profanity against Bragg is entirely justified.)

On November 22, a rebel deserter informed the Union that Bragg was going to evacuate his lines. Deserters often told us lies. In fact, many of them were not real deserters but decent soldiers following orders to spread misinformation among us. But Grant could not wholly discount this latest tale. Some rebel divisions were being moved, perhaps toward Knoxville, which Burnside had turned into a citadel as he continued to keep Longstreet at bay. If Bragg sent more forces to threaten that city, we would have to weaken our hold on Chattanooga in order to chase after him. Bragg considered the four-hundred-foot-high Missionary Ridge to be impregnable, so he must not have been greatly concerned that he now had about forty-three thousand troops to hold back the Union's total of seventy-five thousand.

I had only four divisions under my command; my other units had been sent to reinforce our flanks. But I still had enough soldiers, in Grant's opinion, to threaten the center and perhaps persuade Bragg to call back his forces that were enroute to Knoxville. Grant ordered my twenty-five thousand troops to do so on November 23. He expected that after our demonstration, we would withdraw back to our original positions.

We put on quite a show for our peers from Sherman and Hooker's commands, not to mention our enemies. The flags, bugles, drums, and gleaming bayonets may have made the rebels (those who could read) recall a Walter Scott fantasy. Some of the grayclads stationed in the plain in front of the ridge came out of their entrenchments to watch the impressive spectacle of men in arms with whom they would soon be engaged in mortal combat.

War is not always the hell Sherman has called it. In those minutes of marching, it was splendid.

An hour later, at 1:30 in the afternoon, the pageantry turned back into hell. Three brigades of Union soldiers under Gordon Granger, one of the Chickamauga heroes, swept over the outposts of Orchard Knob and Bushy Knob, at the cost of one thousand Federal men killed and wounded.

When I saw Union banners on Orchard Knob, I had my signal officer waggle his flag to our forces, telling them that "you have gained too much to withdraw; hold your position, and I will support you." I sent two divisions to solidify our gains, even as Grant, surprised by our victory, ordered all the Union troops to withdraw. That was nonsensical. Even Grant's chief of staff, Rawlins, knew this. (Some Union officers considered Rawlins to be smarter than his commanding general. Perhaps he was.) Grant finally countermanded his order, and we kept Orchard Knob.

I rode to the troops and shook hands with the officers and thanked the men. Grant wired Halleck that the Cumberland Army "moved under fire with all the precision of veterans on parade." Perhaps he meant this as a compliment; I sensed shock in his recognition that my troops were as good if not better than Sherman's. Still, Grant lacked respect for us. The next morning he sent Sherman toward Bragg's right and Hooker toward the left, expecting the Army of the Cumberland to be mere spectators when the "real" battle was decided.

Sherman did not play a leading role in this battle. On November 24, Cleburne's solidly entrenched division stopped Sherman's six divisions assaulting it. Hooker also was held up, though eventually he did capture Lookout Mountain in what was called "the Battle Above the Clouds." Hooker's triumph—his redemption —was an impressive breakthrough and added to the pressure on Bragg. Grant always belittled it, likely because it was a victory in which he played little part.

By November 25, Grant was greatly ill at ease as he and I stood on Orchard Knob with our staffs. Sherman could make no progress, and it appeared Bragg was ready to go on the offensive against him. And though seeing the American flag atop Lookout Mountain gave us all inspiration, Hooker could do no more at present. So Grant began looking restlessly at the Army of the Cumberland, idle since our preliminary victory two days before. An advance by our four divisions toward the rifle pits at the base of the ridge might take pressure off Sherman, but Grant knew how dangerous it would be for the Cumberlands. Bragg still had five divisions at the top of what most considered to be an unconquerable position.

As the afternoon wore on, Grant, egged on by the even more nervous Rawlins, inquired of me, "Don't you think it's about time to advance against the rifle pits?"

By way of reply, I continued to gaze about the ridge with my binoculars. Please don't decry me as being petulant for not speaking, as if I were paying Grant back for barely conferring with me during the days when he planned this battle. I only wanted to demonstrate by my silence that it was not my place to debate with him then and there. If he were going to put my men in such a lions' den, let him say so firmly, not like a mugwump.

More time passed. It was 3:30 in the afternoon. Sherman's latest assault on Cleburne failed. Rawlins, nearly frantic now, spoke to his commander again. Grant turned to me. This time with no hesitation, he said: "Now is your time."

At once I sent orders to my commanders, Thomas Wood and Phil Sheridan in the center, Absalom Baird on the far left, and Richard Johnson on the far right, to take the rifle pits. Six guns fired in succession would be the signal for the attack to begin. Just minutes after Grant gave me the order, the first of the six went off. Granger was in his glory as he directed those guns. Shouting like a schoolboy on the Fourth of July, Granger needed a reminder from me to calm himself. He really should have been with the infantry, but I felt he deserved some toleration for his high spirits.

Our goal, at the foot of Missionary Ridge, was nearly a mile away. There were 112 pieces of artillery at the top, all aimed at the advancing two-mile-wide blue wave. The Cumberlands began in a quick march, then broke into a run. The shelling was murderous, yet all it seemed to do was speed the troops on. They were the proud Army of the Cumberland. They knew all Union eyes were upon them, and they wanted to wash away the stain of September's defeat. "Chickamauga!" they shouted in manly Union voices that mocked the rebels' shrill screeching. Even cooks, clerks, and quartermasters found guns and joined the Union charge. The rifle pits were taken easily, with the ridge close at hand.

What to do next? Grant had not ordered anyone to capture the ridge, only the rifle pits at the base. The officers ordered the men to dig in to protect themselves from the next rebel line above them. The slope was so steep that many cannons at the top couldn't aim at the Union men directly, but the butternut gunners were rolling down shells with lit fuses. Staying in the pits seemed suicidal.

Someone—I am told it was a nameless corporal of the Ninth Kentucky Regiment—shouted, "By God, boys, let's go up!" A few followed him, then more and more. At first the officers tried to stop them. Then they realized their men were the leaders on that day. Presently everybody went up.

It was hard going. Besides bullets and shells, the men had to contend with shifting soil and rocks that made it difficult for their feet to find purchase. At least there were stumps, boulders and fallen trees that provided shelter where they could briefly rest before pressing on with their climb. At the top were rebel bayonets.

Grant could see all this from our position back on Orchard Knob. If Bragg's men threw the Federal troops off the ridge, there were no reserves to hold the rebels back.

"Thomas, who ordered those men up the ridge?" he shouted.

"I don't know. I did not," I replied, feeling an urge to smile and using all my strength of will to resist it.

Grant turned his wrath on Granger, asking him if he gave the order to climb the ridge.

"No, they started up without orders," Granger answered with a smile as big as the one I was repressing. "When those fellows get started, all hell can't stop them."

Our commander looked away from us and sulked, promising

that someone would suffer professionally if the Union were defeated. Oh ye of little faith.

He need not have worried so. Nothing could stop the Army of the Cumberland that day. Our best ally was Bragg, who had made a terrible error when laying out the upper line of artillery. He placed the cannons on the true top of the ridge rather than at the locations where the gunners could best see the enemy and fire down upon them.

Bragg also had given orders for those in the lower rifle pits on the ridge to fire only one or two massed volleys, then fall back to positions just uphill. Not all of his soldiers farther up the ridge knew of these orders, so when they saw some of their fellow butter-nuts seemingly retreat under pressure, many became demoralized and ran.

The rout became so widespread, our captives told us, that Bragg himself was forced to ride among his soldiers to plead with them to rally. "Here is your commander!" he yelled to his men. "Here's your mule!" they answered, and kept running. We captured three thousand rebels but not, I'm sorry to say, Bragg. I would have given a year's pay to see him as a prisoner.

Missionary Ridge was ours, at the cost of three thousand casualties, a bloody victory to be sure, but not the annihilation it might have been. Granger rode up to the victors and laughingly shouted: "I'm going to have you all court-martialed! You were ordered to take the works at the foot of the hill, and you've taken those on top! You have disobeyed orders, all of you, and you know that you ought to be court-martialed!"

The only Union general not overjoyed was Grant, who appeared stunned rather than delighted. I've been told that Grant's first response to the victory was, "Damn the battle. I had nothing to do with it!" I hope he didn't express such rubbish—I certainly didn't hear him say it. Still it must be acknowledged that the course of the battle had little to do with what Grant had envisioned. His favorite general, Sherman, was stymied, and men commanded by two generals for whom he had little regard, myself and Hooker, achieved the triumph.

When I rode my bay Billy the 400 feet to the top of the ridge, I was surrounded by some of my old soldiers. They commenced chatting to me as if I were another private, giving me their views of the victory. When I attempted to compliment them for the gallant manner in which they made the assault, one man (as gaunt as a trained runner) very coolly replied: "Why general, we know that you have been training us for this race for the last three weeks."

That was generous of the gaunt soldier, but it was the soldiers' moment, and they made me proud to be their comrade.

When the rebellion was over in 1865, many Southerners still clung to their pride, claiming they only lost the war because they were outnumbered and that the rebels were still the better soldiers. Hogwash, of course. Some of them still say the greatest gallantry of the war occurred on the third and final day of the Battle of Gettysburg, when infantry under George Pickett and others charged across an open field and nearly took Cemetery Ridge before they were thrown back by George Meade's Yankees.

Without disparaging the fortitude of those Southerners at Gettysburg, allow me to make these comparisons between Cemetery Ridge and Missionary Ridge. In both battles, the charges were made across a mile of open field. But at Missionary Ridge, the defenders were on a much higher elevation, and they'd had two months to prepare their entrenchments and gun positions, not two days. And allow me to now make the most cogent observation: The grayclads failed to take a vital ridge; the Union succeeded.

Let the rebels boast about a defeat; I will savor a victory.

CHAPTER 18

IN WHICH ANOTHER INJUSTICE IS
DONE TO ME

Although Grant was merely a spectator at Missionary Ridge, he would gain the most from that victory. He would assume command of all Union armies and go East to challenge Lee. Yet had it been up to the secretary of war, it would have been me, not Grant, trying to conquer Richmond.

Edwin Stanton wanted me to replace George Meade as commander of the Army of the Potomac. Meade had won at Gettysburg but had displeased Lincoln by failing to finish off the defeated rebels and end the war in the East. James Garfield recommended me to Stanton for the position, a job I did not desire.

On December 17, I wrote Garfield, thanking him for honoring me with his advocacy but expressing my dread at the prospect of leading an army so near to the White House. I assumed that Lincoln would always be looking over my shoulder, interfering with anything I proposed and panicking at any minor delay.

"You have disturbed me greatly with the intimation that the command of the Army of the Potomac may be offered to me. It is a position to which I am not in the least adapted ..." I wrote Garfield. "The pressure always brought to bear against the commander ... could destroy me in a week without having advanced the cause in the least."

Instead of me, "Baldy" Smith would be the best choice for the Army of the Potomac, I wrote Garfield. Smith had impressed me mightily during the Chattanooga campaign with his strategy and energy. Stanton still endorsed me, but Lincoln chose Grant. Politics, again, swayed the president. Besides being a Northerner, Grant did Lincoln a favor by not allowing his name to be floated as a possible rival in the presidential campaign coming the next year, 1864. And Lincoln lacked the nerve to put a Virginian in such a prominent military role, though he had implored Lee to take it in 1861.

Even had I wanted the Potomac command, I was sure that Lincoln would not have chosen me. His administration had already honored Grant for the victory at Missionary Ridge, giving him a gold medal for the little he did in Chattanooga. He was hailed as a national hero, and it would have upset many in the North had he not been promoted.

Still, from the vantage point of my writing desk in 1870, I wonder if I should have pressed for the command, regardless of my misgivings.

I know now that Lincoln had a higher opinion of me than I knew then. If Stanton could have convinced the president to give me greater leeway in my strategy, I would have done better than Grant in defeating the South.

Of course my old friend Lee was an exceptional general and would have outfoxed me a few times, as he did Grant and his predecessors. But I would have adjusted as needed, and I would have taken Richmond in quicker order and with far less effusion of blood than Grant. Again, I say this in private with no false modesty, only an honest appraisal of my capabilities. I would not have been the reaper who wasted good men's lives as Grant did at Cold Harbor and other Virginia battlefields.

Instead, Grant was the one who went to Washington as overall Union commander, keeping Meade in place as the figurehead leader of the Army of the Potomac. He also took Burnside with him, leaving a vacancy at the Army of the Ohio.

At least Grant respected some of my Cumberlands, as he took

one of my divisional commanders, Phil Sheridan, east with him to lead the Potomac cavalry. I liked Sheridan when he was under my command, but in the East he would become another Grant acolyte. And from what state did Sheridan hail? That damnable Ohio, of course.

(Frances reminds me that Garfield is also from Ohio, so I should be more respectful toward the Buckeye State. I grunt in acknowledgment.)

Grant's move would happen three months hence as the spring of 1864 approached. During the Christmas of 1863, I was in high feather, still warmed by the memory of the Army of the Cumberland atop Missionary Ridge.

I hosted a holiday dinner with some of the most able generals I knew in the Army, along with my nephew and aide, Captain Sanford Kellogg. Over glasses of brandy, we amused ourselves at Braxton Bragg's expense. We had heard that Jefferson Davis found wisdom enough to give Bragg's beaten army to a better man, Joe Johnston. Bragg was on his way to Richmond as chief of staff to Davis, a curious kind of "promotion." I was sorry to see him go, for I would have taken an un-Christian pleasure in seeing my Cumberlands once more sending him galloping in retreat.

A very Christian general, one for whom I came to have great esteem, was Oliver Otis Howard, who had come to our Western force with Joe Hooker and the other Potomac reinforcements we'd received earlier that year. Being some sort of Protestant revivalist, Howard didn't partake of the Christmas brandy with us. Despite that, I valued his friendship and his advice. Like Rosecrans, he liked to talk of religion but didn't take offense that I simply couldn't manage to show his kind of piety in my every waking moment.

Howard had endured a calamitous war so far, losing an arm fighting Lee at the Battle of Fair Oaks. Then, after he returned to duty, forces under his command broke and ran at Chancellorsville and then again at Gettysburg, perhaps because his soldiers were mostly German immigrants who didn't have the Prussian martial spirit (unlike their countrymen who were with me at Mill Springs).

Howard vindicated himself in Chattanooga, as his new unit performed well on Missionary Ridge.

My only regret that Christmas was that Sanford's favorite aunt, Mrs. Thomas, could not be with me. I simply was not able to leave Chattanooga to see my wife, even at Yule time. Based on past occurrences, I was sure that if I took leave, something important would go amiss. Your letters, Frances, brought me great holiday cheer.

Never far from my thoughts were the brave men who would not celebrate Christmas ever again in this world. I constantly inspected a cemetery on Orchard Knob set aside for the dead of the Chickamauga and Chattanooga battles. It was once a beautiful place and would be again after the scars of war healed. A chaplain asked me if the bodies should be buried in sections according to their home states. "No, no, no. Mix them up, mix them up. I am tired of states' rights," I replied.

As the year 1864 began, I started to worry that we might not have enough troops to take the field. All Union armies were losing soldiers because their enlistments were expiring. It is perfectly understandable that normal men, volunteers in a great cause, might weary of war after seeing the elephant all too often.

Blessedly, many of the men came back, accepting a thirty-day furlough if they would re-enlist for the duration of the conflict. I suspect that most of these returning soldiers, having dreamed so long of home, found themselves vaguely dissatisfied after a few days back with their loved ones. These men knew that the war in which they had given so much was still unsettled, and that their slain comrades had not yet been avenged.

Doubtless, many also came back for the four-hundred-dollar re-enlistment bonus.

There were also a few disgraceful wretches who collected their money from one unit, then deserted and collected money from another unit, and on and on. Many of these rogues were caught and punished, but not enough of them. They were not worthy to be among the noble troopers who fulfilled their duties to the United States.

The return of so many volunteers helped ease the pressures of installing a draft of eligible men for service. Many of the North's wealthy were shamefully able to avoid military duty by paying poorer men to replace them.

Still, the prospect of the draft caused riots in several Northern cities. Many white laborers had no interest in fighting to free black slaves, who they thought would compete with them for jobs. The worst riot was in New York, where mobs of mostly Irish immigrants nearly took over the city, in the process killing many Negro free men and women. The rioters were not put down until the arrival of Federal troops, many of whom had just days before won the great victory of Gettysburg.

I was hardly aware of this New York outrage until Howard, the Gettysburg veteran, informed me of the details. Howard's report impressed upon me the fact that the enemies of the Union were often north of the Mason Dixon line—supposedly Christian gentlemen who in truth were money-grubbing merchants secretly trading with the South or speculating in gold. Others were traitorous Copperhead politicians eager to have peace at any price. The southern parts of Illinois, Indiana, and Ohio were infested with rebel sympathizers, and we already know how close Kentucky, Missouri, and Maryland came to joining the Confederacy.

Nevertheless, it was New York, the heart of Yankee wealth, that was perhaps most packed with Northern traitors, rich and poor. A mayor of that city once urged it to secede from the Union so that its merchants could harvest more mammon from Southern cotton. Such treasonable words gave license to the discontent that emboldened the rioters. To think that brave Union soldiers had to march from a battlefield of honor where they had bested Lee and Longstreet to another battlefield where they were compelled to fire upon the dregs of this Sodom. Nearly one thousand of the rioters were killed before peace returned to the city. Those New York rebels should have taken their chances and enlisted. Better to die valiantly fighting for the Union than to die ignobly fighting to avoid your duty.

Another problem I am loath to admit was desertion across all the Union armies. Thousands skedaddled. Some ran from cowardice, of course, though many were able to regain their manliness and eventually return to the ranks. Men can be brave one day, craven the next, then stalwart at the last. But too many never came back, hiding in cities or in the brush, others escaping west across the Great Plains.

Some deserted because of racial antipathy. For all the virtue in Lincoln's Emancipation Proclamation, it filled countless whites with disgust and fear. Many in the North who hated slave owners also hated the slaves and saw no reason to give them the status of white men. And in the contested border slave states, many Union supporters scorned the prospect of giving up their servants. A few even spurned Lincoln to go over to the rebels.

But thank the Lord, most white Americans loved the United States enough that they were able to put aside their distaste for the Negro—and preserve the nation.

The volunteers, the deserters, and the status of the Africans were all on my mind when I met Colonel Thomas Morgan as he passed through Chattanooga. He was a white man organizing a regiment of free Negroes and former slaves. I saw them drilling and was impressed by their discipline and precision.

"Will they fight?" I asked him.

"Yes, they will fight. They're fighting for their freedom and the freedom of their families," Morgan replied.

"Maybe behind breastworks, at least to start with," I said. "It takes a while for anyone to be a gallant soldier, especially one who's been a slave for so long."

"They'll fight in the open field," Morgan answered.

"I have sincere doubts."

"Give my men a chance, and we will prove it to you."

Morgan's words soon inspired me to write this message about slaves to the War Department: "The Confederates regard them as property. Therefore, the Government can with propriety seize them as property and use them to assist in putting down the Rebellion.

But if we have the right to use the property of our enemies, we share also the right to use them as we would all the individuals of any other civilized nation who may choose to volunteer as soldiers in our Army. I moreover think that in the sudden transition from slavery to freedom, it is perhaps better for the Negro to become a soldier than to be thrown upon the cold charities of the world without sympathy or assistance."

As I thought more about Morgan and his plans, I agreed with him that since the fate of Negroes was the principal reason for the war, it was altogether fitting for them to take up arms in securing their freedom. Some of their white peers in the Union Army would prove as violently opposed to colored troopers as the rebels might have been. Thankfully, other white Union men would come to respect the Negroes' courage — Howard, for one, who had a Christian regard for all men, Negroes included.[*]

Certainly Sherman had deeper doubts than I about the worthiness of Africans. Sherman shared the white Northerners' usual aversion toward Negroes. All he ever wanted them to do was keep their distance and provide labor that white soldiers wished to avoid. He didn't want blacks to fight for their freedom. Asked if Negroes were as good as whites when it came to stopping a bullet, Sherman replied, "Yes, and a sandbag is better."

Most Southerners, on the other hand, may have detested the idea of emancipation for Negroes but were comfortable in their presence, even having affection for some servants the way they might regard a reliable horse or a faithful dog. Shamefully, too many Southern men gave in to their sinful natures and took advantage of their female slaves in a disgraceful manner. (Frances, though you are too discreet to inquire, I must tell you that such wickedness never took place on my family's farm.)

The rebels had always used their slaves for auxiliary military

---

[*]   Editor's note: Oliver Otis Howard would lead the Freedmen's Bureau after the war and helped found what became Howard University, a historically black college named for him.

chores—digging ditches, hauling supplies, and the like. Now a few Southern leaders, out of desperation, were considering using Negroes as soldiers to augment their diminishing supply of whites. Cleburne, the general who had just fought Sherman to a standstill, had proposed such a step — giving slaves their freedom in exchange for becoming volunteer Southern soldiers. It was a suggestion that was initially condemned at the highest level of the rebels' government and kept secret. I didn't hear of it until the conclusion of hostilities. I'm told that Cleburne's suggestion was so offensive to Davis that he refused to promote this general to the higher command he deserved. I'm thankful it was Hood, not Cleburne, who would lead the grayclads at the Battle of Nashville.

Most white Southerners, such as my sisters, would have preferred losing the war rather than winning it with Negro soldiers. Such a victory would have put the lie to everything they believed in. But as the South's defeat became inevitable, a few rebels such as Lee changed their minds and reconsidered Cleburne's suggestion. By then it was too late.

When I was a youth, I had taught some of our servants how to write, and I was aware of their potential to be more than slaves. Our old overseer Sam would have made a splendid sergeant had he lived long enough to wear a blue uniform. Now, colored men were flocking to the Union Army, and when given the chance to fight, they would prove their stature beyond all doubts.

They would fight even though they knew that if captured, the rebels were likely to execute them without mercy. This is what happened at Fort Pillow in Tennessee, where men under Forrest murdered at least three hundred captive black soldiers in 1864. Despite such atrocities, former slaves kept enlisting. Some of them would help me gain my greatest day as a general. My opinion of the race would evolve again.

Another opinion that was evolving was my regard for Sherman, a friend who was becoming a rival. His ascent over me was set in motion during the last days of 1863 and the first days of the new year.

After our victory at Missionary Ridge, we should have advanced quickly on the running rebels. Here Grant deserved my nickname "Slow Trot" for his listlessness, apparently because he was still cross that his favored Sherman had accomplished so little at Chattanooga. Instead, Grant blamed Hooker for letting Bragg get back over the Georgia line with his army intact. This was an injustice; Hooker's men had done all they could do in pursuit. I should have pushed Grant harder to chase after the butternuts, but I knew he still held me in disregard.

The rebels had withdrawn twenty-five miles to Dalton, Georgia, where they entrenched. When Johnston took over from Bragg, he set up additional fortifications for more than one hundred miles, all the way south to Atlanta. He would never have had time to do all this had we been speedily moving toward him. The country was full of mountains and gorges, with three rivers blocking our way.

I told Grant of the enemy's entrenching, urging action before they were solidly dug in. Grant, however, had his eye on the port city of Mobile, Alabama, and sent Sherman and his Army of the Tennessee to threaten it via Meridian, Mississippi.

To keep the rebels from sending more troops to chase Sherman, Grant ordered a small part of my Army of the Cumberland to test Johnston's defenses in Dalton, and to take the town if we could. Johnston, a far superior general to Bragg, was positioned behind the ominously named locations of Rocky Face Ridge and Buzzards Roost Gap. We pushed close to the enemy works, but at this time we were outnumbered, with limited transportation, artillery, and food, and we would not have been able to drive out Johnston with a direct assault. We returned to Chattanooga, knowing the rebels would stay put and not threaten us.

A retreat, you ask? No, merely a strategic withdrawal. The enemy did not drive us away. More importantly, we discovered an unguarded pass called Snake Creek Gap that could be exploited as a hidden route to Johnston's rear when all of the Union's Western armies took the field.

Grant was displeased, apparently because we did not give him another Missionary Ridge miracle. It was not enough for him that we had accomplished his main goal, which was to force Johnston to pull back the troops sent to attack Sherman. Grant didn't seem dismayed by the shortcomings of Sherman who, though he managed to destroy much of the railroad tracks and equipment in Meridian, was bedeviled again by Forrest. Sherman had to retreat from Meridian with Forrest nipping at his heels and did not come close to Mobile.

As spring approached, I made a proposal for our Western armies to use Snake Creek Gap for a flanking maneuver, one I was confident would trap Johnston and open the way to Atlanta. I was also confident that I would be able to run the campaign with the reinforced Cumberlands as the driving force. And of course I was disappointed once again.

On March 17, 1864, Grant assumed command of the armies of the United States, with Henry Halleck shunted aside to be chief of staff. Practically the first thing Grant did in his new position was inform me that Sherman would be in charge of the Military Division of the Mississippi. Although I outranked Sherman by the date of my commission, I would still be the junior to him. He would run the Atlanta campaign.

It was all too similar to what happened to me with Buell and Rosecrans. Another friend who was junior to me was promoted over my head. I said nothing publicly, but I told Howard in confidence that I'd made my last protest against serving under juniors. I would do all I could do to win the war as soon as possible and say nothing about the injustices done me.

Under Sherman's command, I would lead the seventy-two thousand men of the Army of the Cumberland. Teamed with us would be the twenty-four thousand-man Army of the Tennessee led by James McPherson and the 12,800-man Army of the Ohio led by John Schofield, Burnside's replacement.

McPherson, one of the endless supply of Ohio generals in this war, was honorable and competent if a bit overwhelmed by his promotion. He died a hero's death in the Atlanta campaign, a fate I wish had fallen to Schofield instead.

When I renewed my acquaintance with Schofield, I initially had no harsh feelings against him, though I remembered his indecent conduct at West Point and my recommendation that he be expelled from the Corps of Cadets. That was back in 1853, and from what little I knew of him, he had conducted himself honorably since then. I did not then believe he knew of my recommendation against him when I was on the West Point faculty. Many men are able to redeem themselves for their youthful follies, and I hoped Schofield had done so.

I have since learned more about him. He played a role in helping keep Missouri in the Union when that state appeared to be tipping over to secession, and he showed some courage in early combat there, or at least he said so. That was all to the plus side of his ledger. He became a general who stayed mostly in Missouri early in the war, but some minus signs were now appearing in his record. In one incident he was relieved of duty because of altercations with his superior. In another, after he returned to duty, he was the subject of complaints by pro-Union Missourians that he was showing favoritism to the bushwhackers who sided with the rebels. Should that have been enough to disqualify him as a general? In my mind yes, but we were always short of capable generals, especially those with a West Point education.

Still, why was he promoted to the leadership of an army? I know that his family background was in Illinois and Missouri, and that his early patron was Lincoln's old Illinois rival, Stephen A. Douglas, but Schofield must have had some Ohio connection, or why would Grant and Sherman support him so?

Frances tells me I should not be so obsessed by the state of Ohio and its generals. She is right of course. Well, whatever state he was from, Schofield did not plague me yet. I had to deal with Sherman first.

CHAPTER 19

IN WHICH WE DRIVE TOWARD ATLANTA

When the Atlanta campaign began, the city itself was not the goal; wiping out Joe Johnston's army was. But in the minds of the press and the Northern public, capturing the Georgia capital appeared as coveted a prize as taking Richmond.

Sherman was aware of the politics involved. If he and Grant could show no solid gains in 1864, the voters would likely remove Lincoln from the White House and elect some treasonous Copperhead or a scamp like McClellan, who surely would make peace by letting the South become an independent nation. No love for Lincoln I held in my breast, yet I would vote for him over any traitorous Democrat. It would be too bitter to lose this war after so many good Union men had died.

The plan, as we all know today, was for Grant to come to grips with Lee in the East and for Sherman to finish Johnston in the West.

There were many other areas of the war, ones I was aware of but to which I could pay little heed. There were naval battles in the world's oceans as rebel raiders tried to pierce the Union blockade. Armies of the North and South were still matched farther west, on the other side of the Mississippi. Battles had already been fought as far away as New Mexico. And hostile Indians were taking advantage of our depleted Federal forces to threaten pioneers all over the Far West.

All of these clashes were important, but the fates of Lee and Johnston's forces would decide the ultimate victor.

Again I must face this contradiction in my writings. I have utter contempt for subordinate generals who whine that the battle would have been won, or won at less cost, if only the commander had followed that underling's advice. Nonetheless, I must again play the part of that contemptible vassal, at least in these private pages. Though this paradox vexes me, I say that if Sherman had heeded my counsel, or better yet, had I had been in command, we would have annihilated Johnston within a week, or failing that, we would have captured Atlanta in much better than the 113 days it took us to go those 120 miles.

My long friendship with Sherman was severely strained by our different philosophies during the campaign that began that spring. I was naturally careful, which he considered dawdling. He valued speed no matter the obstacle, which I considered reckless.

Before we set out, I gave him this official proposal: "Let me take the Army of the Cumberland, move through Snake Creek Gap, and get in the rear of Johnston. He must come out and fight me, and I can whip him with the Army of the Cumberland. But ... if he should get the better of me, you can come upon him with the Armies of the Tennessee and the Ohio and between us, we can rub him out. His men will take to the mountains, but he must abandon his artillery and trains, and there will be an end to the matter."

Sherman replied, "No, the Army of the Tennessee are better marchers than the Army of the Cumberland, and I am going to send McPherson."

Sherman obviously wanted a fellow Ohio general to gain the glory of bagging Johnston. (I'm sorry, Frances, but I must bring up the subject of the Buckeye State again.) Now I am not without a general's self-regard, but these Ohioans had more than the lion's share when it came to conceit. Not forgetting the favors Sherman did me early in the war, I feared he was becoming, if not insane, then irrational in his support for McPherson. My seventy-two thousand men would not be able to maneuver as nimbly as McPherson's twenty-four thousand, but the Cumberlands would be more than a match for Johnston's fifty-three thousand.

So Sherman won the first of many debates we would have, and on May 6, 1864, we advanced toward the Rocky Face Ridge that I had found too daunting in February. Schofield and I were to hold Johnston's scrutiny while McPherson went toward Snake Creek Gap with the goal of taking railroad tracks vital to the rebels' position.

As my men and Schofield's were diverting the enemy's attention with our frontal assaults, McPherson made it through the gap—only to be halted by a mere four thousand grayclad cavalry who pushed him away from the railroad. While Sherman was befuddled about the hash he and McPherson had made of things, Johnston recognized the trap that was forming and slipped back to the town of Resaca.

Sherman always regretted the lost chance to obliterate Johnston so early in the campaign. "Well, Mac, you have missed the great opportunity of your life," he told McPherson, as if it were entirely the young general's fault. Well, Cump, I thought, you're the one who wanted him promoted. Sherman could seldom reproach himself publicly for anything, but he must have realized he should have sent me, not McPherson, into Snake Creek Gap.

From here on, the campaign would be "one big Indian fight," as Sherman put it. For the rest of May and into June, we inched ever closer to Atlanta, trying to flank Johnston, who would slowly retreat from one strongpoint to another. There were battles with the names of Resaca, Pickett's Mill, New Hope Church, Dallas, Kolb's Farm, and Peachtree Creek. My army took the bulk of the casualties, more than eight thousand dead, wounded, or missing during the first three weeks of our drive, four times as many as the losses of the Armies of the Tennessee and the Ohio combined.

Our steady progress in pushing the rebels back, even during

heavy rains, did not satisfy Sherman, not when he had been so close to total victory. The pressure of command was making him more short-tempered than usual.

Sherman contended I was miserly with ammunition. Though we had few shortages on this campaign, I dislike firing shells to no effect. Doubtless, it's my background in artillery. Sherman wanted me to blast away at any opportunity, even if the enemy might be out of range. One time, Sherman spotted several rebel generals in a high, exposed position scouting us. I was elsewhere, so Sherman ordered Oliver Howard's artillery to fire upon them. The blast scattered the generals and killed one of them, Leonidas Polk, the former Episcopal bishop. I must admit that Sherman made his point on that day.

Cump could still be humorous, as when he noticed my pleasant quarters, with extra tents and a well-equipped adjutant general's wagon. Sherman called my traveling camp "Thomasville," and added that it was "a very pretty place, appears to be growing rapidly." Despite his sarcasm, Sherman accepted my offer of new tents for his own use. He came to the realization that he was living too spartan a life for a commanding general. While I am always ready to "rough it" when necessary, a general should be sure to look to his own comfort after he's seen to the needs of his men.

Less amusing were Sherman's complaints that I was too languid on the march and too avid to entrench when the enemy was in sight.

On May 25, the Cumberlands were near New Hope Church when I learned that the bulk of Johnston's army was just ahead of us. I told one of my staff to ride back to Howard's corps to urge haste in reinforcing us. I also advised this officer to walk his horse slowly until he was out of sight of the men, so as not to cause them undue consternation. This staff officer, Captain Henry Stone, delivered the message to Howard, then came across Sherman, who told him I was being too cautious. "There haven't been twenty rebels there all day," my commanding general said.

Sherman was right, there were not twenty rebels, there were thousands of them, and they gave us fierce combat in thick mud.

It was necessary to entrench, which displeased Sherman when he came up to view the situation. He grudgingly tolerated the entrenchments but ordered me to move my headquarters to the rear.

As I expected, this upset the troops, who always fought with greater confidence when they knew their general was nearby. I decided I would never again place my headquarters too far back from the front line, whatever the consequence to my career. The battle near New Hope Church continued for three days before the rebels fell back. So far the Union casualties on the campaign totaled twelve thousand.

We marched on into June, forcing the rebels to continue retreating. Here Sherman and I were in complete accord as he reopened a rail line so we could establish a forward supply base. On June 15 and 16, the Cumberlands made another advance, breaking through Johnston's fortifications near Pine Hill. All three of the Union armies were under constant fire, making progress despite the continued rains and nearly impassable roads.

Now we were under the shadow of Kennesaw Mountain. The word "Kennesaw" supposedly comes from the Cherokee word for burial place, another example of the foreshadowing we whites always seem to find in Indian languages.

This hulking summit Johnston had fortified with great skill, making it a superior strongpoint fifteen miles north of Atlanta. If Sherman had been in a more sensible mood, he would have noticed the similarities to his missed opportunity at Snake Creek Gap. Surely this time McPherson would be able to slip around Kennesaw Mountain, take the town of Marietta (a gateway to Atlanta) and leave Johnston surrounded.

No, that was not for Sherman, not this time. For he had read the dispatches from Grant's ongoing struggles with Lee. The wasteful shedding of Union blood at sites such as the Wilderness, Spotsylvania, and Cold Harbor kept the nation's attention on Virginia. I believe Sherman was jealous of Grant and wanted the press to throw their attention on him instead. Also, shamefully, he wanted to punish the Cumberlands for what he perceived as my slowness and my soldiers' "softness," as if the mettle they had shown on Missionary Ridge was of no consequence.

Thus Sherman ordered a frontal assault by my Cumberlands, with support from McPherson's Army of the Tennessee. I protested, to no avail, giving Sherman the impression I didn't want to fight. "Nonsense, Billy," I told him, "I'm always willing to fight, but I prefer to do so when we have a chance to win." Even Sherman's pet, McPherson, protested, also in vain. He was told it was necessary to show the country that Sherman's troops could fight as well as Grant's.

My staff officer Captain Stone and I made a reconnaissance to find a possible point of attack, coming as close as we dared to the enemy's picket line. Alas, Johnston had done his work too well. The mountain was well abatised, with felled trees full of sharpened branches facing us. We found no weaknesses. The next day, June 27, we targeted a rebel position whose only advantage was that it was the closest one to our line. It was on Cheatham Hill, south of Kennesaw Mountain. McPherson went for nearby Pigeon Hill.

One last time, I implored Sherman to change his mind, telling him that the rebels' fortifications were so "strong that they cannot be carried except by immense sacrifice even if they can be carried at all." In reply, Sherman simply looked at the top of Cheatham Hill and snapped, "You have your orders."

A colonel in the Cumberlands, Dan McCook, was one of the "fighting McCook brothers" as well as a former law partner of Sherman. McCook used his oratory skills to rally his men before the initial assault, reciting part of Thomas Macaulay's poem "Horatius at the Bridge." I am not much for such florid verse, but I have recently reread the work and feel compelled to repeat Macaulay's words.

"Then out spake brave Horatius
The Captain of the Gate:

To every man upon this earth
Death cometh soon or late,
And how can man die better
Than facing fearful odds,
For the ashes of his fathers
And the temples of his gods."

Soon after he recited this poem, McCook was one of the first of three thousand Union soldiers to fall in the Battle of Kennesaw Mountain. Even as he was about to die, McCook orated dramatically. On an enemy parapet, he slashed with his sword and shouted, "Surrender, you traitors!"

Kennesaw was the second saddest time of the war for me and my Cumberlands—only Chickamauga was worse.

Through the smoke of battle, I could see it all from my headquarters near the bottom of Cheatham Hill. On a day when the temperatures in the Georgia hills reached over 100 degrees, we proved we could die as needlessly as Grant's army. As any West Point plebe could have predicted, our assaults failed. Thrice we attacked, thrice we were thrown back. McPherson had the same results on Pigeon Hill. The rebels may have lost only one thousand men.

At one point, the grayclads called a truce, asking that both sides take time to carry off their wounded and bury their dead, who were becoming disagreeable in the heat. Some soldiers in blue and butternut used the sad interlude to converse in friendship with their enemies and learn how much they were alike. They would soon return to attacking each other with bullets, bayonets, and rocks.

By mid-afternoon, Sherman was still not convinced of his foolishness and ordered a fourth assault. Perhaps he had other law partners he was willing to sacrifice. I lodged a "most earnest protest," and this time he relented.

The only partial success of the day came from Schofield's Army of the Ohio, which was able to advance (with little resistance) to within five miles of the Chattahoochee River, the last natural barrier between us and Atlanta.

In the evening, Sherman thought about doing what he should have ordered in the first place, a flanking movement. He sent me a dispatch asking my opinion. I sent him this reply: "What force do you think of moving with? If with the greater part of the army, I think it decidedly better than butting against breastworks strongly abatised and twelve feet thick."

Sherman may have thought I was being sarcastic. On such a terrible day, I had no place for insubordinate humor, only the truth.

"Our loss is small compared to some of those battles in the East," he later told me. "It should not in the least discourage us."

"We have already lost heavily today without gaining any material advantage; one or two more such assaults would use up this army," I replied.

Sherman never expressed regrets for Kennesaw Mountain, always claiming it proved to Johnston and the world that "I would assault, and that boldly." Not even insanity can excuse such absurdity.

Soon after this catastrophe, we finally made the flanking maneuver, a relatively bloodless action that forced Johnston off his mighty mountain. Had we done this first, we would never have known the butchery of Kennesaw. After witnessing so many misjudgments by my commanding generals, I am reminded of the words of another poet, John Greenleaf Whittier: "For of all sad words of tongue or pen, The saddest are these: 'It might have been!'"

On July 2, the Cumberlands found the enemy's rearguard below Marietta and pushed the rebels to withdraw almost to the Chattahoochee River. On July 5, on a bluff overlooking the river, Sherman and I could see the church spires of the city. For a few minutes of contemplation, we gazed at our goal.

"There it is, Old Tom, Atlanta."

"Not so grand a city as Nashville or Chattanooga, I'll wager."

"Yes, but now it's the great prize, our El Dorado, our Holy Grail. I'm more ravenous for this prize than Sam Grant is for Richmond."

"Billy, I was under the impression that Joe Johnston was our prize."

"All in good time, all in good time."

"Two months so far."

"It won't take another two months to finish the job. Johnston must be on his last legs by now. Kennesaw took it out of him."

"Kennesaw took much more out of us."

"Put that aside, George. We've had that debate already."

"My apologies, general."

"You love the men too much."

"And you love them too little."

Sherman and I glared at each other, our frayed friendship nearly at the breaking point. Then he laughed harshly and rode off. I turned to Absalom Baird and asked him to position artillery in nearby timber so we could shell the city. So close, yet with plenty of rebels still between us and our goal.

That was the end of Joe Johnston's command. Our soldiers on the lines heard the rumors of his coming demotion and reported them to the generals. One Union picket told of yelling to his foe across the line. "Hello, Johnny Reb, who's your commander now?" The man in butternut replied, "Sherman." The sentry in blue asked, "How's that?" The rebel replied, "Well, when you move, we move."

Though I have been critical of Sherman's conduct of this campaign, my disapproval is nothing to what Johnston faced from the Southern leadership in Richmond and the rebel citizens in Atlanta.

Johnston had fallen back a long way, to the gates of the city, always stinging us when he could and whipping us when we errored at Kennesaw Mountain. Yet he could not expect another Union disaster like Chickamauga. With his limited manpower and materiel, Johnston could not be faulted for his strategy of a gradual retreat. His flaw in generalship was that he was worse than I was at keeping the mongrels of the press at bay.

Bragg, Johnston's predecessor as commander, did the Union a crucial favor as we approached Atlanta. Now chief of staff to Jefferson Davis, Bragg visited the Georgia capital and recommended that John Bell Hood succeed Johnston. I believe the phrase Bragg used was that Hood would give the rebels "unlimited satisfaction." Of Bragg's many mistakes during the rebellion, his advocacy of Hood might have been the most ultimately hurtful to the rebels' cause.

A spy verified Hood's promotion, bringing to Sherman a copy of a Southern newspaper from July 18 with the announcement. Sherman wisely sent for John Schofield, who had been Hood's roommate at West Point.

I have little good to say of Schofield, but he gave an accurate prediction of what we could expect. Schofield informed us that Hood was "bold even to rashness and courageous in the extreme." There was also a story that Hood was just as reckless at the poker table, once betting more than two thousand dollars on a hand when he had nothing of value in his cards. I have little interest in gambling, but I know such bluffing seldom pays at either games or battles.

I also knew Hood at West Point, where he was one of my students. I will never negate his many fine qualities. A braver man never put on a military uniform. The loss of a functioning left arm at Gettysburg and the loss of a leg at Chickamauga had failed to keep him from battle—his staff would strap him onto his horse every morning. But I agree with Schofield that Hood's courage was of an imprudent sort that could not tolerate a strategic retreat like Johnston's without a decisive battle.

That is the terrible mistake that Bragg made. What Hood and most of the Southern leaders failed to understand was that any decisive battle at this point was sure to be a rebel defeat. Sane or crazy, Sherman was too competent a general, with too many good men, to be driven all the way back to Chattanooga.

Johnston had also been popular with his men, never risking their lives unnecessarily. They'd fought better for him when he was retreating than they'd fought for Bragg when he was advancing. As I related earlier, a general need not be liked by his men to be successful, but one who is despised often finds that his troops will go into battle with less than their whole hearts. And some in the rebel ranks, we were told, had no love for Hood even before he was given command. Hood also lacked that element a winning general must have—good fortune. He was unlucky in his wounds and unlucky in his battles.

Had Johnston retained command, he likely would have tried to hold us off in a siege extended into November, longer than that of Vicksburg, putting Lincoln's chances for re-election in jeopardy. A defeat of Lincoln would mean final victory for the rebels. Such a scenario should have been obvious to a politician like Davis in 1864, as obvious as it is in hindsight to a simple soldier such as myself in 1870. Of course, if Davis had truly been wise, he would never have led this wicked rebellion.

Rash as Hood could be, he acquitted himself in Atlanta better than we expected. As we learned later, he put into effect a battle plan that Johnston had already devised. The idea was to strike one of our exposed flanks as we crossed the narrow Peachtree Creek, then drive us back to a deep part of the wide Chattahoochee where there was no ford.

On July 19, Sherman told me that the Army of the Cumberland could probably walk into Atlanta, that nothing would be in our path. He expected Hood to attack the armies of McPherson and Schofield, which were busy damaging enemy rail lines vital to keeping Atlanta's rebels supplied.

The next day the Cumberlands crossed Peachtree Creek, with McPherson and Schofield far to our left, leaving a two-mile gap between us. I could sense that Sherman's placement of our armies was a mistake, but I almost relished it, knowing that we Cumberlands would have to act independently.

As the rest of my command crossed the creek, one of my division commanders reported his suspicions that Hood was lurking nearby. Careful as always, I had cannon placed on a hill on our left. At 3:00 p.m., the rebels struck, close to where the cannon were. The grayclads may have been lamenting the demotion of Johnston, but they fought with the dash that Hood was expected to provide. In the next two hours, we repulsed three enemy assaults.

It was a near thing. Once I had to use the point of my sword to urge artillery horses to gallop to position, where I directed the guns' fire. The butternuts soon retreated. We had lost about two thousand men, the rebels between four thousand and five thousand.

While the Battle of Peachtree Creek was at its peak, Sherman sent me a message informing me he still believed there was little to my front. Later he realized his misconception, sending me this: "I have been with Howard and Schofield all day, and one of my staff is just back from McPherson. All report the enemy in their front so strong that I was in hopes none was left for you."

It was Sherman's good fortune that he had been elsewhere, for we Cumberlands did ourselves proud with our autonomy. Cump would only have gotten in our way.

Over the next two days, Hood showed his own ingenuity, pulling back from Atlanta's outer fortifications and fooling Sherman into thinking he had departed the city entirely. On July 22, Sherman's brother-in-law and aide, Colonel Charles Ewing, rode to my headquarters indecently giddy, shouting that the rebels were gone and ordering us to "march right through Atlanta and go into camp on the other side." He rode off before I could ask any questions. I feared he was premature in his excitement. The Cumberlands advanced cautiously.

Thinking Hood's army would be ripe for the taking, Sherman ordered McPherson's army to pursue him. McPherson was killed as he rode forward to direct his line. It was an ambush. A rebel corps led by William Hardee had marched east from Atlanta, detoured around the Union left, then assailed the rear, nearly routing McPherson's army. These Union men did well to hold off the surprise attack, especially with the death of their commanding general. McPherson had done what a good general must always do —go near the front of his lines to know what's ahead of him. The North lost 3,400 men; the rebels lost 5,500.

As the Cumberlands advanced, even Sherman had to admit he was in error and that the city was still occupied. He ordered us to converge toward the outskirts of Atlanta. But Hood and the main part of his army were still sturdy, and a proper siege began. For a month, we could make no headway, almost as if Johnston were still in charge.

Weary of the deadlock, Sherman showed some tardy wisdom and had part of the Union forces move south by west toward the rail center of Jonesboro, knowing that if we could take it, Atlanta would be completely cut off from any supplies and would have to surrender.

On September 1, the Cumberlands stormed Hood's fortifications at the town. Cleburne's division stood in the way, but nothing could stop us this time. I was even galloping on my stout horse, Billy, the pain in my back hardly noticeable as we achieved the victory.

Hood withdrew from Atlanta, burning eighty-one rail cars full of ammunition as he left. It was a tremendous fire, though there would be worse flames to come before the end of the year. Some city fathers who professed to be Union supporters surrendered the city on September 2. The next day Sherman sent a message to Washington: "Atlanta is ours and fairly won." His eloquence would help Lincoln win re-election.

Hood had divided his command as he departed the Georgia capital. Learning this, I proposed to Sherman a plan to pursue them. Atlanta was as wonderful a prize as he had hoped, but bagging Hood would be far better. Yet Sherman was in no mood to chase rebels then, telling me that we had been in constant battle or skirmish since early May and it was time to give our men some rest. The Union had suffered 34,500 casualties during the four-month Atlanta campaign, nearly as many as the rebels' losses. I did not object too strenuously to Cump's decision. Nevertheless, this was a time when "Slow Trot" urged speed and Sherman urged torpor.

Billy and I shook hands in congratulations, our tense feelings over the past few months forgotten, for a time. I didn't remind him of his forecast from July 5, that it wouldn't take us another two months to capture Atlanta. He was right in a way; it was only September 2.

I wonder if Cump will compose a memoir of the war, especially the Atlanta campaign. Such a book would be entertaining, full of his pride, wit, sense of history, and perhaps the truth now and again. He might sound perfectly sane if he proclaims "Veni, Vidi, Vici," but if he publishes a piece of puffery about his strategy at Kennesaw Mountain, I will not let that pass uncontested.

CHAPTER 20

IN WHICH WE PREPARE FOR HOOD

Since Hood couldn't hold the north of Georgia, he decided to capture all of Tennessee and Kentucky instead. Sherman had even grander plans.

Hood was at large, but it was Forrest, or at least the terror of him, that caused my dispatch from Atlanta. The rebel cavalryman's troops were threatening the railroad line that supplied us from Nashville and Chattanooga. Unleashing Forrest was an excellent idea, one that Hood or Johnston should have ordered much earlier, before we even approached Atlanta. Now Grant, who was still grappling with Lee in Virginia, worried that we could be driven out of the Georgia capital if Forrest kept our railroad under pressure.

So it was that on September 29, less than a month after we conquered Atlanta, I was ordered to Nashville to reorganize Union forces in Tennessee. I sent a division to pursue Forrest, but the former slave dealer was able to escape, crossing the Tennessee River and rejoining Hood.

Poor Hood, so crippled in body and so indomitable in spirit. And so rash in strategy.

Not that he had many choices; there was little he could do against the superior forces of Sherman. So, thinking he was at least the equal to Bragg in generalship, Hood decided to follow the same path that Bragg took in 1862, only this time he'd finish the task and drive north all the way to the Ohio River. Such a victorious campaign might encourage (or frighten) thousands of neutral Kentuckians to at last join the rebel cause. With these reinforcements, Hood could turn east and help Lee whip Grant.

A forlorn hope, but in 1864 it did not seem impossible to Lincoln or Grant. The Army of the Potomac, after two months of grievous bloodletting against Lee's forces, had stolen a march on him in June, crossing the James River and putting Richmond and the gateway city of Petersburg in a siege. It was perhaps the only time Grant showed he had the generalship to outmaneuver Lee rather than simply bludgeon him with superior numbers. Yet with Lee bottled up in the East, Grant and Lincoln were fearful of Hood in the West. How they wailed for me to speedily defeat him, even as I was building an army from scratch while Sherman took many of my best soldiers for his jaunt to the port city of Savannah, Georgia.

No, I do not begrudge him his glory for the "March to the Sea." It was a plan nearly as outrageous as Hood's, and it proved as decisive as it was cruel. Sherman's proposal was to ignore Hood to his north and march southeast to the Atlantic. He would lay waste to all in his path, driving home a lesson to Southern civilians that the rebellion could not last much longer and that outrages such as Andersonville, the Georgia prison camp where thirteen thousand Union captives died of starvation and disease, must be answered for. In Sherman's heartless phrase, he would "make Georgia howl."

I was conflicted about the strategy. I had first suggested to him that he stay in Atlanta and I take my Cumberlands toward the sea. But I did not advise the destruction that Sherman envisioned. War is the greatest cruelty, and we could not be gentle in putting down this illegal rebellion, not as gentle as Buell tried to be in Kentucky. But in a message I sent Sherman, "the thing becomes horribly grotesque... when from an ugly feeling ... we visit on helpless old men, women, and children the horrors of a barbarous war. ... We must be as considerate and kind as possible, or we will find that in destroying the rebels we have destroyed the Union."

Sherman snorted in disdain at my concerns. He also snorted when I complained about the prime units he was taking with him on his Georgia quest. Gone were two-thirds of my Army of the Cumberland, the Twentieth Corps, and my beloved Fourteenth Corps, which included the first brigade I had organized at Camp Dick Robinson, veterans who were instrumental in winning the Battle of Mill Springs so long ago. To part with these sturdy men after nearly three years of comradeship was a sorrow.

"These are good soldiers I'm taking from you. I know that, Old Tom," Sherman told me. "But I need them, and I wish I could take more. I have every confidence in you to put together a decent army without them."

"I'm proud to have your confidence, but I need more men, Cump," I answered. "Hang it all. Hood and Forrest will greatly outnumber us until we are reinforced."

"You'll get what you need. Have no doubts," Sherman said. "Whatever Hood has in mind, I'm sure he's not going to Nashville. He'll probably just annoy us by traipsing around the South chewing his cud. I'm tired of chasing Hood. Maybe he'll chase me once I start for Savannah. Right now he's in Alabama, but if he goes toward the Ohio River, I'll give him rations."

"No, send *me* the rations, and the men to eat them," I said.

"Don't fret, don't fret," Sherman said. "Now admit it, George, you've always wanted an independent command, away from my harping, and now you have it. I can only go to Savannah if I know my back is protected, and you're the man I trust to do it. Grant would never have allowed me to head out if I hadn't assured him that you could handle Hood."

"I thank you for that trust, Cump, even if I don't trust Grant."

"Yes, well, Lee's been even tougher than Grant expected, so it's got his insides all in a knot. He'll beat Lee in the spring, though. I'm just glad Sam's not the drinking man he used to be. Otherwise, he'd be guzzling jugs of week-old busthead."

"Let's pray to God for his temperance."

"God or Lucifer, I'm not particular. You heard what one reb prisoner said about me? That Sherman will never go to hell because he'll keep outflanking the devil."

"Heaven help you, Billy, and good luck."

"To hell with luck—we'll go through Georgia like we're Genghis Khan wiping out Russia."

Before I departed Atlanta, there was the matter of selecting the replacement for James McPherson as commander of the Army of the Tennessee. During the battle that was waged after McPherson's death, his army was commanded by General John Logan, a former congressman from Illinois. Political generals rarely impressed me, and while Logan performed acceptably during the battle, his overall record convinced me that an army under his command would bump up against other units and cause confusion and complications.

Joe Hooker would have been acceptable as McPherson's replacement, but Sherman rejected him, causing an angry Hooker to ask to be relieved. I wish he had stayed with us, but my friend went to Cincinnati, where he commanded troops north of the Ohio River. I then urged Sherman to promote Oliver Otis Howard to command the Army of the Tennessee. Thankfully, Sherman agreed with me on Howard's qualifications and gave him the post. I was well pleased but regretted that Howard wasn't coming north with me to Nashville.

For some reason, Sherman took my objections to Logan as a personal animus. I've heard that he said I hated Logan. I have never had any personal dislike for Logan, only a professional's doubts about his qualities as a general. Nonetheless, in a few months, Logan (through Grant) would nearly cause me to have the gravest enmity toward him.

Fortunately, I retained the services of David Stanley and the Fourth Corps of the Army of the Cumberland. Unfortunately, Sherman inflicted Schofield on me, the price I had to pay to receive what was left of his Army of the Ohio, ten thousand men. During the Atlanta campaign I had started to have doubts about Schofield's worthiness. He had not excelled, and I had heard that he was critical of me, repeating the old accusation that I was slow. And worse, he was intriguing to have some of my Cumberland divisions assigned to his army.

Whatever Schofield's drawbacks, I needed his ten thousand men. In late September, I had only thirty-one thousand total. I would have to wait weeks before I could receive my main reinforcements, two divisions under General A.J. Smith that had been fighting in Missouri. Until then, my thin force would be spread out across the Tennessee River area, watching to see which way Hood or Forrest would go.

Despite my concerns about the rebels' intentions, I sent for Mrs. Thomas to visit me in Nashville that autumn. The city seemed safe for the present, and three years away from you were three too many, Frances. I was in rapture when I saw you step off the train that October.

Our happy reunion was too short, thanks to Forrest. In early November, he captured several small boats in Johnsonville, a river town ninety miles west of Nashville. The cavalryman then turned sailor, using the craft to attack a small fleet of gunboats and barges loaded with Union supplies. When he was finished wrecking the floating property, he turned his attentions to warehouses on shore. Altogether, he destroyed Union food and other goods worth nearly two million dollars and revived my painful memories of the hungry days in Chattanooga.

I decided it was time for Mrs. Thomas to return to the haven of New York. Reading this, Frances reminds me she wanted to stay with me to face the danger. Her courage was always understood. But she knew that her presence would weigh on my mind at a time when I needed to focus all my concentration on the war.

When Schofield arrived in Nashville on November 4, I did not allow him to linger but hastened him and his men on in pursuit of Forrest. The cavalry chieftain again was too quick to be trapped, and went south to rejoin Hood in Gadsden, Alabama. I then dispatched Schofield to Pulaski, a town seventy-five miles south of Nashville that was near the Alabama border. There he combined forces with Stanley's and waited for the rebels to reveal where they were headed. I would have preferred Stanley to be in overall command of the thirty thousand men in Pulaski, but Schofield had seniority. His job was to hold off any rebel advance as long as he could, then fall back.

On November 8, a non-military event occurred that was as important as anything Grant, Sherman, or I could accomplish. Abraham Lincoln was re-elected, with my patron Andrew Johnson to become his new vice president. It meant the Union would accept nothing less than complete surrender by the rebels. The news cheered us all in the Union Army. If the butternuts were disheartened by Lincoln's triumph, we were not apprised of it.

Sherman made his move on November 16. While Atlanta underwent a second, more engulfing fire, he and his soldiers began their march toward Savannah. Did Sherman truly want all of Atlanta in flames? He has always denied it, and I believe he only meant for military sites to be consumed. Yet his soldiers were eager to put everything to the torch, and Sherman has told me he did not feel the need to discipline men for going beyond their orders. This lax practice would continue through the march, as some troopers became "bummers" who went out of their way to destroy Georgians' food and dwellings.

It showed how military strategies can change drastically. The original idea had been to destroy Johnston's army. Well, that army, now under Hood, still existed—beaten but unbowed. Sherman would leave the destruction of this rebel army to me while he would cause destruction in much of Georgia.

As if to answer Sherman, Hood left Alabama on November 21 with his eye on Nashville. He had sixty thousand men.

What did I have then? Besides the thirty thousand in Pulaski, I had five thousand men from the quartermaster's department who had been placed on the defense line. I had several thousand troops returning from leave, plus convalescents. There were also recruits just out of training camp, railroad guards and black regiments not yet tempered by combat. I had lost about fifteen thousand men whose enlistments had expired or who were still on the leave they had taken so they could vote in the presidential election. I'm sure they nearly all voted for Lincoln, and he needed every ballot, but how I wanted them in my defense line in Nashville. And I had gotten word that the arrival of A.J. Smith's divisions would be delayed.

At least Sherman sent me a splendid cavalry officer from Grant's staff, twenty-seven-year-old James Wilson, whom I sent to Pulaski to take command of Schofield's cavalry. There were about twenty-seven thousand other Union troops scattered all over Tennessee and Kentucky, guarding the rail lines and the river depots. I longed to pull them into my force, but they were needed where they were to resist enemy raiders.

When I knew of Hood's movement, I sent Schofield a message telling him to prepare to fall back to Columbia, Tennessee, so he would not be trapped by enemy flanking movements. Schofield hesitated, however, and his thirty thousand men were nearly surrounded. Despite bitterly cold and wet conditions, the rebels marched more than eighty miles in a week to Columbia, a town forty-five miles southwest of Nashville that was a vital crossing on the Duck River. Schofield was tardy in recognizing Hood's maneuver and in a thirty-mile march barely got to Columbia in time to cross the river ahead of the grayshirts.

And an even greater jeopardy awaited him. Forrest was loose again, besting young Wilson in a cavalry skirmish and nearly cutting off Schofield's line of communications back to me in Nashville. And Hood was trying to steal another march on Schofield, heading north to Spring Hill and hoping to trap him. Wilson sent me a warning of a heavy rebel movement across the Duck. Even from forty miles away, I could sense enemy strategy better than Schofield, and so before Forrest could completely isolate the befuddled Union general, I ordered him to withdraw to Franklin, where he could throw up fortifications only twenty miles south of Nashville.

But Schofield was a doltish slug. Rebel forces were already

along the road that he must take, and had they attacked in what was a perfect flanking position, the Union forces would have been annihilated. I am told that Schofield even considered the ignominy of surrender.

A craven laggard he might have been, but on the night of November 29, Schofield was blessedly lucky. God took pity on the Union men and allowed them to creep through the night practically unmolested. Stanley told me it was like "treading on thin ice over a smoldering volcano." Through incredible happenstance, the rebels, whether because of exhaustion, incompetence, sloth, or drunkenness, did not attack. This astonishment has never been satisfactorily explained. Rebel officers would barely speak of it after the war. Some of my staff speculated that Hood, in constant pain due to his terrible wounds, had been medicated so strongly that he couldn't recognize what was happening that night. On an occasion when Hood's planning had been quite sound, his army let him down.

And then Hood let his army down. The fortifications the Union troops put up that night were stout, yet Hood must have looked at them with the same hubris that Sherman had when he gazed at Kennesaw Mountain. Or perhaps Hood was angry at his men for the missed opportunity from November 29. The next day, he ordered his troops to storm the works, and they did so, nearly winning a battle that, on a smaller scale, was as terrible as Kennesaw. Only a charge led by Colonel Emerson Opdyke of Stanley's corps impeded the butternut assault. The enemy suffered six thousand casualties, 1,750 of them dead. Six of the slain were generals, including the best in Hood's army, Cleburne.

The Union casualties totaled more than two thousand, one of whom was Stanley, wounded by a bullet in the neck. Schofield had left command of the combat to Stanley, the real "victor" of the Battle of Franklin. The wounded general would win the Medal of Honor for his actions that day. (Frances asks me what state Stanley hails from. Ohio, I sheepishly admit. Another exception to my prejudice against Buckeye generals.) Thankfully, Stanley would recover and return to duty.

Where was Schofield during this fight, the one he is so proud of, the one he dares suggest nullifies any credit I won at Nashville? That yellowbelly was two miles away with a reserve division. As was his wont, Schofield did not put himself within range of a hostile gun. It is a mystery to me that he apparently had a reputation for fortitude when he was in Missouri. Did he have only a finite amount of gallantry and thus exhausted it too early in the war?

Though I asked Schofield to hold on to Franklin for at least three days, he rushed back to Nashville before the smoke cleared from the battleground. Under the rules of engagement, Schofield's hurried retreat might have made him the official "loser" at Franklin. And the cur still had more dastardly tricks to play on me and the rest of the Union forces.

CHAPTER 21

IN WHICH WE TRIUMPH AT NASHVILLE

For all the odium I now feel toward Schofield, and my disappointment then that he didn't stay longer in Franklin, I was pleased to see him and his men in Nashville on December 1. But I didn't greet him as joyously as I did General A.J. Smith when he and his troopers, on that same day, finally arrived from Missouri. I fear I embarrassed Smith with my hearty embrace, almost like a father grasping his prodigal son. With the forces of those two generals, I now had enough soldiers to defend the city.

Smith's rugged men were especially welcome. One proclaimed: "We're A.J. Smith's guerrillas! We've been to Vicksburg, Red River, Missouri and about everywhere else ... and now we're going to hell if General Smith leads us there!"

With such men and the fortifications we'd thrown up, the Tennessee capital was as secure as any city in the North or South. Even if Hood tried to march around Nashville, we had Union Navy gunboats patrolling the Cumberland River to discourage any advance. Grant and Lincoln should have realized this and let me go about my duties without interference. Hood should have seen that and retreated. And Schofield should have done his duty and acted the role of an officer and a gentleman.

Hood felt he had no choice in the matter—to retreat would be to finalize the defeat of the rebellion in the West. To storm our entrenchments would inflict a far greater loss of life than he suffered at Franklin. Bypassing us and marching north would only leave a superior force in his rear, and we now had enough soldiers to keep our supply line open despite rebel raids. Hood's one hope, even more forlorn, was to draw the Union troops out of Nashville, defeat us, and press north to the Ohio, still expecting a surge of martial spirit among the uncommitted Kentuckians.

So Hood encamped in the hills south of Nashville, waiting for deliverance. Knowing my numbers were growing, he sent Forrest away to block any more reinforcements. Though Forrest did his best, Hood would have been better off had he kept him close at hand.

My own cavalry was being built up, despite my having to detach some units to chase after Forrest and other raiders. Wilson was seizing every beast that could carry a man, be it the equines of a streetcar company or a circus. Even the carriage horses of Andrew Johnson were impressed into duty, which annoyed the vice president-elect. The necessity of war, I told him. I was still thankful to Johnson for the support he gave me early in the war, and eventually he gave his blessing to the loss of his fine horseflesh.

I had every confidence that Wilson would soon have a formidable cavalry, and on December 1, I wired this conviction to Halleck: "If (Hood) remains until Wilson gets equipped, I can whip him, and will move against him at once."

This should have reassured Washington, but my cursed nickname of "Slow Trot" was never more of a detriment than now. Halleck took my message to mean I was being hesitant, using Wilson's search for horses as an excuse to do nothing. I'm told that Lincoln expressed fears I might prove as unworthy for independent command as McClellan. Stanton, once a supporter of mine, was nearly unhinged, and in an exchange of wires with Grant, said: "Thomas seems to be unwilling to attack because it is hazardous (as if all war were not hazardous). If he waits for Wilson to get ready, Gabriel will be blowing his last horn."

Who was inspiring such mistrust in me? I was sure it was Grant, who took time from his Virginia struggles with Lee to wire me to assail the rebels before they could entrench. From 800 miles away, he thought he knew the situation better than I did. He could not comprehend that there was no purpose in moving against Hood until we had the cavalry and the rest of the men prepared for a decisive victory instead of another Cold Harbor massacre. In my reply to Grant, I reminded him that he had left me the most understrength units of Sherman's army and that my reinforcements had been delayed.

Only when I, as commanding general, was convinced of our fitness for battle did I pass the word for us to attack within two hours. That was on December 8. Then came a melodramatic change in the weather—fog, followed by freezing rain. The ground was covered in ice, which would have been disastrous for any offensive. I recalled my order with the greatest regret.

Grant apparently blamed me for the weather, assuming I had willed the ice storm so I could stay warm and snug in my hotel room. The foolish son of a tanner was ready to strip me of command and give my duties to Schofield, or so I was later informed. Here I must commend Halleck, usually not my greatest admirer, who on this occasion did me a service by convincing Grant not to relieve me just yet.

Grant then sent me a wire that said in part, "I have as much confidence in your conducting the battle rightly as I have in any other officer, but it has seemed to me you have been slow, and I have had no explanation of affairs to convince me otherwise. ... I hope most sincerely that there will be no necessity of repeating the order (to dismiss you), and that the facts will show that you have been right all the time."

The next day I replied: "General Halleck informs me you are very much dissatisfied with my delay in attacking. I can only say that I have done all in my power to prepare, and if you should deem it necessary to relieve me, I shall submit without a murmur."

Not a murmur, but with melancholy. Luck was seemingly

forsaking me. If we could achieve this victory, I would prove myself once and for all as a commander and as a loyal Union soldier in service to my country and my oath of office. Yet it appeared that the forces of nature looked down at me with the same contempt I received from Grant, Bragg, Stuart, the state of Virginia, and my own blood relations. Never had I felt so despondent, even as I kept my outer composure. My only true solace was from the letters of Mrs. Thomas. The memory of your recent visit still lingered, Frances.

What of the soldiers, the men who were waiting for my command to advance? They were not despairing at the weather. They always cheered me as I inspected our battle lines. Unlike the skittish hens in Washington, the soldiers knew that victory would be ours as soon as the ground thawed.

On December 10, I invited my corps commanders to the St. Cloud Hotel and told them what I knew, including Grant's lack of confidence in me. All of them, except for a silent Schofield, agreed with my decision not to attack until there was a thaw, including Wilson. Though young, the cavalry commander was a man of sound, mature judgment, someone in whom I could confide. After the other generals left the meeting, I called him aside.

"The Washington authorities treat me as if I were a boy," I told him. "They seem to think me incapable of planning a campaign or of fighting a battle. If they will just let me alone till thawing weather begins, I will show them what we can do. I am sure my plan of operations is correct and that we shall lick the enemy if he only stays to receive our attack."

The press was part of the problem. Since the beginning of autumn, the Northern newspapers had been panicked by the threat to Nashville, raising alarms that after taking that city, Hood would cross the Ohio and imperil the safety of Northern farms and cities. This must have contributed to the impatience in Washington. And Grant and the forces of nature continued their harassment of me. The frozen ground still constrained us. The Union's commander in chief was more fearful of Hood than he was of Lee, though Hood was as hampered as we were by the ice.

On December 11, Grant wired me this insult: "If you delay attacking longer, the mortifying spectacle will be witnessed of a rebel army moving for the Ohio, and you will be forced to act, accepting such weather as you find. Delay no longer for weather and reinforcements."

I replied as respectfully as I could: "I will obey the order as promptly as possible, however much I regret it, as the attack will have to be made under every disadvantage. The whole country is covered with a perfect sheet of ice and sleet, and it is with difficulty that the troops are able to move about on level ground."

Why was Grant so convinced that I was a malingerer, so unwilling to do his duty? More subtle minds than mine began to suspect an imp in Nashville was using the wire to belittle me. William Whipple, my chief of staff, was the first to ask the question. It was answered by James Steedman, one of my corps commanders. He found a message in the telegraph office that had been sent to Washington. It read: "Many officers here are of the opinion that General Thomas is certainly too slow in his movements."

Steedman gave this missive to me for inspection. Wearing my glasses, I recognized the writing as Schofield's. Blindly, I asked Steedman, "Why does he send such telegrams?" Steedman smiled at me as would a father to a young son who asks a childishly simple question. "General Thomas, who is next in command to you, and would succeed you in case of removal?"

"Oh, I see," I replied, my eyes opened at last.

My outrage at Schofield was cooled by the knowledge that I could not demote him or relieve him of duty, not now when the battle was so close to being joined. If I ousted him at this time, it would have caused great uncertainty among his men and turmoil when we could not afford it. I must put up with him for the present.

What made me especially angry at his treachery was that he knew the reasons for our delay were reasonable. And more importantly, he knew the soundness of my battle plan and that once we were on the move, we would destroy the rebel army. Schofield wanted to use my strategy to take all the credit for himself. He was not the greatest scoundrel I ever met (I reserve that dishonor for Twiggs back in the old Army), but Schofield was a vile serpent in my garden. My greatest fear was not that he would receive acclaim for my Nashville plan, only that he would prove incompetent at putting my strategy in operation, thus allowing the grayclads to triumph or escape unscathed.

Perhaps Grant had similar misgivings about Schofield. Though he earlier had ordered the cur to relieve me and then changed his mind on Halleck's recommendation, Grant had second and then third thoughts. He ordered General John Logan, then in Virginia, to travel to Nashville and take my command if battle had not yet been joined. Logan I have already described, a political general who was not qualified for that rank.

Nevertheless, Logan never arrived in Nashville, getting only as far as Cincinnati on December 14, the day the weather lost much of its chill and the ice began to melt. That night I gave orders to attack in the morning.

On December 15, the day we were to attack, Grant traveled from Virginia to Washington, where he met with Lincoln, Halleck, and Stanton. He told these three of his determination to oust me from my command, and to their credit, all three tried to convince Grant not to do it. The general was not swayed.

Lincoln should then have ordered Grant to retain me, but the president had put too much faith in this now-agitated general to back away now. Grant himself was going to come to Nashville and take charge, no longer trusting either Logan or Schofield. He drew up an order dismissing me and gave it to Major Thomas Eckert, the superintendent of military telegraphs. Eckert won my everlasting gratitude when, on his own responsibility, he decided to delay sending the wire and wait for developments from Tennessee.

Blissfully, I was unaware of Grant's ultimate insult to my capabilities. At 5:00 a.m., not long before he met with Lincoln and the others, I checked out of the St. Cloud and rode to my field headquarters. The melancholy of the past few days was replaced by relief and anticipation.

Before I got to my headquarters, I remembered a debt that should be paid. During the cold weather of the past few days, I had depleted my personal store of coal and needed to borrow some from a neighbor at the hotel. Knowing I might forget this matter when the battle commenced, I asked one of my staff to make sure that replacement coal was sent to the neighbor. The other staff members smiled and shrugged at what outsiders might consider a trivial matter. My staff knew I was not daft, only responsible in settling my obligations. We rode on to put my battle plan into operation.

The strategy was not complicated. It would be a turning movement. A holding action would focus the enemy's attention on one point, while a stronger force would hit another sector. Steedman's corps, including a good portion of Negro soldiers, was on the Union left and would feint at the enemy, making Hood believe his right was the target of the main assault. Thomas Wood's corps would drive at the center while Smith's corps, on the Union right, would strike the enemy's left side. Schofield's corps would be in reserve in the center. Wilson's cavalry would also strike the enemy's left; the troopers would fight dismounted until they had the opportunity for pursuit. Commissary troops and armed civilian employees would hold the interior lines. All in all, a makeshift collection of fifty-five thousand men that would prove a mighty army.

I estimated the enemy, weakened by desertions, had forty thousand troops, but in a piece of good fortune for the Union, Forrest's men were thirty miles southeast near Murfreesboro, leaving Hood with thirty thousand. Still, if Hood had entrenched his five-mile line of rolling hills properly, they would be a formidable defensive force.

Fog delayed our first assault but also hid our movements. At 8:00 a.m., I ordered Steedman to attack. His men made a good account of themselves, their feint causing Hood to move troops from his center. "The issue is settled! Negroes will fight!" I would later shout at my staff. Steedman reported that they advanced "with cool, steady bravery."

Wilson's twelve thousand cavalry rode well on the thawed ground as they went to their position, and they did even better when dismounted, firing their new seven-shot carbines.

In the center, Schofield was slow in getting into place, and I took quiet pleasure in ordering him to speed up. Wood's corps was fast off the mark—Wood still felt shame for his role in Chicka-mauga, when his following the unclear instructions to "close up" on another unit opened the gap that led to our defeat. This time there would be no stain on his record. His men in the center took Montgomery Hill, a key position.

The assaults thinned out Hood's lines as he was forced to extend them. The feint had worked. By the end of the short December day, our army had taken two thousand prisoners and pushed the rebels two miles back to their second line of defense, another series of fortified hills.

I returned to Nashville that night to send wires to the men in Washington who had doubted my fitness for command. "I attacked the enemy's left this morning and drove it from the river, below the city. ... The troops behaved splendidly, all taking their share in assaulting and carrying the enemy's breastworks. I shall attack the enemy again tomorrow, if he stands to fight and, if he retreats during the night, will pursue him, throwing heavy cavalry forces in his rear, to destroy his trains, if possible."

Grant, who had abruptly turned back from the Washington train station when told of our advance, sent a nag. "Much is now expected" was the crux of it.

Hang it all, the tanner's son was still a man of little faith, his message to me so sullen that he reminded me of the townspeople of Nashville, nearly ninety thousand, most of whom desired a Union defeat. They packed the rooftops and hills behind us, a natural amphitheater that allowed them to witness the dashing of their rebel hopes.

One official in Washington was especially gratified by our first day's success. Eckert, the major who had delayed sending Grant's wire relieving me, had received the first of many telegrams telling of the Union advance. Stanton told me later how Eckert appeared at his door with the good news, and the two of them rode to the White House to inform Lincoln. On the way, Eckert gave Stanton a copy of Grant's never-delivered order.

"Did you send this?" Stanton asked.

"No, sir. Mr. Secretary, I fear I have violated a military rule and have placed myself liable to be court-martialed," Eckert replied.

"Major, if they court-martial you, they will have to court-martial me," Stanton said, putting his arm around Eckert's shoulder.

Lincoln also approved of Eckert's inaction. What Grant thought of it is unknown to me.

The road back to Nashville was filled with butternut prisoners. Some of them were from that most traitorous state of South Carolina. They moaned to me, complaining that they would rather die than be guarded by colored soldiers. I replied, "Well, you may say your prayers and get ready to die, for these are the only soldiers I can spare."

December 16, the second day of the Battle of Nashville, is a date I will always remember with personal pride and gratitude to the soldiers who built on the success of the first day and achieved the final victory. I have never doubted my decision to honor my oath of loyalty to the Union, but these men validated my choice by their valor.

As I departed the hotel for the battlefield early that morning, my thoughts were interrupted by a nearby noise that was definitely not the sound of guns. It was the slamming of a window by a young woman who was staring at me with a face of fury. I smiled at her and rode on to my headquarters. Another Nashville civilian who knows her side is losing, I thought. As it happened, the young lady would eventually marry a Union officer in my army. Love can be stronger than hate.

My attention turned back to what awaited us on the battlefield. I must reluctantly give Schofield some credit here. He had warned me that Hood wouldn't willingly retreat after the first day's setbacks, and he was right. In some ways the rebels were in better condition than the previous day. Their defensive line was more concentrated, and there were heights on both flanks. The most imposing was on our right, Compton's Hill (which Tennesseans later called Shy's Hill, after a fallen rebel). On the other side was Overton Hill, also solidly entrenched.

Again we attacked Hood's left obliquely, waiting for Wilson's cavalry to get at the rebels in another turning movement so I could order a general assault from the center. Wood had the hardest going. His men, assisted by a brigade of Negroes, went for Overton Hill. Twice they were driven back, but they persisted.

By the middle of the afternoon, Wilson's dismounted men had put Hood's forces in peril. We got our hands on a captured dispatch from Hood telling a subordinate: "For God's sake, draw the Yankee cavalry from our left and rear, or all is lost."

The time had come to strike the decisive blow. Smith and Schofield's two corps were to launch a frontal attack as Wilson's men pressed the enemy's rear. Now Schofield made me doubt the wisdom of not dismissing him for his disloyalty. Just before the attack was to begin, he implored me to give him reinforcements from Smith's corps. Smith rightly refused to weaken his own forces. I had to send Whipple, my chief of staff, to see if Schofield truly needed reinforcements. He didn't, Whipple informed me. So I went myself to Schofield to accelerate him.

As Schofield continued to beg for more troops, Wilson rode in and reported his cavalrymen were doing their part, flooding into the enemy's works. Indeed, Wilson, though he had climbed down from his horse, was jumping up and down as if he were still in the saddle, urging me to send the infantry forward. I confess I acted a bid ponderously, for Schofield's benefit, using his field glasses to confirm with my eyes what Wilson had just told me, that a direct assault would crumble the rebels.

I also saw that one of Smith's divisions, led by General John McArthur, was already attacking. He had asked Smith for permission to move against an enemy point that was jutting out and looked vulnerable. Getting no immediate response, McArthur decided the silence must mean approval. His division pushed the enemy out of the salient.

I turned to Schofield and said, "General Smith is attacking without waiting for you. Please advance your entire line." Schofield did so with little ardor, perhaps hoping that the battle would be over before he got close to the enemy guns. Wilson jumped back on his horse and returned to his cavalrymen.

Our artillery started firing all along the line. The forces of Smith, Wilson, and Schofield then shattered the rebels on Compton's Hill, Schofield's men showing none of the reluctance of their commander. The collapse on Compton's Hill helped Wood and Steedman's corps push the rest of Hood's army off Overton Hill. Wilson's cavalry made it impossible for the rebels to rally. Suddenly the battle was a rout.

When I rode up to confer with Smith, I saw hordes of butter-nuts coming down Compton's Hill. "General, what is the matter? Are your men being captured up there?" I asked him. "Not by a damn sight," Smith answered. "My men are capturing them—those are rebel prisoners you see." I laughed as if were New Year's Eve.

Even Hood would later admit, "For the first and only time, a Confederate army abandoned the field in confusion." (Hood was in error on this point. He hadn't been at Missionary Ridge or Mill Springs, where the rebels also ran like scalded dogs.)

I could hear the manly cheering of the Union troops. "That's the voice of the American people," I said to my staff. Later I rode to the top of Overton Hill and became more emotional. I lifted my hat to the Union men and exclaimed, "Oh, what a grand army I have! God bless every member of it!" When I saw Negro soldiers marching, their ranks thinned by the battle, I faced them and kept my head uncovered to honor them until they had passed by.

Those are noble sentiments to express, and I did so with a general's composure. Yet I also made a spectacle of myself with some boorish boasting, galloping my poor horse Billy and shouting at my young cavalry general, "Dang it to hell, Wilson, didn't I tell you we could lick them, didn't I tell you we could lick them?"

Wilson grinned in agreement, even as he and his cavalry tried to chase down the remnants of Hood's army.

"Follow them as far as you can tonight and resume the pursuit as early as you can tomorrow," I told him, an order that he didn't need because that was what he was already doing. We had won a great battle, but there was still much work to do before the war would be over.

CHAPTER 22

IN WHICH THE UNION ACHIEVES
FINAL VICTORY

The Northern press, so often my enemy, now hailed me by an overly heroic nickname, "the Sledge of Nashville." As sobriquets go, it was kind and generous. The men under my command, who truly wielded the sledgehammers in the battle, still referred to me as "Old Pap" and "Uncle George."

Grant, however, refused to think of me as anything other than "Slow Trot." His adherence to the notion I was sluggish was as ingrained as the way many people continued to regard him as a drunk. Grant and Halleck kept sending wires implying that I was not diligent in hunting down the remnants of Hood's fleeing army.

As I told Halleck, we did all within my imagination: "General Hood's army is being pursued as rapidly and as vigorously as it is possible for one army to pursue another. We cannot control the elements. I am doing all in my power to crush Hood's army and, if it be possible, will destroy it, but pursuing an enemy through an exhausted country, over mud roads, completely sogged with heavy rains, is no child's play."

I must salute young Wilson and his cavalrymen for the determination of their chase. His troopers wore out six thousand horses in their ten-day race to head off Hood. Through the wintry weather, without rest, they rode on, never being cowed by Forrest's raiders nipping at their flanks.

The rebels threw down many bridges and crossings, hampering our pursuit. How I missed my Cumberland regiment of bridge builders, one of the many plums Sherman took with him, along with our pontoon train. Before the battle, we had started making a replacement for the pontoon structure in the expectation that we would soon be on Hood's trail. However, it was accidentally sent down the wrong road when an aide miswrote an order, and valuable time was lost until the pontoon was shipped in the right direction.

Throughout these pages, I have not been falsely modest in relating my wisdom in military matters, especially strategy and tactics. Now I must be equally candid when describing an error in judgment on my part. I should have detached part of Wilson's cavalry to try cutting off the enemy's rear. I was so intent on chasing the grayshirts down the main road from Nashville that I did not divide our forces for better speed on parallel routes. Had I done so, would we have bagged more of Hood's dwindling command? We will never know.

Our cavalry's chase ended only when Hood and a few thousand of his men were able to cross the Tennessee River at Muscle Shoals, Alabama. Still, some Union cavalry were able to cross the river and capture the last of Hood's wagon trains.

Grant and others in his circle said my "slowness" allowed Hood's army to escape. The tanner's son has never been so wrong. He must have been reading Southern newspapers, which tried to hide the fact of Hood's loss. The newspapers in Richmond and elsewhere in the rebel states said that Hood's army had barely been scratched and was still lurking in parts unknown.

Here is the truth that the Southern press didn't dare report and that Grant refused to accept. When Hood went north, he had sixty thousand men. When he crossed the Tennessee after his defeat at Nashville, he had no more than fifteen thousand and probably as few as eight thousand. My men did as I promised Halleck—we crushed and destroyed Hood's army, both in the battle and in the chase. His army never took the field again, though a few of the men drifted into other rebel units. Hood resigned his command in January and never led soldiers again.

Where did the rest of Hood's men go? As best as we can tell, in the Battles of Franklin and Nashville, nearly four thousand were killed and twelve thousand wounded. At least thirteen thousand were made prisoners. And many others, yeomen tired of fighting and yearning for home, simply skulked away.

As I've already written, desertion was a constant problem for the Union armies, but it was far worse for the rebels throughout the war. The South simply couldn't find enough men. In every one of the seceded states there were regions of Union loyalty that provided refuge for those who had no interest in the war. Some of these Southern deserters even kept their arms and fought against the rebel government that had sent them to war.

The slaveholders' rebellion was, as Southern yeomen often told us, "a rich man's war and a poor man's fight." Many of the wealthiest slaveholders were excused from serving in the rebels' army on the assumption that they must stay on their plantations to keep their Negros under control. That angered those other Southern men who owned few slaves or none at all. While they despised and feared the idea of freedom for Negroes, they despised and feared death even more. And no, I'm not implying that all the rebel deserters were cowards; they had simply exhausted their courage in a terrible cause.

At Nashville, the Union lost 387 killed, 2,562 wounded and 112 missing. Though mourning the dead, I was happy and proud that our losses were so light, especially since we were attacking fortified positions. No Cold Harbor here, where Grant took seven thousand casualties, including two thousand dead.

Yet Lincoln, still haunted by Meade's lost opportunity at Gettysburg, both congratulated and hectored me in his wire when he heard of our smashing victory: "Please accept for yourself, officers and men the nation's thanks for the good work of yesterday. You have made a magnificent beginning; a grand consummation is within your easy reach. Do not let it slip."

Others were more magnanimous.

Secretary of War Stanton wired me: "I rejoice in tendering to you and the gallant officers and soldiers of your command the thanks of this department for the brilliant achievement of this day." Treasury Secretary Chase told me: "We all feel profoundly gratified to you and your gallant Army for the great success over Hood. I rejoice that you were in command."

I published Stanton and Chase's messages in general orders to my army and added my own words of thanks: "The general commanding with pride and pleasure ... adds thereto his own thanks to the troops for the unsurpassed gallantry and good conduct displayed by them in the battle."

Though I was a major general of volunteers, I was still only a brigadier general in the Regular Army. On Christmas Eve, Stanton sent me this wire: "With great pleasure I inform you that for your skill, courage, and conduct in the recent brilliant operation under your command, the president has directed your nomination as a major general in the United States Army, to fill the only vacancy in that grade. No official duty has been performed by me with more satisfaction, and no commander has more justly earned promotion by devoted, disinterested, and valuable services to his country."

I was on duty at my field headquarters in Tennessee when I received the telegram. I looked at it a long time before handing it to an aide, Chief Army Surgeon George Cooper.

"What do you think of that?" I asked him.

"Thomas, it is better late than never," Cooper replied.

"I suppose it is better late than never, but it is too late to be appreciated," I said. "I earned this at Chickamauga."

Later I observed, "There is one thing about my promotions that is exceedingly gratifying. I have never received a promotion they dared withhold."

I regret my cynicism was so often validated. They had passed me over so many times before. Even Phil Sheridan, an Ohio man with thirteen years less experience than I had, had already received a regular major generalship for his work in Virginia.

Despite Stanton's words, it seemed as if they had promoted me grudgingly, after my near loss of command at Nashville and then my smashing victory, and as if they could think of no one else to fill the vacancy. I learned later that Grant had initially opposed the promotion, still believing I had not done enough to capture Hood. Lincoln, perhaps feeling a twinge of conscience for the many slights he had paid me, overruled Grant.

I was still pondering the lateness of my promotion when I received a message Christmas Day from Sherman, glorying in his capture of Savannah. He praised me, of course, though he was rather more pleased with himself:

"I have heard of all your operations up to about the seventeenth, and I do not believe your own wife was more happy at the result than I was. Had any misfortune befallen you, I would have reproached myself for taking away so large a proportion of the army and leaving you too weak to cope with Hood. But as events have turned out, my judgment has been sustained. But I am nonetheless thankful to you. ... Here I am now in a magnificent house. ... The old live oaks are beautiful as ever, and whilst you are freezing to death in Tennessee, we are basking in a warm sun."

I tossed his wire aside. Old Cump, I thought, you took the best part of my army, left me what you called "trash" to replace them, had an easy if destructive excursion toward the Atlantic, and now you're a gentleman of leisure. Had it not been for the bravery of my "trash" in Nashville, you would have been grievously exposed in Georgia, trapped deep in enemy territory, and faced with a disaster not witnessed since Napoleon's retreat from Moscow.

My bitter thoughts faded with the return of Mrs. Thomas to Nashville. Being a husband again was better than any belated military promotion.

In a refreshed mood, I thought my army deserved a brief rest after its victory, with some recuperation for a few weeks in winter. Grant thought differently and ordered my new army to be broken up, with many of its divisions sent to other commanders. My supposed slowness was still on his mind, even as Grant himself was practically immobile in his siege of Richmond and Petersburg. He meant for me to be a major general with only administrative duties, not on the front lines.

At least Schofield would soon be gone; he and his corps were going to North Carolina to join Sherman's army. Let Billy deal with the serpent.

In early 1865, there were still rebels in Alabama to contend with. Grant gave Wilson command of an independent cavalry force sent to dispatch them. Now Wilson well deserved this responsibility, and I was happy and proud for him. But this promotion had the taint of a Grant sneer at me.

No matter, Wilson still considered me in charge and conferred with me on strategy. He was sure he could capture the last arsenals and weapons factories still operating in the South. I approved his operation, as did Grant. By March, Wilson was accomplishing just what he had promised, defeating Forrest outside Selma and crippling the rebels' ability to arm themselves.

Other cavalry units commanded by capable men such as Edward Canby and George Stoneman, though nominally independent as well, also looked to me for leadership from my headquarters in Nashville. I am not saying that I was watching over every detail of their command, only that they all reported to me and sought my guidance on major matters through the telegraph wire.

The rebellion was nearing its end that March. Wilson was taking Montgomery, Alabama's capital; Canby was moving against Mobile on the Alabama coast; and Stoneman was riding into Virginia and western North Carolina, pinching off railroad lines supplying Lee in Petersburg. Stoneman also was creating a diversion for Sherman, who after departing Savannah had been devastating the Carolinas.

With his supplies running out, Lee left his entrenchments in Petersburg and abandoned Richmond. His best hope was to link up with rebel forces in North Carolina, but Stoneman blocked that option.

Grant, who except for his badgering of me had been motionless all winter, roused himself from his stupor and got the Army of the Potomac marching again, dogging Lee's tracks. The tanner's son trapped Lee near Appomattox, and my old friend surrendered on April 9, 1865. Other rebel forces soon gave up as well.

With all my complaints about Grant's slights and my delayed promotions, I am losing sight of the main goals of all the bloodshed —victory, the preservation of the Union, and the end of slavery. All these things were achieved, thank heaven.

At least being in Nashville, I was spared duty in my home state as the war ended. There would have been little joy in my witnessing my friend Lee humbled at Appomattox, and I would have been heartbroken if, after his signing the surrender documents, he had shunned me. Yet had he not surrendered, if the war had gone on, I would have been willing to keep battling across Virginia to bring the state to heel, even if my sisters' abode had been in my path.

Thank God Lee was honorable enough to end the war in a civilized manner, not turning the conflict into a national guerrilla war, the horror of Missouri spread wide and everlasting across the continent. And Grant showed a surprising amount of wisdom in giving Lee good terms for the surrender.

I remember the relief and satisfaction that we who were faithful to the Union felt when the surrender was announced in Nashville. You clasped my hands, Frances, and told me our sacrifices had not been in vain. I was so thankful that we could share this time after all our years apart.

And then came the dismay of Lincoln's assassination, so soon after the surrender. Frances told me that day that his death amid the exultation of victory shows that while virtue is rewarded in the hereafter, there is no such guarantee in life. Regardless, she said, we must carry on with God's eye upon us.

I would like to have met Lincoln, so he could have taken my

measure face to face and known that I was just as strong for the Union as he was. Stronger, for I had to give up more than a law practice in Illinois to fight for it. Yes, he gave his life for his country, but I risked life every day, as did all the men who followed me in war.

My wife encourages me to bury my bitterness over Lincoln's snubs and forgive him. I have mostly done so, I assure her. Five years after his death, I recognize his inherent nobility and that my grievances against him diminish when set against all the good he did and the good he would have done.

The rebels were defeated, but there was no peace for me. Not with Reconstruction ahead, not with Forrest and the Ku Klux Klan, and not with Grant.

CHAPTER 23

IN WHICH THE NATION HAS AN
UNEASY PEACE

Lee had surrendered, Davis had not.

We knew the rebels' president was heading south and west, perhaps desiring to escape to Texas and continue the rebellion from there as a Western Confederacy. There were even rumors that the last holdouts might sail for Cuba to create a Caribbean slave empire. Not for Davis the nobility and grace of Lee's surrender.

I ordered all the cavalry units under my jurisdiction to search for him, and I told Grant that if Davis escaped, "he will prove himself a better general than any of his subordinates."

On May 10 in southern Georgia, Wilson's troopers captured a man traveling with his wife. The man, apparently wearing her shawl as a disguise, was Davis. Some have ridiculed him for his choice in apparel, questioning his courage for wearing such a feminine garment. This is unjust. His courage was always a given; his treason was the issue.

Under heavy guard, Davis was sent to me in Nashville, where we treated him with courtesy as we waited for Grant to tell us where to send him. I visited the rebel leader while he was in my care.

"Mr. Davis, I am General Thomas of the United States Army."

"President Davis, if you please. Yes, I remember you. I saved your life at Buena Vista."

"Yes, you and Braxton Bragg. I remember that day, and I thank you again for my life, sir."

"And yet you betrayed your own state."

"And you, sir, were a great statesman who betrayed his country. ... Please, sir, let's don't bicker. We have just fought a terrible war over these questions. We both consider ourselves patriots and men of honor. Let us leave it at that for now. Are you comfortable?"

"As well as could be expected. How is my wife?"

"She is safe and well."

"That is good. When may I see her?"

"Soon, I hope."

"So what will be done with me?"

"That is up to General Grant."

"That butcher?"

"He is my commander, and he is also the victor. He will decide where you shall be kept while your future is decided."

"Very well, I await my fate. Forgive me for saying this, general, but I regret putting you in the Second Cavalry so many years ago."

"Good day, President Davis."

As it happens, Grant was dilatory in responding to me, so on May 15, I had Davis sent to Washington under heavy guard. He was imprisoned in chains for two years, finally winning a pardon from President Andrew Johnson. The other rebel politicians and generals have faced little in the way of punishment for their traitorous actions.

I experienced no exultation at the imprisonment of Davis, nor did his jibes at me sting. Davis didn't hate me; he was only disappointed in me. The hatred that many others in the South still express toward me has been expected and is of no import. Except for my sisters and brothers, and perhaps Lee, I am impregnable to the South's disregard.

The disregard some in the Union Army had for me was another matter. Of the six major generals of the Regular Army, I was the only one who would not command a military division in the new government being established in the South. I was assigned only a department under Sherman. This would not do.

I asked my friend General John Miller, the Nashville commander, to go to Washington and speak on my behalf to President Johnson. I told Miller that "during the war I permitted the national authorities to do what they pleased with me; they put my juniors over me, and I served under them; the life of the nation was then at stake, and it was not then proper to press questions of rank, but now that the war is over and the nation saved, I demand a command suited to my rank, or I do not want any."

Miller made a good case for me, though Johnson already knew my worth. He gave me a division of five states: Alabama, Georgia, Kentucky, Mississippi, and Tennessee. Sherman wasn't pleased by my new assignment, but I was.

My duties were nearly as challenging as my war service; indeed, I knew that the threat of renewed hostilities was always present. Despite the bitter attitudes of most whites, I worked to ensure the progress of former slaves. When I could, I settled them on the estates of their former owners and gave them equipment so they could make good on their own. It encouraged me that many former slaves were also advancing not only as farmers but as merchants and mechanics. I insisted that the Southern states eliminate laws that discriminated against Negroes.

In this I had the support of Tennessee Governor W.G. Brownlow, a former newspaperman and Methodist preacher from Knoxville. Like me, he was a Southern-born supporter of the Union who was hated in much of the South. Though he was too much of a fire-and-brimstone speaker for my taste, I liked the man. I even tolerated his past life as a journalist.

There were other good Union men from east Tennessee who were now rebuilding the state's government, and they made

Frances and me feel welcome. But many in the state were uncivil. A next-door neighbor made a point of pretending I didn't exist when we both took the evening air on our verandahs. Finally, after six months of snubs, he deigned to approach me to shake my hand. I brushed him aside. "Too late, too late, sir; you have sinned away your day of grace," I told the crestfallen fellow. The Methodist governor smiled when I told him this story.

The resistance of the whites across the failed "Confederacy" almost made me wish I could bring Sherman and his "bummers" to burn out their property as a proper chastisement. As I wrote earlier, I didn't want to punish children and old people, but what in heaven will it take to prove to their traitorous families that they lost the war and the world has changed? Some Southerners are claiming they weren't truly defeated, only "overwhelmed" by superior numbers and resources. Damn their lies—they were beaten by valiant Union soldiers.

I often had to use military tribunals to try white ruffians because the local courts would refuse to convict them for attacking Negroes. When local civic officials in my division of the South approved anti-black laws, I threatened them with detention until they backed down. And when an Episcopalian bishop refused to include the president of the United States in the federally prescribed prayers in the South, I deprived him of the right to preach the Gospel. We want no more treason in the pulpit or anywhere.

As I reported to Washington: "With too many of the people of the South, the late civil war is called a revolution, rebels are called `Confederates,' loyalists to the whole country are called damned Yankees and traitors, and over the whole great crime, with its accursed record of slaughtered heroes, patriots murdered because of their true-hearted love of country, widowed wives and orphaned children, and prisoners of war slain ... they are trying to throw the gloss of respectability. ... Everywhere in the states lately in rebellion, treason is respectable and loyalty odious."

I also warned Washington about the Ku Klux Klan, a group of defeated rebels who sought to achieve in white robes what they could not do in gray uniforms. This nest of vipers was led by our old cavalry nemesis, Forrest. The former slave dealer apparently wanted to resuscitate his lamented profession and spread terror among the freed Negroes. I emphasize that whites should have little fear of their former slaves. I have heard of no murderous Nat Turners seeking revenge against their old masters, only that the Negroes are an emancipated race learning to use their liberty in a responsible manner. Yet the Klan wants to slash away their most basic right, the right of free men to vote. I did what I could to safeguard the polls, sending troops so that many freedmen could cast their ballots. But I never had enough troops to do all that was needed.

I've heard recently that Forrest has withdrawn from the Klan, disgusted that it's become wicked far beyond his initial schemes. If this rumor is true, I would tell that hellcat what I told my Nashville neighbor—you have already sinned away your hope for grace.

As much as I am thankful to Johnson for his support of me during and after the war, he was a disappointment to me as president. He appeared to loathe the freed Negroes as much as he detested their former owners. I did not favor his impeachment, though lately I've grown to respect the arguments of his political foes, the radical Republicans who want a heavier hand on the Southern states. I fear that the Federal government will need to station troops there for several generations before the stain of treason and racial animosity fades. Still, whatever his faults, Johnson was a better president than Buchanan.

Oh, but surely this Reconstruction would have a greater chance of ultimate success had Lincoln lived.

Grant has been president for only a year, so I will reserve judgment on his record in the White House. I pray he is more honorable as president than he was as my commanding general. However, I applaud that he has taken strong action to limit the Klan. If only he would do more for the Negroes' advancement. It will take time for the regeneration of the colored population, but I feel they have been purified by the terrible ordeal of slavery and will assume an honorable position in the ranks of Americans.

Soon after the war ended, I went to Washington at the request of Stanton. The secretary of war wanted to meet with me personally after four years of knowing each other only through telegraphed messages and letters. We shook hands in his office, and he immediately told me a falsehood: "I have always had great confidence in you."

"Mr. Stanton, I am sorry to hear you make this statement," I replied, glaring at his mendacity. "There were times when your support of me was not evident."

Yes, he was a supporter of mine, but at least four times he allowed Lincoln to promote lesser men over me. And I heard no encouraging words from him before the Battle of Nashville.

He smiled at my rebuke and took no visible offense.

"General Thomas, I know that some in Washington did not value you as highly as we should have," Stanton said, "and last December, I admit to some nervous days and nights while we awaited news from Nashville. If I have been amiss in my conduct toward you, please forgive me. If God had spared him, President Lincoln would express the same sentiments to you."

"I thank you for that, Mr. Stanton, and please forgive me if I seemed intemperate just now. I know that you helped Mr. Lincoln carry a mighty load these past four years."

"Of course, general. Now tell me how we can lighten the load for President Johnson."

Johnson and Stanton would soon become enemies over the president's preference for a less harsh treatment of the defeated South. When Johnson attempted to remove Stanton from his cabinet, it led to a presidential impeachment. Johnson survived a Senate vote, but his weakened political condition opened the door for Grant to win the presidency in 1868.

Stanton would be nominated by Grant to the Supreme Court the next year, but he would pass away before he could take his seat.

I mourn for him. As unsteady as his support for me was, I know that Stanton did me far more good than harm. He was as stalwart as Lincoln in his love for the Union.

Some former rebels proved to be men of vision in remaking the Union. James Longstreet, for example, became a Republican and has worked to truly reconstruct the nation. Unfortunately, many Southerners now despise him as much as they do me. I conferred with him and gave him as much help as I could. We also talked of military matters and exchanged compliments over our philosophies. As much as I esteem Lee, I believe Longstreet was the better general. This I told Longstreet. With a smile, he said he was only a mortal but Lee had become a god to the vanquished.

John Bell Hood did not go so far as to join the Republicans, but he asked to visit me when I was in Louisville. Beholding him coming to my door on crutches, I threw my arms around him and helped him to a chair.

"Thank you, General Thomas," Hood told me. "I'm averse to accepting such assistance from most men, but from you I'll take it gladly. I usually get along adequately on these accursed crutches."

"I see that," I replied. "My friend, despite all you've endured, you look well indeed. This is the first time I've see you since we were in the Second Cavalry in Texas."

"Yes, though I tried to spy you with my field glasses at Atlanta and Nashville, without success. We had proud days when we were cavalrymen in Texas. I wish you had come with me then to serve the Confederacy. You would have been loved in the South."

"Perhaps. I would have been proud to have you as a comrade in any army, regardless."

"Thank you. We had insurmountable differences on states' rights, but I always knew you to be a man of honor. How I wish you had been with me at Nashville instead of with the Yankees. But the fates were against me."

I was tempted to correct Hood on his reference to states' rights, as if that issue, not the peculiar institution, was the breaking point for our nation. Had I been uncharitable, I might have reminded him that freed slaves fought bravely against him in Nashville. Yet I felt no urge to renew old arguments with him; I was so glad we could be friends again.

Hood and I talked for an hour on many matters. Mostly we spoke of the comrades we had known in the old Army, the ones who survived the war and those who had not. He asked after you, Frances. A good man, Hood, a good man despite his rebellion. He's a cotton broker now, with a young wife and children.

If Lee should ever ask for a similar meeting with me, I would rush to Virginia, where he is president of a college, and proudly shake his hand. I understand that he is urging our fellow Virginians to come to terms with their losses and to be good Americans. God bless him.

I would also be pleased if I ever had a chance to break bread with Joseph Johnston, our great foe in the Atlanta campaign. When Lee surrendered to Grant in Virginia, Johnston was leading a weak rebel army in North Carolina and making no headway against Sherman. After a week of negotiations, Johnston surrendered most of the butternut forces still resisting east of the Mississippi. Sherman, like Grant, was very merciful to the defeated, giving them rations and horses.

Davis, still in flight from Richmond at that time, had no criticism of Lee's capitulation but considered Johnston's submission to be an act of treachery because his army had not yet been annihilated by Sherman's. Well, Davis and Johnston had never been close. If they had been friends, Johnston would never have been relieved from command in Georgia, and Sherman and I might still be knocking on the door to Atlanta. Johnston is now selling insurance in Savannah. I would consider buying a policy from him if he called on me.

What of Bragg? I've heard he's selling insurance in New Orleans. He might be desperate enough to sell even me a policy. Goodness, that makes two defeated rebels from whom I am willing to purchase insurance. It's the least I can do for national reconciliation.

Jeb Stuart, the Virginian who wanted to hang me as a traitor to our state, was killed in May 1864 near Richmond. When he died, I was six hundred miles away with Sherman as we were approaching Atlanta. Though Cump and I were not on the best terms at that time, he was jovial when he informed me of the rebel's death.

"Good news, Old Tom, it looks like you're not going to be strung up after all. Jeb Stuart just died. "

"God forgive him. Did he die in battle?"

"Yes, indeed. Phil Sheridan's boys sent him to his Maker. Some big cavalry fight. That's going to be a big help for Grant, not having to wonder where Stuart is lurking. Lee depended on him as much as anyone."

"Yes, as much as Grant depends on you."

"Hmm, well, maybe. I remember you telling me that Stuart was one of your students at the Point."

"Yes, in cavalry tactics, among other subjects."

"I'll wager he was one of those cadets who called you 'Slow Trot,' wasn't he?"

"Sadly, yes. I also taught him how to charge, at the quickest possible speed."

"You taught him too well, then. He was almost as good as Forrest. Well, God forgive him, as you say, but I won't. One more dead rebel."

"Yes, one more former friend."

One of my brothers has reached out to me, and we've made peace with each other. Sadly, my sisters back at my family's farm are still at war with me. Learning they had become poor with the loss of their slaves, I attempted to send them money. Rejected, of course. I still pray for a reconciliation. I know not the fate of my other siblings. I pray for them as well.

For all the slings and arrows I have received, the honors I was given after the war were some compensation. I learned to not efface myself when my usual public modesty would serve no purpose other than to disappoint my friends and admirers who wanted to show me their regard. The official thanks from Congress were most welcome, and the applause given me when I visited the House of Representatives was unnerving even as it was cherished.

The finest honor was being elected the first president of the Society of the Army of the Cumberland. When this august body was formed in Cincinnati, I gave a speech at the final banquet of the session. No exceptional speaker am I, but meeting my worthy Cumberland comrades again made me forget my nervousness and salute their gallantry and persistence. Complain as I have about Ohio generals, their home state was most welcoming.

The city of Cincinnati then sought to give me a fine house, one I had to refuse because it went against my personal code of ethics. Whatever services I gave, they were rendered to the country itself. When admirers raised money for me, I told them to give it to the widows and orphans of the war. My pay as a general has been more than enough for Frances and me.

Grant continues to do me little injuries—jealousy may be the reason. When he and I were on the same stage together in Chicago for a military reunion, the applause for me rivaled what he had received—and he had just been elected president of the United States. There had already been talk of my seeking the presidency, a job for which I lack the proper temperament. I prefer to give orders, not speeches of persuasion.

Still Grant must fear I will be a future challenger. As president-elect, he named Sherman to succeed himself as general of the Army and promoted Sheridan to take Sherman's position as lieutenant general. Many thought that I, not Sheridan, deserved this elevation. By seniority, I deserved it, but seniority had never served me well. The irony is that Andrew Johnson, in his last year as president, knowing Grant was a political rival to him, tried to demote the general and put me in his place. I turned Johnson down, not wishing to be promoted in such a political fashion. Did Grant thank me for this courtesy? Must you ask?

Another Grant stab at me is my current posting as commander of the Military Division of the Pacific. It's a place of exile, one where Grant had sent Henry Halleck previously. I had hoped to be transferred to the Military Division of the East, where Frances could be closer to her friends and family in New York and I could be near at hand in the event my sisters ever bestow their forgiveness on me. No, the Eastern post went to Grant's pet, Sheridan.

Well, San Francisco is a lively city, and Frances has made friends here. She only wishes I did not have to make so many tiresome inspections all over the frontier. Visiting our new territory of Alaska was fascinating, however. I was able to renew my study of nature, a beloved avocation I had to relinquish during the war. Despite my constant travels, I continue to gain weight. Frances tries, unsuccessfully, to reduce my meals.

Even in peacetime, I still feel under siege by my enemies in the U.S. Army. Some newspapers early this year printed a statement by Halleck about how narrowly I held on to my command before the Battle of Nashville. "Old Brains" was gossiping in 1870 like an old woman about matters in 1864 that should have remained a military secret. I already knew that Schofield and Grant had intrigued against me before the battle, but Halleck confirmed it for all the world to see. What had been one of my proudest accomplishments in service to my country has become a humiliation.

Soon after Halleck's statement was reported, the *New York Tribune* published the anonymous letter that gives Schofield the bigger credit for the defeat of Hood in Tennessee. It said that after the Battle of Franklin, "the enemy had been whipped until there was very little fight in him."

The letter was obviously written by Schofield or one of his minions. Perhaps he was embarrassed by the Halleck story and felt compelled to justify the machinations against me in Nashville more than five years ago.

However, I'm sure the letter was also inspired by Grant, still concerned that I might run for president against him.

Thank goodness for the many soldiers who have written in newspapers across the nation to defend me and proclaim that the rebels still had plenty of "fight" in them after Franklin. One of them is General David Stanley, who has just published a reply in the

Tribune that puts the lie to Schofield's claim. Stanley, after all, was the true victor at Franklin, a talented soldier who showed gallantry where Schofield did not. Stanley won the Medal of Honor for Franklin, not Schofield.

I must send Stanley a note of thanks for writing this: "No one who knows what that army was and what its failings were will dare dispute the fact that Thomas's removal would have proved a great if not fatal error, and that a very large part of the enthusiasm, vim, and heartiness with which the Battle of Nashville was fought was due to the fact that in the current words of the men in the rank: 'This is Old Pap's fight, and we're going to win it for him.' "

Why didn't Sherman write a defense of me as well?

I will now write my own reply to the *Tribune*, and these memories that I have put to paper have been a boon to me as I consider my response. Though I will salute Stanley and others for their courage at Franklin, I will be diplomatic and not question Schofield's leadership and valor, at least in public. But the next time I see him I shall be tempted to box his ears. I may do the same to Grant when his presidency ends.

Frances thanks me for these stories of my military career. Again, I stress to her that I do not mean for these remembrances to be made public; they are too personal. I have endeavored to be publicly impervious to the injustices done me by the Union's leaders, and I do not desire anyone but my wife to know all the pain I've withstood. It is also best that Americans never realize how two-faced such exalted men as Lincoln, Grant, and Stanton could be. And I hope Sherman never suspects that my friendship and respect for him have waned.

Hood was right on one point. Had I chosen Virginia over the Union, I would today be admired in my home state and all over the South, even in defeat. My sisters would love me. Bragg would tolerate me. And I would have enjoyed the wartime company of Lee, Longstreet, and Hood far more than that of Grant, Halleck, and Schofield.

But I chose well, if painfully. I'm sure that had I gone to the

South, the traitors would have won, and there would now truly be a Confederate States of America.

My sacred oath of loyalty to the United States was paramount, as were the love of my wife and my disapproval of slavery. I know that time and history will do me justice.

EPILOGUE

My husband, General George Henry Thomas, died on March 28, 1870, soon after he finished writing this private memoir. The letter he was composing as a reply to Schofield was unfinished. Thank goodness for the letters by David Stanley and others who gave George the tributes he deserved for the great Union victory at Nashville.

My husband's poor health finally proved fatal after the many pressures and dangers of a military life. His untimely passing at age fifty-three was also caused by the strain and anguish brought on by the recent underhanded efforts of U.S. Grant, John Schofield, and Henry Halleck to demean him. They were more deadly enemies to George than the rebellious South.

Some justice has been done, however. Schofield has been widely condemned in public for his attempt to steal my husband's glory. That cur, as George called him, had the effrontery to be one of the pallbearers at my husband's funeral. As a major general and a former secretary of war, Schofield must have felt he was entitled to this honor. I did not formally object to his presence, but I ignored him as best I could. George would have told me to keep a brave face, and I did so to honor my husband.

I could not ignore the president of the United States. Grant was at the funeral, and I gave my respects to his office, if not the man. The president was very civil to me—how I wish he had paid the same courtesy to my husband during his lifetime. Sherman, Rosecrans, Meade, Hooker, Granger, and other generals, as well as the governor and many other government officials, also attended the last rites at St. Paul's Episcopal Church in my hometown of Troy. More importantly, thousands of his soldiers were there, the men he most loved and respected.

A special train had carried his body to upstate New York from California. Mourning crowds were at every rail station. Flags were at half-staff all over the country, at least in the North.

Of all the tributes given George, the one by Joseph Hooker was especially kind. He called George "the ablest, the most just, and the most beloved man I ever knew. I never shall know his equal. I never supposed a man of his merit could live."

Whatever tensions there had been between them, William T. Sherman was gracious in his salute to George, remembering his "honesty, integrity and honor ... the *beau ideal* of the soldier and gentleman. Though he leaves no child to bear his name, the old Army of the Cumberland, numbered by tens of thousands, called him father, and will weep for him many tears of grief."

Though Sherman had asked me to have George buried at West Point, I wanted to be near him, even in death. George found Troy to his liking the few times he was able to visit. The people of the state of New York were as proud of him as if he had been a native son.

His sisters and brothers were not in evidence when he was buried. A pity they were so blind and misguided. Their brother, my husband, was a great man. He did as much as any man to end slavery. As Oliver Otis Howard told me, "George was the best general in the Civil War, North or South." If Lincoln had realized this, the war might have been won much sooner and with much less bloodshed.

To respect George's wishes, I will not release these writings to the public, but I will save them in memory of him. I will be a tigress in defense of his reputation as a soldier, so Schofield and Grant should beware.

I bless my luck that I had such a husband. The nation should bless its luck that it had such a general.

Frances Kellogg Thomas

AUTHOR'S AFTERWORD

How much of this novel is fiction?

I've tried to keep to the known facts, letting the characters do what they really did, in the correct places and on the correct dates.

Many of the quotations by George Thomas are from the official documents he wrote and the memories of his fellow soldiers and friends, as recounted in several biographies of the general and many histories of the Civil War. Though most of the novel's conversations are from the author's imagination, I hope I've allowed Thomas to speak for himself in what I believe to be a fair representation of his voice with his nineteenth century insights and prejudices.

But a few liberties were taken.

Did a teenage George Thomas help warn his Virginia neighbors of Nat Turner's advance? Perhaps, though the record is unclear. Regardless, I believe a bit of embellishment can be allowed in a novel. Thomas and his family barely escaped the uprising, and it's a certainty, given his history of heroism, that he would have been a young Paul Revere if needed.

There was no embellishment about his record in combat as an American soldier.

Before the Civil War, was Thomas as strongly anti-slavery as he appears in this novel? His Northern friends would say yes; his Southern enemies would say no. General Oliver Otis Howard, who did a great deal of research into Thomas' early life, insisted that his friend never held any respect for slavery and never held any hatred for Africans. There is no doubt about Thomas' uncompromising support for black Union soldiers during the war and for extending civil rights to former slaves during Reconstruction.

Did John Schofield send U.S. Grant telegraph messages undermining Thomas in Nashville? After the war, Schofield denied it, but his veracity should be questioned.

Was Grant the villainous nemesis to Thomas that he is in this novel? The opinions of biographers and historians vary. What's sure is that the future American president would have done well to give Thomas the same level of trust, if not friendship, that he gave to Sherman.

Was Thomas the best general in the war? That's for military experts and historians to debate, and I am neither. With all due respect to the U.S. armed services, I've never been a soldier, and I am not a Civil War buff, though I've learned much about the conflict in the time I've worked on this book. Did Howard actually say Thomas was the best general in the war? Call it a novelist's prerogative.

Thomas' early death in 1870, and the autobiographies of his Union rivals, Grant and Sherman, helped put him in the shadows. Sherman was a good writer, Grant a better one, and their books, published after Thomas' death, are worth reading, despite some inaccuracies and half-truths. Though these two generals wrote of their respect for Thomas, they still hectored him in print for being slow. I suspect that in spite of their greater fame, Grant and Sherman knew that many Union veterans considered Thomas the better soldier and the better man, and they feared that future historians might come to the same conclusion.

Another reason for Thomas' post-war obscurity was the 1877 end of Reconstruction, when the Virginia-born Yankee hero became an insulting embarrassment to the "Lost Cause" of

Southern mythology and a political inconvenience to Northern hopes for a lasting, peaceful reconciliation. But the reputation of Thomas, who was always held in high regard by historians of integrity, has been rising in most recent studies and biographies.

As for his decision to remain loyal to the Union, I believe Thomas must have struggled with it more in real life than he did in this novel. His sense of honor and his oath to the United States were the deciding factors, but the love of his Northern-born wife likely played a bigger role than the general would ever admit, in life or in fiction.

What's beyond debate is that George H. Thomas was a great American, a needed example for the twenty-first century.

Conrad Bibens

BIBLIOGRAPHY

Blight, David W. *Race and Reunion: The Civil War in American History*. Cambridge, Mass., and London: Belknap Press of Harvard University Press, 2001.

Bobrick, Benson. *Master of War: The Life of General George H. Thomas*. New York: Simon & Schuster, 2009.

Bordewich, Fergus M. *Congress at War: How Republican Reformers Fought the Civil War, Defied Lincoln, Ended Slavery, and Remade America*. New York: Anchor Books, 2020.

Catton, Bruce. *The Coming Fury, Terrible Swift Sword* and *Never Call Retreat*. Garden City, New York: Doubleday & Company, 1961, 1963 and 1965.

Chernow, Ron. *Grant*. New York: Penguin Books, 2017.

Cleaves, Freeman. *Rock of Chickamauga: The Life of General George H. Thomas*. Norman: University of Oklahoma Press, 1949.

Connelly, Thomas L. *The Marble Man: Robert E. Lee and His Image in American Society*. Baton Rouge: Louisiana State University Press, 1977.

Cozzens, Peter. *No Better Place to Die: The Battle of Stones River*. Urbana: University of Illinois Press, 1990.

Donald, David Herbert. *Lincoln*. New York: Simon & Schuster Paperbacks, 1995.

Engle, Stephen D.: *Don Carlos Buell: Most Promising of All*. Chapel Hill: University of North Carolina Press, 2006.

Foner, Eric. *Reconstruction: America's Unfinished Revolution*. New York: History Book Club by arrangement with HarperCollins Publishers, 1988.

Foote, Shelby. *The Civil War: A Narrative*. 3 vols. New York: Vintage, 1986. (First editions published in 1957, 1963 and 1974.)

Freeman, Joanne B. *The Field of Blood: Violence in Congress and the Road to Civil War*. New York: Farrar, Straus and Giroux, 2018.

Grant, U.S. *Personal Memoirs*. New York: Da Capo Press, 1982. (First edition published in 1885.)

Hess, Earl J. *Braxton Bragg: The Most Hated Man of the Confederacy*. Chapel Hill: University of North Carolina Press, 2016.

Levin, Kevin M. *Searching for Black Confederates: The Civil War's Most Persistent Myth*. Chapel Hill: University of North Carolina Press, 2019.

McDonough, James Lee. *William Tecumseh Sherman: In the Service of My Country*. New York, London: W.W. Norton & Company, 2016.

McPherson, James M. *Battle Cry of Freedom*. New York: Oxford University Press, 1988.

Monaghan, Jay. *Civil War on the Western Border: 1854-1865*. New York: Bonanza, 1955.

Nolan, Alan T. *Lee Considered: General Robert E. Lee and Civil War History*. Chapel Hill: University of North Carolina Press, 1991.

Oates, Stephen B. *The Fires of Jubilee: Nat Turner's Fierce Rebellion*. New York: Harper & Row, 1975.

Paul, Joel Richard. *Indivisible: Daniel Webster and the Birth of American Nationalism.* New York: Riverhead Books, 2022.

Phillips, Christopher. *The Rivers Ran Backward: The Civil War and the Remaking of the American Middle Border.* New York: Oxford University Press, 2016.

Piatt, Donn and Van Boynton, Henry. *General George H. Thomas: A Critical Biography.* Cincinnati: Robert Clarke & Co., 1893.

Raines, Howell. *Silent Cavalry: How Union Soldiers from Alabama Helped Sherman Burn Atlanta — and Then Got Written Out of History.* New York: Crown, 2023.

Reid, Brian Holden. *The Scourge of War: The Life of William Tecumseh Sherman.* New York: Oxford University Press, 2020.

Schecter, Barnet. *The Devil's Own Work: The Civil War Draft Riots and the Fight to Reconstruct America.* New York: Walker & Company, 2005.

Sherman, William T. *Memoirs.* New York: Penguin, 2000. (First edition published in 1875.)

Silber, Nina. *The Romance of Reunion: Northerners and the South, 1865-1900.* Chapel Hill: University of North Carolina Press, 1993.

Sword, Wiley. *Confederacy's Last Hurrah: Spring Hill, Franklin & Nashville.* Lawrence: University of Kansas Press, 1992.

Thomas, Wilbur. *General George H. Thomas: The Indomitable Warrior: A Critical Biography.* New York: Expository, 1964.

Vardon, Elizabeth R. *Longstreet: The Confederate General Who Defied the South.* New York: Simon & Schuster, 2023.

Weber, Jennifer. *Copperheads: The Rise and Fall of Lincoln's Opponents in the North.* New York: Oxford University Press, 2006.

Wert, Jeffry. *General James Longstreet: The Confederacy's Most Controversial Soldier.* New York: Simon & Schuster Paperbacks, 1993.

Wills, Brian Steel. *George Henry Thomas: As True As Steel.* Lawrence: University of Kansas Press, 2012.

Woodworth, Steven E. *Manifest Destinies: America's Westward Expansion and the Road to the Civil War.* New York: Vintage Books, 2010.

ACKNOWLEDGMENTS

My thanks to Steve Sanderson, Rosalie Massery Sanderson, Paul McGrath, Ernie Williamson, Mike Riepen, Ronnie Crocker, Janet Elliott, and Roger Bibens for reading early drafts and making helpful suggestions; Ken Ellis for designing the cover; and Loren Steffy for publishing this novel. And special thanks to my wife, Becky Massery Bibens, and our daughters, Anna and Allison, for being patient with me.

ABOUT THE AUTHOR

Conrad Bibens worked at newspapers for more than forty years—as a copy editor, wire editor, city editor, and reporter—including twenty-eight years at the *Houston Chronicle*. A 1977 graduate of the University of Kansas, he grew up in St. Joseph, Mo., and lives in the Houston area.

Looking for your next book?
We publish the stories you've been waiting to read!

Check out our other titles, including audio books, at
StoneyCreekPublishing.com.

For author book signings, speaking engagements, or other events,
please contact us at info@stoneycreekpublishing.com

Printed in the USA
CPSIA information can be obtained
at www.ICGtesting.com
LVHW050949300924
792480LV00002B/4